SHARON SALA

"Sala's characters are vivid and engaging."
—*Publishers Weekly* on *Cut Throat*

"Perfect entertainment for those looking for a suspense novel with emotional intensity."
—*Publishers Weekly* on *Out of the Dark*

"[Sala] takes readers with her on an incredible journey of overcoming adversity and increased self-awareness in every book."
—John St. Augustine,
Power!Talk Radio, WDBC-AM

"Chilling and relentless."
—*Romantic Times BOOKreviews* on *The Chosen*

"Veteran romance writer Sala lives up to her reputation with this well-crafted thriller."
—*Publishers Weekly* on *Sweet Baby*

"[Sala has a] rare ability to bring powerful and emotionally wrenching stories to life."
—*Romantic Times BOOKreviews*

"This is Sharon Sala at top form. You're going to love this touching and memorable book."
—Debbie Macomber on *Whippoorwill*

SHARON SALA

SALA

BAD PENNY

MIRA®

MIRA

ISBN-13: 978-0-7783-2596-3
ISBN-10:   0-7783-2596-2

BAD PENNY

www.MIRABooks.com

Printed in U.S.A.

The heroine in this story is strong and independent. She is a woman who takes care of business and takes care of herself with no excuses or apologies to anyone for how she does it.

It has long been my belief that while God made most men physically stronger, it was the women to whom he gave the greatest strength.

The ability to endure and persevere.

For all my readers who know how important the dedications in my books are to me, I want you to know that I thought long and hard about who to honor by this story. Each time a group, or a special person in my life, or an event came to mind that I thought I might name, in the end I couldn't bring myself to a decision because of this heroine—because of Cat Dupree.

So it comes to this.

In her name, and in the names of all the women like her—women who have been victims of unspeakable crimes and who walk through life without justice—I dedicate this book to you.

In your darkest hours, in your saddest days, in the endless years that pass you by, when you think you are in this world on your own—know that the God who gave you the strength to survive is with you and within you, and that you are never alone.

One

Jimmy Franks smelled a rat.

It wasn't until he opened his eyes and saw the dark beady eyes and whiskers twitching near his nose that he knew he'd hit a new low. He swung a weak fist at the varmint, which merely scuttled behind a pile of empty boxes in the alley where he had just spent the night.

The taste in Jimmy's mouth was a perfect accompaniment to the stench in the alley. Gagging between breaths, he staggered to his feet. It took a few moments for him to gain his footing; when he did, he took the first good look at his surroundings. It wasn't the Hilton. He wasn't sure how he'd gotten here or even exactly where "here" was, but he was definitely in a garbage-filled alley between two abandoned buildings.

Groaning softly from the aches in his bones and the roiling in his belly, he swiped a shaky hand across his face and stumbled toward the street, anxious to find a bathroom. As he did, a gust of wind rushed through the redbrick canyon, whipping dirt into his eyes. He turned away from the blast just as a couple of sheets of old newspaper wrapped around his ankles. Thinking the paper would be useful to use for toilet paper, he grabbed the pages and headed for the open doorway of the building on his right. He was halfway over the threshold when his gaze fell on a headline in the middle of the page. He stopped.

Local Bondsman Survives Murder Attempt

As he read, he began to curse. His attempt at revenge for himself and his brother, Houston Franks, had gone south. This was pathetic. He couldn't even shoot a man and make it stick. His need for a bathroom forgotten, he wadded up the paper and headed for the street.

He couldn't believe it! He'd made a vow to make Wilson McKay pay for having him arrested for assault, so he couldn't bail Houston out of jail. He had pumped numerous bullets into McKay as payback and had been so certain the deed was done. But McKay was alive and, according to the reporter who'd written the piece, healing nicely.

"Damn it! Damn it all to hell!" Jimmy yelled, as he stomped out of the alley and down the street.

He was so angry he could hardly think. He needed to talk to Houston, but Houston had already hightailed it out of Texas. It was a disgrace. Jimmy still couldn't believe his own brother had left him stranded like this. He didn't have any money. He didn't have a place to stay. And even worse, he needed to find a dealer.

Sick to his stomach and shaking with every step, Jimmy began looking for familiar territory and faces. He was, by damn, going to finish what he'd started with McKay.

But first he needed to find himself a fix.

Luis Montoya was a short, stocky Latino with the blood of his Aztec ancestors strong on his face. His eyes were dark, and his mouth was wide and full. He had a stubborn cut to his jaw and a head of thick, black hair that he wore in a short ponytail at the nape of his neck. He'd been a part of the Mexican police department in Chihuahua for eleven years, the last five as a detective in Homicide. He was a proud man who didn't play favorites, and he was not influenced by people with money.

This morning, he'd had a fight with his wife, Conchita, a flat tire on his car and had burned his tongue on his first sip of coffee. All that, and it wasn't even eight o'clock. Then he'd gotten to work only to be handed a case no one wanted—one with no new leads.

All he knew was that the victim's name was Solomon Tutuola. His body had been found in the debris of a home fire. According to the records, Tutuola had purchased the mansion only days before his death. But Tutuola hadn't died in the fire. According to the coroner, it was the multitude of bullet wounds in his body that had done him in. The fire had only added insult to injury.

Someone had committed murder. It was now his job to find out who.

Montoya picked up the file, patted his pocket to make sure his cell phone was there and headed for the door. He had an appointment to meet with Chouie Garza, the Realtor who'd sold Tutuola the mansion. The man had already given a statement the night of the fire, but Montoya liked to question his own witnesses.

He glanced at his wristwatch as he slid behind the wheel. A few moments later, he was pulling out of the parking lot and into traffic. The hunt for a killer had begun.

Thirty minutes later, he'd found the location, pulled off the highway and started up the drive leading to what had once been a grand home. Now there was nothing left but ruins. A small white

Honda was parked near a saguaro. There was a man leaning against the hood. Chouie Garza, he hoped.

Montoya pulled up beside the Honda, then got out with his cop face on.

"Chouie Garza?"

The little man came forward, nodding nervously. "*Sì. Sì,* señor."

"Detective Montoya. I want to ask you a few questions about Solomon Tutuola, the man who died here. You sold him the house, did you not?"

Garza nodded again. "About three days before the fire."

Montoya began to make notes. "Was anyone else with him when you met with him?"

"No. He was alone."

"What was your impression of him?" Montoya asked.

Garza's eyes widened. *"El Diablo."*

Now it was Montoya's turn to be surprised. "How so?"

Garza made the sign of the cross, then glanced over his shoulder, as if merely speaking of the man might resurrect his ghost.

"There were strange tattoos all over his body...even his face, which had recently been burned, I think. The skin was still pink and healing, and he had no hair on that side of his head."

Montoya frowned. "Can you describe the tattoos?"

"Geometric designs, you know, like something on an old pottery. His teeth were filed into points, and when he smiled, it was like looking at a lion."

Montoya remembered the picture that had come into their office. It was true: the man had a devilish appearance, and Garza's description verified the identity again.

Montoya glanced up, eyeing the burned-out rubble.

"To your knowledge, was he living here alone?"

Garza shrugged. "I think he had hired a cook and a yard man, but I never saw them. I only saw him... and his money." He shifted nervously from one foot to the other before smoothing his hands over his thickly pomaded hair, then wiping them on the legs of his pants.

Montoya arched an eyebrow as he watched Garza fidgeting. He didn't think the man was lying, but his actions did explain the slightly shiny appearance of the legs of his suit pants. It wasn't from pressing marks; it was grease. His interest shifted as he resumed his interrogation.

"You say Tutuola had money. What kind of money are we talking about?"

Garza began motioning with his hands. "When he decided he would buy this house, he wanted to take possession immediately. I told him that was impossible, that papers had to go through a process. So he offered to pay the owners whatever they wanted to let him take immediate possession. When they agreed, he opened up the trunk of his car. There was the bag, like a suitcase, and it was full of money. I never saw so much money in my life."

"He paid you cash?"

Garza nodded. "By the handful."

Montoya smiled. Motive. Now things were beginning to make sense.

McKay Ranch—outside of Austin, Texas

Morning came softly, without warning or fanfare. It broke on the eastern horizon with little more than a hint of the warmth to come—a flourish of light bathing the sky in hues of pink and yellow. A jet trail running from north to south took on the appearance of a hot-pink comet as the sun continued its arc.

Cat Dupree watched the display from the back porch while her coffee went cold in the cup. She'd been here before—to the ranch where Wilson had grown up. Only that time, she'd been the one who'd been recovering. This time it was Wilson, who, unlike Humpty Dumpty, *had* been put back together again—by the skill of the surgeons at Dallas Memorial Hospital.

If she thought about it, she could still feel her panic as she'd stood at Wilson's bedside and watched him flatline. She'd screamed. First in shock, next in rage, then, finally, in denial. She'd refused to let him die.

So he hadn't.

And now they were together again, figuring out where to go from here.

The family cat came trotting up the back steps, then leaped into the porch swing beside Cat and head-butted her elbow. She set down her cold coffee, freeing up her lap.

"Well, what are you waiting for?" Cat asked.

The old tomcat chirped once, hopped up into her lap, sniffed the two buttons on the front of her blue chambray shirt, then curled up on her legs and began cleaning his paws.

Cat was scratching at a spot between his ears when she heard the back door open.

She glanced over her shoulder. The man coming out was pale and a good ten pounds thinner than he had been the month before. But the thick, spiky hair, the single gold earring and the gleam in his eye were still the same.

"Wilson. I didn't know you were up," she said.

"I couldn't find you," he said.

Cat shook her head, then patted the empty spot beside her.

"You should have known I wouldn't be far."

Wilson eyed the cat in her lap. "Is there room?"

She grinned. "Stop pouting and come sit."

Wilson eased himself into the seat beside her, then gave the cat an additional scratch before sliding his arm around her shoulders.

"Why are you up so early?" he asked. "Couldn't you sleep?"

"Didn't want to miss the show," she said, pointing to the sky, which was slowly turning to day.

Wilson looked up, then sighed softly. "Oh, yeah. I see what you mean."

Cat put a hand on his leg, grateful for the pulse of lifeblood as it flowed through his veins.

"Living in a city makes you forget things like sunrises."

"Living in a city makes you forget all kinds of things," he added. "Like how to enjoy life without buying into the rat race."

Cat leaned against him, making sure not to put weight on any of his still-healing wounds.

"A person could get used to this."

"Definitely," Wilson added, then, like Cat, let himself in on the light show breaking in the east.

As Wilson sat, he looked down at the woman in his arms. The defiance that had been with her for so long was gone. Losing the fury that came with the need for revenge had made room for his love. It seemed like a lifetime ago that he'd first seen her, carrying an unconscious man over her shoulder and out of a burning building. He hadn't known then that she was a bounty hunter, but he knew it now. The woman was fierce beyond belief. She'd tracked down the killer of her best friend with relentless determination, then dragged him kicking and screaming back to Dallas to stand trial.

And no one but Wilson knew the depths to which she'd gone to exact retribution from the man who'd killed her father, then cut her throat and left her for dead. After endless years of looking, she had finally found him, trailed him through the Mexican desert to Chihuahua, and ended what she'd begun to fear was a hopeless quest.

When Tutuola died, Cat's rage had died with him. And their relationship, which Wilson had sometimes feared was one-sided, had begun to flourish. Then he'd been shot. And according to Cat, his heart had stopped when he'd come out of surgery. He didn't remember much about that, but he did remember hearing Cat screaming at him, begging him not to die on her, too. She was a formidable woman to oppose.

And now here they were. They'd both been given a second chance at life and didn't want to waste it.

"Do you have any plans today?" Wilson asked.

"I'm going to drive into Austin and run some errands for your mother. She said there's a funeral at her church and she's helping serve food for the family."

Wilson nodded. "Yeah, Dad told me old Henry Daughtery died. He was one of the church deacons when I was a kid. I think Dad said he was ninety-two when he passed."

"I'd call that a good run," Cat said.

"Do you want me to go with you?" Wilson asked.

"No. I'm fine. It's just some extra groceries for Sunday dinner."

"Sunday dinner. Mom looks forward to that almost as much as the rest of us do. No matter what's going on through the week, she gets to catch up on all her kids and grandkids when they come for Sunday dinner."

"I remember," Cat said, thinking back to the first one she'd experienced after Wilson had found her near death in Mexico. He'd brought her back to Texas, then to his family home. It was here at the McKay ranch that she'd begun to believe she still had something left to live for besides revenge.

The old tomcat suddenly leaped down from Cat's

lap, and ran off the porch and out into the yard just as Wilson's dad, Carter, came outside to join them.

"Good morning to the both of you," Carter said. "I'm going to the barn to feed. Dorothy's already making breakfast."

"I'll go help her," Cat said and, after a pat on Wilson's leg, went into the house.

"Mind if I tag along with you?" Wilson asked.

His dad grinned. "Oh, I suppose I can find a way to put up with you."

Wilson stood up carefully, wincing a bit from the healing surgery; then, together, he and his dad walked off the porch and out into the morning.

It was just after nine o'clock when Cat set off for Austin. Wilson had gone with Carter to the south pasture to feed cattle, and Dorothy was already on her way to the church. Cat had checked her messages before leaving and noticed she'd had a call from Art Ball Bail Bonds. Art Ball was her employer. She'd been hunting bounty for him for years, but she'd come to a decision a few days back that was going to change all she knew about life.

She wanted a family. She wanted babies with Wilson, and she wanted to be the kind of mother that her mother had been to her—like Wilson's mother was to him and his brothers and sisters. She wanted to be as far removed from the dregs of society as she could get, which meant no more hunting bounty. Not for Art Ball. Not for anybody. And she was ready to put as much passion into a family as she had into avenging her father's murder. All she needed was the chance. After she returned from Austin, she would give Art a call.

As she drove, she couldn't help but notice how clear the air was and how blue the sky. That blue was echoed by the bluebonnets blooming in the pastures and along the roadsides. Calves dotted the fenced-in fields, as did the new foals tottering on long, shaky legs as they ran alongside their mamas.

It was spring. A time of renewal. Cat felt it in every facet of her being.

A short distance ahead, she noticed an old car on the side of the road. When she passed, she saw it was empty and thought nothing of it. But no sooner had she passed than she realized someone was on foot on the shoulder ahead.

Most likely the driver of the car.

It wasn't Cat's habit to pick up hitchhikers, but the person on foot was a young teenage girl carrying a small suitcase, so she changed her mind.

The girl was wearing blue jeans so old that they looked gray, a long-sleeved white T-shirt and a pair of tennis shoes. Her hair was red and short, and when Cat began to slow down, the girl suddenly stopped and turned. There was fear on her face—and something else that set Cat's teeth on edge.

Cat hit the brakes and rolled down the window of her SUV before the girl could panic.

"Hey…need a lift?"

Cat could tell that the girl was torn between the need for aid and a fear of the unknown.

"My name is Cat Dupree," Cat added. "I'm visiting Carter and Dorothy McKay."

Cat saw that the girl recognized the names, which seemed to ease her distrust.

The girl glanced over her shoulder and seemed to come to a decision. She smiled briefly at Cat, put her suitcase in the backseat, then got in. She eyed Cat carefully, taking note of her dark hair and pretty face, but when she saw the scar on her throat, she bit her lip and quickly looked away, as if she'd been caught staring at something forbidden.

Cat saw the look. It wasn't the first time someone had been startled by the twisted adhesion.

"It's just a scar," Cat said.

"I'm sorry for staring. Thank you for the ride. I'm Shelly Green."

Cat eyed the dark bruise on Shelly's cheekbone, the dried blood under her nose and the black eye, then shifted focus.

"Nice to meet you, Shelly Green. Where were you heading?"

"The bus depot, but if it's out of your way, just drop me off wherever you're going."

Cat put the car in gear and started driving. Now that the car was moving at a fast clip, she keyed in on the girl's wounds.

"So you said your name is Shelly?"

The girl nodded.

"Who hit you?"

Shelly flinched, then shrugged, but Cat saw her lower lip tremble.

She tried another question—one that wouldn't be so difficult to answer.

"How old are you?" Cat asked.

"Seventeen."

"Was it one of your parents who hit you?"

Shelly shook her head. "No, ma'am. I ain't got no folks."

"Yeah, me neither," Cat said, then gave the girl another quick glance. Shelly was wiping tears and snot with the back of her hand. "There are some tissues on the backseat. Help yourself."

Shelly looked startled, then glanced over her shoulder into the backseat, saw the box of tissues, and grabbed it and put it in her lap. Without comment, she blew her nose twice—hard—wadded up the used tissues and stuffed them in her jeans pocket, then put the box on the seat beside her.

"So…are you going to tell me who hit you?"

Shelly sighed, as if realizing Cat wasn't going to stop until she got an answer.

"My old man. I pissed him off because I wouldn't screw him this morning before he left for work."

The skin crawled on the back of Cat's neck as rage filled her.

"Your old man as in…?"

Again Shelly shrugged. "His name is Wayne. Wayne Bedford. We ain't married, but I've been with him since I was fifteen." Then she sighed, and it sounded to Cat as if the kid was carrying the weight of the world. "He didn't used to be this way, but now… Anyway, I told him last month that if he didn't quit hittin' on me, I was leaving."

"So this is the day?" Cat asked.

Shelly nodded.

"Where are you going?" Cat asked.

"Wherever a hundred and five dollars will take me," Shelly answered.

Cat nodded without comment, but she felt sick to her stomach. This kid reminded her of herself at the same age. The only difference was that while Cat had been hurt many times in her life, it hadn't been by someone who was supposed to love her.

"If you had a choice, where would you go?" Cat asked.

Shelly's expression changed. Her eyes widened, and the tone of her voice lifted.

"Seattle, Washington."

Cat grinned. "Why Seattle?"

"The trees and the mountains. I ain't never lived anywhere that had mountains and trees, and I think it would be pretty close to heaven up there."

Cat sighed. So young. Even after her living in hardship, life hadn't taken the joy out of this kid's world.

"If you got to Seattle, what would you do?"

"I'd figure something out. I'm a good waitress and—"

"Shelly, if you spend all your money on a bus ticket, where will you live when you get there?"

Shelly shrugged. "I've been homeless before. I'll figure something out. I always do."

Cat didn't answer, because there was nothing to say.

A few miles farther down the road, Cat noticed a pickup truck coming up fast behind her but thought nothing of it. The road was straight and flat, and there was no other traffic in sight. The driver could pass her without a problem.

Only he wasn't slowing down or trying to pass. He was riding her bumper so close that she could see the three-day-old whiskers on the driver's face when she looked in her rearview mirror.

"What's that crazy trying to do?" she muttered, more to herself than to Shelly, but Shelly turned around to see what was happening.

"Oh lordy!" she screamed. "It's Wayne! He found me! *He found me!*"

At that moment the truck rammed the back of Cat's SUV. Shelly screamed again as Cat frantically tried to keep the car upright and on the highway.

"He's going to kill me!" Shelly cried, and then began sobbing.

"Shut up and hold on," Cat said sharply, then stomped the accelerator.

She sped forward, putting a good twenty yards between her car and the pickup. But the distance didn't last. Wayne sped up, too, and within seconds, he rammed the SUV again.

This time it skidded and went sideways before Cat got it back under control. She floorboarded the accelerator at the same time that she pressed the emergency button on her GPS program. Within moments, the dispatcher's voice came on.

"Good morning, Miss Dupree...how can we help you?"

Cat had to shout to be heard above Shelly's wails.

"This is an emergency. Someone is trying to run

me off the road. Track my location and contact the county sheriff's office immediately."

"I have you on track. We're contacting the sheriff's department right now. Are you injured?"

"No. Not yet," Cat said, and then winced when the pickup hit her again.

Shelly's shrieks elevated.

It occurred to Cat that this could very well be the last day of her life—and all because she'd picked up a young girl with a black eye and a bloody nose.

The more she thought about it, the angrier she got. She wasn't willing to give up her future for a jerk who couldn't control his anger.

"Shelly, stop screaming," Cat said firmly.

Shelly upped the level of her wail, so Cat went her one better. The roar that came out of Cat's mouth was startling, even to her.

"Shelly! Shut. The. Hell. Up."

Shelly had been conditioned to respond to fear, and right now she didn't know who to be afraid of first: Wayne, who was trying to run them off the road, or this wild-eyed woman with the scar on her throat. She hiccupped as she caught her breath, then put her hands over her mouth.

Now the only sounds in the car were the dispatcher's voice assuring them that help was on the way and the sound of their engine as they went flying down the highway.

Cat's fingers were numb from the death grip she had on the steering wheel, but her mind was racing. She couldn't outrun him. She'd already tried. If help didn't get here soon, she was going to have to rethink her options. When the truck suddenly rammed them again, she lost it.

She opened the top of the console, throwing CDs out into Shelly's lap until she reached the bottom of the compartment, then pushed hard. The bottom popped up, revealing the 9mm handgun she kept hidden beneath. Without missing a beat, she put it in her lap.

"Brace yourself!" she yelled, and then stomped on the brakes.

Tires squalled.

Rubber burned.

It was the last thing Wayne Bedford expected. The air bag went off in his face when he crashed into the back of Cat's SUV. Her air bags went off, too, but she was ready for that.

Once she could concentrate after the bone-jarring crash, she jammed her car into Park, then fired a shot into the deployed bag, deflating it instantly. When she jumped out, her gun was aimed at the driver.

"Get out of the car!" she yelled, and then to

emphasize her point, fired a shot over the top of the truck.

Suddenly Wayne's fury at finding his girlfriend missing morphed into pure panic. He didn't know who this woman was, but he realized he'd made a really bad move.

"Don't shoot! *Don't shoot!*" he screamed.

"Get out!"

"I can't. I'm stuck," he wailed.

Cat yanked the door open and fired another shot, this time into the air bag in Bedford's truck.

Wayne was screaming as the bag deflated.

"Oh lord, oh lord, I'm sorry. Don't shoot me. Please, I don't want to die."

"You should have thought of that before you tried to wreck us!" Cat yelled, as she grabbed the man by the back of the collar and dragged him out of the seat.

He hit the blacktop face-first, then grabbed his nose as blood spurted.

"My nose! "

"That's nothing compared to what you did to your girlfriend's face. Your ass is next if you don't shut the hell up," Cat told him.

Like Shelly, Wayne chose the safe road and gritted his teeth against the need to bawl.

At that point Shelly made her way out of Cat's

car and staggered over to the truck, which was spewing steam and water all over the highway from a busted radiator.

"Wayne Bedford…what on earth is the matter with you?" Shelly yelled, and kicked the bottom of Wayne's boot. "You almost got us killed."

"She's got a gun," Wayne said.

Shelly gave her Good Samaritan a nervous glance.

"Yes, I see that, and she looks pissed enough to use it."

"I'm right in front of you, so you can both quit talking as if I wasn't here," Cat muttered.

Shelly sucked in her lower lip.

"I don't feel so good," Wayne said.

Shelly sighed and looked at Cat.

"Are you gonna shoot him?"

"I haven't decided," Cat said. Then she began to hear sirens. She glanced down at Wayne. "I guess not. Looks like you'll live to screw up again another day."

Two

After the way Wayne Bedford's morning was going, he was more than happy to be handcuffed and on his way to jail. The crazy woman who'd pulled a gun on him wasn't anything like Shelly. He didn't know how to handle women who hit back.

Meanwhile, Cat had assessed the damage to her car and considered it well spent. But she certainly couldn't drive it.

The tow trucks were on the way.

A second deputy had arrived to work the scene, while the first one hauled Bedford into booking. Cat was forced to accept the fact that she was going to have to call Wilson and tell him what happened.

She punched in the numbers, then cleared her throat as she waited for him to answer, which he did on the third ring.

"Hey, baby…what's up?" he asked.

"I need a ride," she said.

The tone of Wilson's voice changed slightly. "What happened? Are you having car trouble?"

Cat eyed her smashed SUV and sighed.

"In a manner of speaking."

Wilson heard the hesitation. "What the hell happened?"

"I had a slight accident, but no one is hurt."

Wilson's heart skipped. "I'll be right there. Where are you?"

"I'm about fifteen miles from the ranch, toward Austin."

"You sure you're not hurt?"

"I'm fine. Just mad."

That was when Wilson knew there was more to the story than what she'd told him, but knowing Cat, she'd said all she was going to say until he got there.

"I'll be right there."

Cat dropped her cell phone back in her pocket, then turned around. Shelly Green was watching her from the side of the road.

"Are you all right?" Cat asked.

Shelly touched her already swollen face, then nodded and said, "Them air bags are a bit startling, but they do the job, don't they?"

Cat stifled a grin. Little Shelly did have a way with words.

"Yes, they do."

Shelly sat down on her suitcase, then braced her hands against her knees.

"I heard you call someone named Wilson. Is he one of Carter and Dorothy McKay's boys?"

"Yes. Do you know him?" Cat asked.

"No, ma'am. I know some of their kids, but I don't know him."

"He lives in Dallas," Cat said.

Shelly nodded, then looked away, toward a small flower blooming up against the fence across the road.

Cat studied Shelly's face, and as she did, realized that Shelly reminded her of her best friend, Marsha, when Marsha had been about that age. A quick shaft of pain came and went as she tried not to remember what Marsha's dead and crumpled body had looked like, hanging in the broken boughs of the trees growing out of the side of the ravine— right where Mark Presley had tossed her.

She swallowed past the knot in her throat, then closed her eyes and took a slow breath. This was no time to get maudlin.

"I'm real sorry about your car," Shelly said. "If

you hadn't picked me up, this wouldn't have happened to you."

Cat swiped at her eyes, then looked up.

Shelly's hands were clenched into fists in her lap, and there were tears running down her cheeks. Add the black eye, the bloodied and swollen face, and she was a sight to behold.

Once more, Cat's empathy kicked in.

"Honey, meaner men than your Wayne have tried to bring me down without success. Besides, if I had it to do over again, I wouldn't change a thing."

Shelly sighed. "I have to say, I'm right glad I didn't have to go back with him."

"So am I," Cat said, then patted the girl on the shoulder. "Next time you go hunting for a boyfriend, maybe you'll choose more wisely."

Shelly rolled her eyes, then winced from the pain.

"There ain't gonna be a next time…at least, not any time soon."

Cat shook her head. "Never say never, kid." Then she looked up the highway. "And here comes Wilson."

Shelly stood up, then began smoothing her hands down the front of her shirt.

"I look a sight," she said.

Cat grinned. "You're fine. Besides, I'm the one who's gonna catch heck."

"But you didn't cause this," Shelly said.

"When I'm in trouble, Wilson loses sight of extenuating circumstances. All he wants is for me to be safe, and I keep getting myself into trouble."

Shelly sighed. "That's the kind of man I'm looking for."

Cat laughed. "You just told me there wasn't going to be another boyfriend."

Shelly looked a little startled, then grinned shamefacedly. "Well, not for a bit, anyway."

At that point Wilson pulled up. Cat and Shelly watched as he exited his truck. For someone who was still recovering from surgery, he was moving fast.

"Honey… Lord have mercy, what happened?" he asked, as he wrapped Cat in a big embrace.

"It was sort of my fault," Shelly said.

Wilson had been so focused on Cat, he'd barely noticed the other woman until she spoke, but when he turned and saw her face, he frowned.

He looked at her long and hard, then turned to Cat. "Talk to me."

Cat sighed. "It's simple, really. I passed an abandoned vehicle, then I saw her walking, carrying a suitcase. I took one look at her face and picked her up, okay?"

Wilson eyed the state of Shelly's face, and his expression stilled.

"I take it that didn't all happen in the wreck," he said.

Shelly sighed. "No, sir."

He looked at Cat, then nodded. "It's very okay."

"It was Wayne who caused the wreck," Shelly said.

Wilson frowned. "Wayne? Who's Wayne?"

"Wayne Bedford. He is…was…um, I lived with him for the past two years."

"Not Shirley Bedford's younger brother?"

"Yes, that's Wayne's sister. Do you know her?"

"I went to school with her." Wilson pointed at Shelly's face. "Did he do that to you?"

"Yes, sir."

Wilson's frown deepened. "Where is he now?"

"On the way to the slammer," Cat said, then watched Wilson's eyes narrow.

"I might need to have a word with him," he said.

"The sheriff will deal with him," Cat said, then pointed up the road. "Here come the wreckers, and I don't know where to tell them to take my car."

"I do," Wilson said. "Let me take care of it."

"Gladly," Cat said. "In the meantime, Shelly and I are going to get in your truck and wait. Oh…and we need to drop her off at the bus station before we run your mother's errands."

"Yeah, sure," Wilson said. "But are you sure you're up to all that?"

"I'm fine," Cat said.

"Thanks to them air bags," Shelly added, grinning.

Cat grinned, too. Wilson didn't know that she'd precipitated the wreck, and she didn't intend to tell him.

"Yeah. Air bags," she echoed.

They were both still grinning as they headed for Wilson's truck.

The bus station was a study in measured chaos as Wilson pulled into a parking place.

Shelly started to get out when Cat stopped her.

"I'm coming in with you," she said.

"Thank you, ma'am, but there's no need," Shelly said.

But Cat didn't listen. She got out and headed toward the entrance with Shelly in tow. When they got to the ticket counter, Cat stepped in front of her.

"How much for a one-way ticket to Seattle?"

The cashier entered the destination on her computer while Shelly stared in disbelief.

"I can't afford that," she said.

"Maybe not, but I can," Cat said, and pulled a credit card out of her hip pocket.

Shelly eyes widened in disbelief, and then tears welled and spilled as Cat paid for the ticket. She glanced at the itinerary, then handed it and the ticket to Shelly.

"The bus leaves in an hour and a half," Cat said, then emptied her wallet of cash and gave that to Shelly, as well. "You're going to need this until you can find yourself a job. Don't fall for someone promising easy money. It isn't worth it," she added.

Shelly hugged Cat fiercely, then clutched the money to her chest.

"Oh, trust me. I'm not the kind to turn tricks. I ain't afraid of hard work, and I *will* pay you back."

"I don't want it back," Cat said. "But if the opportunity ever comes to you, maybe you can help someone else just like I've helped you."

Shelly was dancing from one foot to the other. "I will. You'll see. Oh lordy…I never dreamed in a million years that when I lit out this morning with my suitcase in my hand that I'd be living a dream."

"Yeah, well, I've recently learned that it's never too late to change your life. So…you be careful, Shelly Green," Cat said.

"You know it," Shelly said, and then added, "You know, you have a pretty short fuse yourself. Maybe you should be a little careful, too."

Cat grinned. "Absolutely."

Then she strode across the lobby, only to find Wilson standing at the door with his arms folded across his chest and a smirk on his face. She paused, a little startled that he'd been watching.

"So how long have you been standing there?"

"Long enough to find out that my woman isn't nearly as tough as I thought she was."

"I just—"

He shook his head and pulled her into his arms.

"You don't have to explain yourself—ever. And by the way, just so you know, I'm pretty damn proud of you."

"You are?"

"Yes."

Cat sighed, then wrapped her arms around Wilson's neck and kissed him—hard—and with thanksgiving that she was still alive to do it one more time. When she finally pulled back, he had a glint in his eye that she recognized all too well.

"Save it for later," she said.

Sunlight caught on the gold hoop in his ear as he lowered his head and whispered, "You are in so much trouble."

Cat swung out of his arms, then gave him a wink and a swift pat on the rear, which made him grin.

"Let's get moving," she said. "Your mother will

be waiting for her groceries, and I need to make a trip to the ATM. I just gave away all my money to a stranger."

Jimmy Franks was leaning against a wall inside the doorway of Angels Mission, waiting for them to start serving the meal. The cops had picked him up yesterday for drunk and disorderly, and had turned him out less than an hour ago. When the priest who'd been standing outside the drunk tank had grabbed his arm and started praying for his immortal soul, Jimmy had been so startled that he'd actually stood there and listened.

The experience had reminded him of his childhood back in Horny Toad, Texas—sitting in church with his brother Houston and his mama, while Baxter Masters preached hell and damnation to his East Texas congregation. The street preacher's words had struck a chord deep enough that Jimmy opted for food at the mission, rather than hunting up another meth dealer.

And so he waited, watching as a line began to form near the dining area, and thought about what he was going to do when he got his head on straight—how he was going to find Wilson McKay and blow *his* head clean off his shoulders.

"Welcome, brother. Have you come to eat with us?"

Jimmy eyed the small, wizened woman who was shuffling past him pushing a walker with yellow tennis balls on the legs in lieu of wheels.

"Yes, ma'am, I have," Jimmy said, and then eyed the purse she was carrying over her arm. "Maybe you would allow me to help you to a seat?"

The old woman beamed. "Why thank you, brother."

"Don't mention it," Jimmy muttered, and aimed her toward the nearest chair. As soon as he got himself some food, he was out of here—and dessert was going to be how much meth he could score with whatever she was carrying in her purse.

Luis Montoya shifted his stance as he bent over the table in the crime lab. He'd already been through what they'd confiscated from the fire. The coroner had found several entry and exit wounds during the autopsy, but the fire had been so intense that they'd never found any spent bullets and only a couple of casings.

What he was focusing on now were the contents of the box in front of him. Inside were all the items that the crime lab had taken from Solomon Tutuola's car. They were the only things belonging to the victim that had not burned. He was hoping that something in here would give him a place to start— maybe clues as to a possible accomplice. A bagful of money had to have come from somewhere, and the items he had on the table were all he had to go on.

There were the usual things one would expect to find in a car. A couple of matchbooks had been found in a console. One from a café in Nuevo Laredo, the other from a café in Austin, Texas. Neither of them meant anything other than at one time Tutuola had been there.

There were a handful of coins: some pesos, some American. A map of Texas and a half dozen postcards of various locations in Tijuana. Nothing had been written on them. Who knew why a man such as Tutuola would buy postcards? From what Montoya had seen on Tutuola's rap sheet, he couldn't picture the man maintaining a cordial correspondence with anyone.

Then Montoya came to the duffel bag. Within moments, he knew that the contents had never belonged to his victim. These clothes would have fitted a man less than six feet tall and weighing no more than one-hundred-eighty pounds, and according to the coroner and Tutuola's rap sheet, he'd been close to 300 pounds and five inches over six feet tall. Montoya's heart skipped a beat. Maybe this was the first clue he was looking for to the accomplice.

He dug through the pockets and then checked all the labels, looking for a name. Nothing turned up until he looked in an inside jacket pocket and found a business card for Mark Presley of Presley Implements in Dallas, Texas.

Montoya frowned. Something about the name and business rang a bell, but he couldn't remember if it was something he'd read or something he'd heard, much less what it was.

A few minutes later he was finished. He took down the name and phone number of the implement company, then returned everything to the evidence locker and headed for his desk. The first order of the day was to call Presley Implements. But when he asked to speak to Mark Presley, the silence on the other end of the line was telling.

"Hello? Are you still there?" Montoya asked.

"Oh. Yes. I'm sorry. Um…Mr. Presley is no longer here. Mrs. Presley is acting CEO. I'll put you through."

Luis Montoya prided himself on being able to read people. He knew when they were lying, or when they just weren't being as forthcoming as they should have been. It was the latter that he picked up on this time.

A moment later the call was answered.

"This is Penny Presley. How can I help you?"

"Ms. Presley, my name is Luis Montoya. I'm a homicide detective in Chihuahua, Mexico, investigating the death of a man named Solomon Tutuola. There was a card belonging to Mark Presley of Presley Implements found with his belongings, and I'm trying to find out how or if they knew each other."

He heard a sharp, indrawn breath and then what sounded like a hiss before he got an answer he hadn't expected.

"God! I not only don't know anyone named Tutuola, but during the past few months, it became apparent to me that I didn't know the man I'd married all that well, either. Mark is in prison, on death row, awaiting execution for the murder of his pregnant girlfriend. Needless to say, we are divorced. I suggest you speak to the Dallas Police Department for all the sordid details."

"Have you or your husband ever been to Chihuahua?"

Sarcasm was thick in Penny Presley's voice. "I can't say I've had the pleasure, but it has become blatantly obvious to me that I had no idea what Mark was doing. He could have been to the moon and back and I would have been the last to know. Is there anything else?"

Montoya sighed. Divorce was often ugly. This one had obviously been over the top.

"No, señora. Thank you for your time."

The click in his ear was her only goodbye.

He hung up the phone, made a couple of notes on his file, then dialed Information for the Dallas Police Department. From one cop to another, he was expecting his reception there would be warmer than the one he'd gotten from Presley's ex-wife.

He dialed again, absently tapping the end of his pen against the desk as he waited for the call to be answered. A few moments later, a soft-spoken female picked up.

"Dallas Police, how may I direct your call?"

"Homicide Division."

"Thank you."

This time his call was answered on the first ring.

"Homicide, Detective DeWitt."

"My name is Luis Montoya. I am a homicide detective in Chihuahua, Mexico, investigating the murder of a man named Solomon Tutuola."

"Yeah, so how can I help you?" DeWitt asked.

"We found some property that we think might have belonged to a man named Mark Presley. It was in a car belonging to my victim. I've been told Presley was convicted of murder, and I'm assuming it was your department that ran the case."

DeWitt's attention suddenly sharpened.

"You need to talk to Detective Bradley. He's the one who had the case. Hang on a minute, I'll put you through."

Again Montoya was put on hold, but only briefly, and this time the man who answered was more than ready to help.

"Detective Montoya…this is Bradley. How can I help you?"

Again Montoya explained the reason for his call, telling him about the murder, then about finding the card and the duffel bag full of clothes.

"So…here's my question," Montoya asked. "Was there any question about Presley acting on his own? Did you ever suspect he had hired someone to kill his girlfriend?"

Bradley frowned. "No. As far as we know, he acted alone. Believe me, if there had been someone else to blame, Presley would have done it. Why do you ask?"

"We have information that Tutuola was carrying a very large amount of money on him before he was killed. I'm trying to figure out where it came from. Someone might have wanted it bad enough to kill for it, but I need to know who else knew Tutuola had it."

"What kind of money are you talking about?" Bradley asked.

Montoya remembered the Realtor's description of a "bagful of money" and took a wild guess. "We have reason to believe there could have been as much as a million dollars in American money, maybe more."

"Presley was worth a hell of a lot more than that," Bradley said. "But when he was turned over to the American authorities at the border, he didn't have anything on him."

Montoya's heart skipped a beat. "He was arrested in Mexico?"

"Technically, he wasn't arrested there. It's a little complicated, but here's the deal. Mark Presley's private secretary was a woman named Marsha Benton. Her best friend was a woman named Cat Dupree. When Benton went missing, it was Dupree who suspected foul play. We didn't have any proof of Dupree's accusations against Presley, so she made it her business to do some investigating on her own."

"What do you know about this Cat Dupree?" Montoya asked.

"Oh, she's sort of a local legend here in Dallas. She works as a bounty hunter for a Dallas bondsman named Art Ball."

"Really," Montoya said, and made another notation.

Bradley sighed. He remembered all too well how disgusted Dupree had been with them for not going after Presley sooner. He had to admit, the man could easily have gotten away with murder if she hadn't been tracking him.

"Yes. It all came out in Dupree's statement when she turned him over to the Texas authorities at the border."

Now Montoya was impressed. "So it was this Cat Dupree who tracked Presley into Mexico?"

"Yes. She and another bounty hunter trailed Presley to an abandoned hacienda outside Nuevo Laredo. If I remember correctly, there was an explosion and then a fire during a gun battle. I believe Dupree stated that there was another man on the premises, but that he was an unknown who'd died in the fire."

"Ah…the fire," Montoya said, more to himself than to Bradley. That would have explained the healing burns that Realtor Chouie Garza had mentioned seeing when he sold Tutuola the property.

"So do you know where I can reach this lady bounty hunter?"

"Call Art Ball Bail Bonds. Hang on, I'll give you the number," Bradley said.

Montoya waited, then wrote down the number,

thanked Bradley for his help and disconnected. Just as he was about to make a second call to Dallas, all hell broke loose.

There was a loud explosion; then the desk at which he was sitting actually moved a good foot across the floor. Outside, he could hear screaming, and then the sounds of sirens.

"Madre de Dios!" he cried, as he ran to the windows.

Even though he had a clear view of what had happened, he found it difficult to believe his eyes. Three buildings less than two blocks away were on fire, and the flames were already jumping to the adjoining rooftops. Something had blown up. Whether it was an accident, arson or an attack remained to be seen.

He ran back to his desk, grabbed his gun from a drawer and headed out of the building as fast as he could run. Solomon Tutuola's murder would have to wait.

Three

The morning dawned gray and overcast and, as the day wore on, it continued to worsen. The air was sultry—barely stirring—and there was a gray-green cast to the clouds that warned of the possibility of hail accompanying the gathering storm.

Carter and Wilson were at the barn working on a hay rake. Every so often, one of them would stop and glance up at the sky before returning to work.

Cat was on her way to Austin with the radio on her favorite country station, while thinking of Shelly Green's hasty exit from Texas and her abusive boyfriend, Wayne.

She thought back to earlier that morning, when she'd received an unexpected call from the girl....

"Hey, Cat, it's me, Shelly Green."

Cat absently pushed up the sleeves of her yellow

shirt as she sat down to take the call, relieved to hear the girl's voice.

"How are you doing?" she asked.

"That's why I'm calling," Shelly said. "I just wanted you to know that I got me a job working at one of them Seattle coffee shops. They're all over the place, and you wouldn't believe how many ways they got to make a plain old cup of coffee."

Cat laughed. "Good for you. Did you find a safe place to live?"

"Yep. Nice little efficiency apartment over the garage of a retired dentist and his wife. I'll be fine. I just wanted you to know that and to tell you…to say…"

Cat heard the catch in Shelly's voice and knew she was trying not to cry.

"You're welcome," Cat said, then heard Shelly sigh before she managed to continue.

"I won't ever forget what you did for me, and I remember what you said. One day I'll pass the favor on, right?"

"Right," Cat said.

"So, I guess I'd better go. I don't want to be late for work. Thank you again, Cat Dupree."

"You're welcome," Cat said.

When the dial tone sounded, she disconnected,

then glanced at Dorothy, who was at the sink peeling potatoes.

"That was Shelly Green," Cat said. "She made it to Seattle, and she already has a job and an apartment."

Dorothy frowned. "Thanks to you," she said. "I don't know what might have happened to her if you hadn't come along. Wayne's family is just horrified by his behavior. I heard at church that his daddy is sending him to Michigan to live with his brother Joe, who's a cop up there."

Cat thought of the man who'd come close to ending their lives and decided that spending a few winters plowing through the Michigan snow would be good for him.

"Life is always a surprise in the making," Cat said, and then began washing her hands. "Want some help?"

Dorothy could tell Cat wasn't going to discuss her Good Samaritan act again, but it didn't matter.

Once, she'd feared her eldest child would wind up an old bachelor, but no more. She already had an opinion of the woman her son was in love with and she was thoroughly convinced the girl had been worth the wait.

"I'm making pie crusts," Dorothy said. "If you'll peel these apples, it will cut the prep time in half for me."

"Consider it done," Cat said, and happily began the task. Working in tandem with anyone, especially a woman, was new ground for her, and she was liking it.

A short while later, they had two pies in the oven and were cleaning up the kitchen when Wilson and Carter came in the house.

"Something smells good," Wilson said.

Carter winked at Cat as he moved past her and gave Dorothy a quick hug. "Honey, you make coming home a pleasure," he said softly, and kissed the side of her cheek.

Dorothy beamed.

"Come outside," Carter said. "I've got something to show you."

"What is it?" Dorothy asked.

"The old barn cat had herself some kittens, and she's gone and brought them all up to the house. I heard them mewing inside the old doghouse."

"Oh my goodness," Dorothy said, and hustled outside with Carter in the lead.

Cat sighed. The love between them was palpable. She glanced at Wilson, who was washing his hands at the sink, and thought how happy she was at this moment and how close she'd come to ruining their relationship. If Wilson had quit on her—if he hadn't come to Chihuahua, Mexico, looking for her—she would have died from the beating Solomon Tutuola had given her, and she knew it.

Suddenly she realized Wilson was watching her. Old habits made her want to shut down her emotions and turn away. Instead, she took a deep breath and forced herself to meet his gaze. The love she saw took her breath away. Her vision blurred.

Wilson saw the tears and quickly spoke.

"The parts Dad ordered for the hay baler are in. Would you mind picking them up? I'd go, but I don't want to leave Dad to lift the machinery we're working on by himself, and if I left, I know he would."

Cat frowned. "You'd better be careful of what you're lifting, too, mister. You haven't been out of the hospital long enough to impress me."

Wilson grinned. "I promise not to lift anything too heavy. So, do you mind going?"

"Of course not, but I'll have to drive your truck. My SUV is still in the shop."

Wilson slid his hands down her back, then cupped her backside and pulled her closer, settling her right between his legs.

"Now you know how I felt when I got that phone call from you in Chihuahua."

She sighed. "We sure haven't come to this place by an easy route."

He grinned. "There wasn't anything about you that was easy, but I can honestly say you're worth it."

Cat arched an eyebrow, then picked up her wallet.

"So where am I going in Austin?"

"The John Deere dealer. We passed it the other day when we were going out to dinner. Do you remember where it was?"

"I do. Do I just ask for Carter McKay's order?"

Wilson nodded. "That'll do it. Here's Dad's credit card. He's already called them to okay you signing for it."

"Good. I'm off, then. See you soon."

"Drive safe," Wilson said, and stole one last kiss.

Cat sighed when he pulled away, then headed outside, where she saw Dorothy on her knees beside the doghouse, with Carter squatting down beside her.

"How many?" Cat called.

"Five," Dorothy said. "And they're the cutest things. You'll have to help me name them when you get back."

"Count on it," Cat said, and waved goodbye.

Cat pulled herself back to the present as she walked into the equipment dealership, pausing in the doorway to orient herself. After spying the parts department sign, she headed that way. The man behind the counter was sporting the remnants of a sunburn and a fat lip. She knew enough about men not to mention either one. Instead, she pulled Carter McKay's credit card out of her pocket and leaned her elbows on the counter as the parts man gave her the once-over.

"Hello there, missy…exactly what can I do for you?"

"I came to pick up some baler parts for Carter McKay."

The leer morphed into courtesy so fast that Cat almost believed she'd imagined her first impression.

"Yes, ma'am. Right away, ma'am."

Then he yelled at someone standing halfway down the aisle behind him. "Hey, Junior. Wilson McKay's girl is here to pick up his dad's baler parts."

Cat's breath caught in the back of her throat as an old memory slammed into her so hard it brought tears to her eyes. All of a sudden she was seven years old again and standing at the checkout beside her father as an old woman leaned over the counter and looked down at her.

"Well, would you looky here," the old woman said. "It's Justin Dupree's little girl, Catherine."

Cat took a deep breath and made herself focus on the green and yellow John Deere logo painted on the wall, instead of on the emotions sweeping through her at the realization that for the first time in a long, long time, she belonged to someone again.

"Here you go, ma'am," the parts man said, and set a small box on the counter in front of her.

Not trusting herself to speak, she managed a smile as she slid the credit card forward. She signed her name, pocketed the card and the receipt, and picked up the box as the parts man glanced down at her signature, then back up at her.

"Real nice to meet you, Miss Dupree."

Cat smiled. "Call me Cat."

Her smile was a knockout, just like the woman who wore it. The parts man was toast. He watched her all the way out the door and then as she got into Wilson McKay's truck, all the while reminding himself it was a sin to covet another man's woman.

Cat was still smiling as she passed the Austin city limits sign, but her smile disappeared as she began noticing the rapid change in the weather. The sky had gone from partly cloudy to dark and threatening. It didn't look too good.

Thankful that she was on the way home instead of just starting out, she increased her speed. Spring in this part of Texas was beautiful, but it could also be deadly. Rain was expected, but tornadoes often accompanied spring storms, and those could get a body killed.

As she drove, she kept glancing up at the sky. The wall of clouds in the southwest was growing bigger and getting darker as the wind continued to strengthen, making it harder and harder to keep the truck on the road.

Stephanie Goodman was on her way to the pediatrician with her twin three-year-old boys when she topped the hill south of their home. One moment she'd been worrying about what could have caused their fevers to spike, and the next thing she knew it started to rain. She turned on the windshield wipers, and less than three minutes later was horrified as the raindrops turned into hail, hammering down like bullets.

Both boys started crying. Before she had time to calm them down, she drove out of the hail. Her relief was short-lived when she glanced to her right and saw a dark snake of whirling cloud drop out of the clouds. It appeared to be about a quarter of a mile away, which, in the grand scheme of storms, was too damned close. She glanced in her rearview mirror at her twins and felt a surge of fear unlike anything she'd ever known.

"Oh, God…oh, Jesus, please don't let this happen," she whispered, as she made a U-turn and stomped on the accelerator, praying she could make it to the McKay place.

* * *

Today was Billy Joe Culver's seventeenth birthday and, so far, the best day of his life. He'd awakened to the scent of blueberry pancakes and a set of car keys on his pillow.

"Oh shit, oh shit…no way man!" he yelled, and bounded out of bed with the keys in his hands. He ran out of the house wearing nothing but his underwear, piled into the brand-new red Dodge four-by-four, and drove it around the house and barns a half-dozen times before his mom waved him into the house to eat breakfast.

Then, because it was his birthday, she'd let him skip school.

Later that morning, he'd begged his dad to let him drive his new truck into Austin to pick up the horse feed. The last thing his dad had told him was to drive safe.

But Billy Joe had been unable to resist the urge to see what the truck could do, and because he was going ninety-five miles an hour when he topped the rise in the road, it took him a few moments to register the tail of a twister tearing through old man Waller's pasture. The first thing he thought of was that his brand-new truck was going to be ruined, and then it dawned on him that the situation didn't bode well for him, either.

With nothing but flat, nearly treeless land stretching out between him and Austin, he slowed down enough to turn around, then pushed the accelerator all the way to the floor just as it began to rain. The road to the McKay ranch was just a couple of miles back. He could take shelter there.

Cat was reaching for the cell phone to call Wilson and ask him about the weather when she drove into rain. It quickly turned to hail, which didn't make her feel any better. It was common knowledge to those versed in the ways of tornadoes that they were often concealed by hail or a rain-wrapped wall cloud.

She was only a couple of miles away from the turnoff to the ranch. Suddenly, the wind was so strong that it shifted the truck into the wrong lane of traffic.

"Oh lord…please help me get home in one piece."

Then she tightened her grip on the steering wheel and jammed the accelerator all the way to the floor.

One mile passed, and then she saw the turnoff and took it without slowing down. The rain was hitting the truck like bullets, and she was no longer ahead of the storm. She was driving parallel to it, the wind buffeting the truck so hard it was almost impossible to keep it on the road.

Suddenly her cell phone rang. She jumped but ignored it when a small tree flew past the hood of the truck. Her heart dropped. The only thing that would uproot a tree and then send it flying was a twister. She didn't know how close it was to her, but she didn't think she was going to beat it to the ranch, and she didn't want to die just when she'd found the best reason to live.

Wilson. Oh God. Wilson.

It was the last thing she thought before the truck went airborne. Cat started to scream, but the sound was lost in the roar of wind and rain. She had one glimpse of a rooftop sailing past her line of sight, and then a pig flew by upside down. After that, everything went black.

Wilson glanced at his wristwatch, then laid down the wrench and walked out of the toolshed. He looked up at the sky, then up the driveway. Cat should have been back by now. The wind was rising, and he could smell the rain. He was well aware that Cat could take care of herself, but that didn't stop him from worrying. All he needed was to hear her voice and he would be fine. He took his cell phone out of his pocket and had just started to call her when his mother came running out of the house carrying a laundry basket.

"Wilson! Wilson! The weatherman said there's a tornado on the ground and headed this way. Get your Dad and get to the cellar."

He saw his mother heading for the doghouse and realized she was going to get the old cat and the litter of kittens, and take them to the cellar with her.

"Dad!"

Carter had heard Dorothy yelling but didn't know what she'd said until he came out of the barn.

"What's wrong?" he asked.

"Mom says there's a twister on the ground and to get to the cellar."

Carter glanced toward the house. "Oh lord, she's after those cats." He took off running toward her.

Wilson was punching in Cat's number when he heard the sound of an engine coming fast. *Thank God.* He turned toward the driveway, but his relief was short-lived. It wasn't Cat. Moments later, the car came to a sliding halt at the front fence and he recognized Stephanie Goodman. When he saw she was trying to get two little kids out of the backseat, he ran to help her.

Stephanie was shaking so hard that she couldn't unlock the seat belts on their car seats.

"Here, I've got them," Wilson said, then pushed her aside, got one boy out and handed him over. Seconds later, he got the second one out.

"There's a tornado on the ground!" Stephanie cried. "We've got to get to the cellar."

"Follow Mom and Dad!" he said.

Stephanie grabbed her boys by the hands and began running as the first edge of the gust front hit. It knocked both boys off their feet and dragged Stephanie to her knees. Her scream alerted Carter, who saw her and ran to help.

Once she was safely in his parents' hands, he tried calling Cat's number again, but before he finished dialing, another vehicle came over the hill. His relief turned to panic when he saw it wasn't her, either. He didn't recognize the truck, but he knew the kid who got out. It was Jordan Culver's boy.

"Tornado! On the ground!" Billy Joe screamed.

At that moment the hail hit. The boy shrieked, then wrapped his arms over his head for protection. "My truck! It's gonna ruin my new truck!"

Wilson yanked him toward the cellar as hail slammed into their faces, dialing Cat's number as they ran.

"Quit worrying about your truck and worry about your hide. Run, boy!" Wilson yelled. "Get in the cellar—now!"

Then they both heard the whine—a high-pitched scream of wind and power that sounded like an approaching freight train.

"Oh, no!" Billy Joe screamed, and bolted for the cellar.

Wilson was right behind him with the cell phone

held to his ear. All the way to the cellar, then down the steps and into the concrete-walled room, he kept listening to the ringing and waiting for the sound of Cat's voice. It never came.

It was the silence after the din that brought them all up out of the cellar. Wilson went first, praying that his truck would be back now, with Cat sitting in it, wondering where everyone had gone. Dorothy was carrying one of Stephanie's boys. Stephanie carried the other. Carter had the basketful of cats and was coming out behind Billy Joe, who vaulted up the steps, anxious to see what damage had been done to his birthday present.

The house was still standing, as were the shade trees and the barn, but debris was everywhere. A tree branch was hanging half in and half out of one front window, but the roof appeared intact.

Billy Joe ran to his truck, bemoaning the broken back window and the hail dents in the hood. Wilson saw his father put the cats back in the doghouse, then began helping the kid clean the glass off his truck seats.

Dorothy was walking Stephanie to her car, which had survived the storm with nothing but some hail dings. He watched her help the young mother buckle the boys back in their car seats and wave her off.

Billy Joe finished brushing the glass off the

driver's seat and started to get inside when his cell phone began to ring. Wilson heard him telling his mother where he'd been, and that he was fine and heading for home.

Wilson stared down at his own cell phone, as if willing it to tell him where Cat was. But there were no missed calls or voice messages waiting to be listened to. He started to dial her number again, then changed his mind and dropped the phone in his pocket.

"Dad, I need the keys to your truck. Cat isn't answering her phone, and she should have been back long before now. I'm going to look for her."

"I'm going with you," Carter said.

Dorothy glanced at the tree branch through the window.

"What about that?" she asked.

"We'll deal with it when we get back," Carter said as he palmed his keys. "Get in, Wilson. I'm driving."

Wilson didn't care and didn't argue. All he wanted was to get moving.

His stomach was already in a knot and, as they started up the driveway toward the highway, worry turned to fear. Destruction was everywhere.

"Oh, no…Dad…where the hell is she?" he whispered.

Carter glanced at him once, then gritted his teeth and focused on avoiding the debris on the road.

"Don't borrow trouble, son. She could have taken shelter almost anywhere."

"She would have called."

Carter sighed. It was hard to argue with the truth.

They had topped the hill and started down when Wilson glanced over into the pasture on his right.

"The fence is down, Dad."

Carter nodded. "It's okay. I moved the cattle out of there last week. We'll fix it later."

As they neared the highway, a news van was coming toward them. Wilson could see the passenger hanging out the driver's side window filming the evidence of the destruction. Then he heard the familiar whap-whap sound of helicopter rotors and glanced up. Another news crew.

"How do they get out and about so fast?" Carter muttered, more to himself than to Wilson.

Wilson heard his father's voice, but couldn't make out the words. His mind was trying to get past the sight of a truck bed sticking out of the north end of the stock pond. He grabbed the dash with one hand and the door handle with the other.

"Stop," Wilson said.

"What's up, son?" Carter asked.

"Dad! Stop! Now!"

Wilson was already opening the door before Carter hit the brakes, and he was out and running as

Carter slammed the shift into Park. Carter was yelling at him to be careful, but Wilson didn't hear. His heart was pounding so hard he couldn't hear himself breathe as he cleared the ditch and kept on running.

Carter cursed beneath his breath. Wilson wasn't in any shape to be jumping stuff. Dorothy would have his hide if he brought their eldest son back to the house in any condition other than safe. Still, he knew Wilson well enough to know something must be wrong. He shifted into four-wheel drive and drove off the highway across the ditch, then through the break in the fence where the wire was down. He didn't know the news crew had noticed the same thing Wilson had until he glanced up in his rearview mirror and saw them following.

He frowned, then glanced up at the chopper overhead.

"What the hell?"

It wasn't until he saw the back bumper and part of a truck bed sticking out of the pond that he panicked. God in heaven, it looked like Wilson's truck.

Catherine!

Wilson didn't know or care that his hasty exit had started a parade of vehicles trailing him to the pond. But he knew now why Cat hadn't answered the phone.

The sky was clearing. Patches of blue were showing through the swiftly moving clouds, which seemed wrong. How could the weather be improving when his life was going to hell? Rain had collected in indentations in the ground, and now it splattered up and onto the legs of his jeans as he ran. The body of a steer lay up against what appeared to be a piece of someone's roof, but he didn't give the macabre scene so much as a glance.

Even before he reached the pond, he knew it was his truck. Seeing the plate number only confirmed his worst fear. By the time he reached the water, he was shaking. Without hesitation, he pulled off his boots, dropped his cell phone inside them and went into the water, then began feeling his way along the truck body until he reached the door. He took a deep breath and went under, desperately pulling at the handle, but no matter how hard he yanked, the door wouldn't budge. It was wedged too deeply into the mud.

God…please don't do this now…not after everything we've been through.

Out of breath, he was forced to emerge. He paused only long enough to take a deep breath, then went back under.

He was feeling his way along the truck body to the other side, trying not to think of the obvious implications. He found the other handle, but that door wouldn't give, either. He pulled and pulled until his lungs were bursting. In fear and frustration, he shot to the surface.

Carter was in the water a few yards away.

"Wilson! Is she there?" he yelled.

Wilson didn't answer. He was already going back under, even though he knew too much time had passed. Even though he knew she might not even be inside. Even though…

His mind was racing as he began to move along the length of the truck again—this time aiming for the hood. He felt the curve of metal, then the place where the windshield should have been. To his horror, it was gone. He pulled himself up and inside the cab, operating entirely on touch. He found the steering wheel first, then felt the back of the seat. Desperate to find her, but dreading the first moment of contact, he kept searching until he realized that she wasn't inside. Scared out of his mind that she was somewhere on the muddy bottom but also hoping against hope that she might have made it out under her own power, he was forced to surface once again.

He came up gasping for air, then drew a breath and let it out in a roar of pain so pure that tears came to Carter's eyes. Believing that Wilson must have found her body, he started toward his son, wading as quickly as he could through the muddy pond.

But Wilson wasn't waiting for comfort. He dragged himself out and onto the bank, then pulled himself upright before looking back into the pond.

Except for the ripples his exit had caused, the surface of the water was almost placid, unlike his thoughts.

Carter came out of the water and ran to him.

"Son?"

"She wasn't inside."

They both stared at the muddy water, imagining her lifeless body lying somewhere beneath.

"I'll call the sheriff," Carter offered.

Wilson covered his face and then dropped his hands to his sides. The sound that came up from his throat was physical heartbreak.

Carter flinched; then his vision blurred. There was only one thing worse than being hurt himself, and that was watching someone he loved suffer.

Wilson grabbed his boots, dumped the cell phone out onto the ground, and then put them on as his father was making the call.

He pocketed his phone, then began talking to himself. "This isn't happening. I don't believe this is the way Catherine Dupree is supposed to die. She survived death three times at the hand of man. I do not buy the premise that nature takes her out."

Carter slid a hand on Wilson's shoulder.

"The sheriff is already out surveying damage. They relayed the message to him."

Wilson turned, his anger obvious.

"Relayed? As in…he'll get to it when he gets time?" Then he hit the sides of his legs with his fists.

Carter was sick at heart. The pain on his son's face was terrifying. "Wilson…son. We have no control over—"

Wilson turned on his dad, his rage evident.

"No! Not like this. Never like this."

Before Carter could stop him, Wilson started walking.

"Wilson, wait! Where the hell are you going?"

But Wilson wasn't listening. He started circling the pond, looking for anything to give himself hope. With the windshield missing, she could have climbed out of the truck on her own. All he needed were some tracks coming out of the mud at the edge. He was halfway around the pond when he paused to survey the backside of the dam at the far end. Suddenly his heart skipped a beat. A boot! There was a boot down the slope lying next to a rock.

Without caution, he headed down, running and slipping in the wet muddy grass as he went.

Four

Wilson's stomach knotted. Even before he picked up the boot, he knew it was Cat's. He'd watched her put her boots on—and take them off—far too many times to be mistaken.

The cold leather and the water inside it gave him a sick, empty feeling. He dumped out the water, then began scanning the land, searching for any sign of the woman who held his heart.

In the distance, he saw something yellow fluttering from the branches of a piece of scrub brush and started toward it, still clutching the boot. The closer he got, the more certain he was that it was a piece of the shirt she'd been wearing. He took a slow, shaky breath and kept moving, using the small bit of color as his anchor to sanity.

As he trudged through the pasture, it became

evident that he wasn't as fully recovered from his gunshot wounds and surgery as he'd believed. After three dunks in the pond, and now this, the muscles in his legs were beginning to ache. His heart was pounding as he moved closer to the bush. It wasn't until he picked up the fabric caught on the thorns that the horror of what he was holding began to sink in and he knew for sure. If the storm had ripped the windshield out of the truck, Cat could have gone with it. He couldn't let himself think of finding her in pieces, as he was finding her clothes.

He brushed the bit of yellow cloth against the side of his face, swallowed past the knot in his throat, and then put the fabric in his pocket and kept on moving.

There had been a small grove of trees about a hundred yards from the dam. They were gone. Ripped up by the roots. He paused, staring down at the holes in the ground like a man in a trance, as if their absence was a clue to Catherine's whereabouts.

Tears were streaming down his face, but he didn't feel them. He was numb from the inside out to everything but fear. Finally he looked up and turned around.

Another dead pig lay a short distance away. Already a swarm of flies was beginning to gather. He gritted his teeth as he looked away. Focusing on death wasn't an option. Not yet. Not until he was faced with the undeniable proof.

A shadow passed across the ground in front of him. He tilted his head, suddenly aware that the news chopper was still there. Then he saw the cameraman waving wildly and saw him pointing out into the pasture beyond where he was standing.

He turned to look, and that was when he saw it.

Movement.

In the distance.

His heart ricocheted against his ribcage with a sharp, painful thud. Someone in brown clothing was walking toward him—no, staggering. Suddenly the figure disappeared, and for a moment Wilson thought he'd imagined it. But when the figure reappeared on the horizon, he realized that whoever it was had just fallen down and was in the act of getting up again.

He started walking, his stride long and measured. The closer he got to the figure, the more anxious he became, but it wasn't until he realized it was a woman and saw her long dark hair that it hit him.

Catherine!

She'd done it again. Survived when the odds were against her.

He dropped her boot and began to run—forgetting that their reunion was about to be caught on tape by the film crew in the air.

The closer he got, the faster his heart beat. She was

covered in mud and leaves, and her hair was plastered to her face and neck. There wasn't a stitch of clothing left on her body, but she was in one piece, and all he could do was praise God for the miracle. When he got close enough for her to hear him, he began calling her name.

Cat had come to, flat on her back in the middle of a pasture, lying on top of what appeared to be a windshield and staring up at a scattering of clouds partially covering a pale blue sky. She took a breath and then moaned. Everything hurt, but she couldn't remember why.

When she tried to sit up, the world went crazy, dipping and swaying and turning in circles. She grabbed hold of the only available stability—the windshield on which she was lying—and held on for dear life until the spinning stopped.

When it finally did, she realized that, except for a layer of mud and leaves, she was naked. There were streaks of blood mixed with the mess—which explained the burning sensation she was feeling all over her skin—but she still couldn't remember what had happened.

It wasn't until she got to her feet and saw the debris left by the tornado's aftermath that understanding dawned. She remembered turning off the highway and starting down the long road leading to the ranch when she'd gotten swept up by the storm.

Her thoughts went immediately to Wilson. What if the tornado had hit the ranch?

She needed to find him. She needed to see his face. All she had to do was put one foot in front of the other, but as soon as she tried, it became apparent that it was easier said than done.

Movement caused pain—and pain caused confusion. She didn't know which direction to go, or even if she could stay upright. But she had to find Wilson, and to do that, she had to move.

She stumbled through the pasture, falling to her knees more than once. It was the overwhelming need to survive that kept driving her to get back up and keep going. Too dizzy to focus and too determined to stay upright, she was oblivious to everything but the effort needed to keep walking until, in the distance, she thought she heard a helicopter— and beneath that, the sound of someone yelling. Someone calling her. But who? Where? Then she saw movement in the distance.

Someone had found her! Someone was coming to help. A few steps farther and she realized she knew that voice—and the man behind it. She began to weep.

She could see him clearly now and began to

shake, her heart hammering against her eardrums until she thought her head was going to explode. It never occurred to her to be concerned that she was naked. She couldn't have cared less if the whole world saw. All that mattered was the man who caught her up into his arms and swept her off her feet. The man who loved her. She heard him thanking God for sparing her right before he buried his face in the curve of her neck and began to cry.

Cat felt the tremors in his body as sharply as the ones in her own. She couldn't find the words to say what she was feeling. All she could do was hold on.

Finally Wilson lifted his head, running his fingers over her face, then her body, oblivious to the transfer of mud from her to him. He saw some abrasions and scratches, but in the grand scheme of things, they didn't matter. All that mattered was that she was still in one piece.

"Catherine…Catherine…oh, God…I thought I'd lost you."

He shook his head, then pulled her to him again.

"I don't know what happened," Cat said.

"It doesn't matter, baby," he said gently. "In fact, it's just as well. Revisiting hell is never a good idea."

Cat stifled a sob as Wilson resisted the urge to tighten his grip. He couldn't tell if or where she was hurt and didn't want to make things worse. But what he did know was that her presence was a miracle.

Once, when he'd been a kid, he'd seen a whole house taken completely off its foundations and dropped into a pasture a half mile away, while leaving a cup and saucer completely intact on the kitchen table back where it once had stood. The fact that this tornado hadn't skinned her alive was enough for him.

All of a sudden he remembered the helicopter overhead and the approaching vehicles behind him. He popped the snaps on his shirt, yanked it off and then helped her put it on. His hands were shaking as he struggled to fasten it back up. The shirt covered her to mid-thigh. It would have to do.

When he'd finished, he hugged her again, then laid his cheek against the crown of her head.

"The truck is in the pond. I thought you were in it."

Cat shuddered, then closed her eyes as he held her.

"I tried to tell myself it would take more than an act of God to take you down." Then he stood back and fixed her with a pointed look. "You have, however, just used up your fourth life. I'm asking you to be a little more cautious with the last five."

His reference to the old wives tale about a feline having nine lives was not lost on Cat.

She'd survived the car wreck that had killed her mother when she was six; then, at the age of thirteen, she'd lived even after having her throat cut as she watched her father being murdered. Less than two months ago, she'd been beaten to the edge of death by Solomon Tutuola. Now this. Wilson was right. She was pushing her luck.

Behind them, she heard someone honking a horn. Startled, she flinched, then swayed.

Wilson quickly steadied her.

"Hang on to me, baby."

Reality was beginning to surface. People were approaching, and she was a disaster in progress. She felt her hair, then her cheeks, before peeling a leaf from her neck.

"My clothes…I don't know what happened to my clothes."

Wilson cupped her face, then bent until their foreheads were touching.

"They're in pieces all over the damned pasture," he said. "I was afraid you were, too."

Cat leaned against him as the sound of an approaching vehicle became louder. Wilson watched his father driving across the pasture, dodging debris as he went. In his wake were the camera crew and their van.

"It's Dad," Wilson said.

Cat turned to look; then her eyes widened. "The others? Who are they?"

"News crews. They're all over the place, filming the destruction. Dad and I ran into them when we were looking for you."

Carter came to an abrupt stop, slammed the shift into Park and got out on the run. He'd been so sure Cat was at the bottom of the pond... To see her alive and standing was more than a miracle.

"Lord have mercy, girl...you're okay. You're okay."

He wanted to hug her but was afraid he would hurt something beneath all the mess, so he settled for a soft pat on the back. "Come on to the truck, honey. We need to get the both of you home. Wilson went in the water after you three times. Last time he went under, I didn't think he was gonna come up. I was already planning on where to hide, because I knew I couldn't go home and face Dorothy without our kids."

At that, Cat began weeping openly again.

"Lord, don't do that," Carter muttered, as he swiped at his eyes. "You're gonna have all of us bawling like babies. So let's get in the truck before those newspeople get here and want an interview."

"I'll get the seats filthy," Cat said.

"I don't give a damn," Wilson said as he swept

Cat off her feet and carried her to the truck. He sat her on his lap as Carter started the engine, his arms around her shoulders, hoping to cushion the ride as the truck took off, bouncing across rough ground on the way back to the road. They passed a news crew that tried to flag them down.

"Don't stop," Cat begged.

"Don't worry, honey. I won't," Carter said.

As they drove past the pond, Cat gasped.

"Is that your truck?"

Wilson wouldn't even look at it. He just kept looking at her.

"I thought you were in it," he said.

Cat heard the break in his voice and shuddered. But for the grace of God, she would have been. Then she closed her eyes. She'd seen all the tornado damage she cared to.

By the time they cleared the field and got out onto the road, the news crew had obviously decided what they had on film was enough and went in the opposite direction, off to the next scene of disaster.

It was none too soon for Wilson. But when they reached the ranch, the yard was full of vehicles. The limb that had gone through the living room window was gone, and his brother Charlie was nailing a piece of plywood over the opening, while two of his sisters were sweeping up glass. He could see one brother-in-law down at the corral nailing up a broken panel and another throwing debris into the back of his pickup.

"Looks like Mom made a few phone calls," Wilson said.

Then Dorothy came out of the house carrying a blanket.

Carter sighed. "Yeah, and I did, too. I called your mom after you found Catherine. If she's still crying, don't say anything. It'll only make her cry harder."

Wilson gave Cat a quick kiss on the cheek. "You know the routine," he said. "Just let her fuss. You'll both feel better."

The thought of facing everyone in this condition was daunting. Cat clutched Wilson's hand. "Don't leave me."

He just shook his head. "Don't worry, baby. After all this, you'd have to kill me to get rid of me."

Cat exhaled shakily as Dorothy reached the truck, took one look at Cat and burst into tears.

Carter frowned. He couldn't bear to hear a woman crying, especially one of his.

"Now, Dorothy, don't cry. She's gonna be all right."

Dorothy began swiping at her tears as she wrapped the blanket around Cat's shoulders, then held her close.

"I've never been so scared. We thought we'd

lost you. Thank God. Thank God. As soon as we get the both of you cleaned up, we're heading for the emergency room."

Cat wouldn't—couldn't—argue. She was overwhelmed by the depth of everyone's concern, and when the rest of the family began crowding around her, all talking at once and marveling at what had happened to her, she couldn't stop the tears. She glanced back once, just to make sure Wilson was still behind her. When she saw him, her gaze went straight to his wet, muddy clothes and his bare chest. The healing bullet wounds were still an angry red. He didn't look any better than she felt.

She pushed her way through the crowd and reached for him. Wilson grabbed her hand, then stepped up beside her. She patted his chest.

"You need to warm up and get into some dry clothes," she said, then looked to Dorothy for confirmation.

"And so do you," Dorothy added.

Cat nodded. As long as they were on the same page regarding Wilson's recovery, everything was good.

The family followed them down the hall, stopping short at the door to their bedroom.

"If you need something, give a yell," Dorothy said, then kissed Cat on the cheek. "Thank the lord you're all right."

Then she shooed everyone away, leaving Cat and Wilson to tend to their own cleaning up. They went inside, and for a moment simply savored the silence. After the desolation they'd witnessed outside, the familiarity of their neatly kept bedroom seemed surreal. But the longer Cat stood, the stiffer and colder she was getting.

Wilson saw her shiver.

"Into the shower with you," he said gently.

"You first," Cat said, concerned about the exertion he'd suffered.

"No, baby. Together. You're shivering, and I can already see bruises beneath the mud. Let's get clean and warm, then we'll deal with the rest of it."

Cat sighed.

Together.

It had taken her a long time to accept it, but as long as they were together, she knew she could face anything.

The trip to the emergency room had been brief. Wilson was given a thumbs-up quicker than Cat. The staff had taken X-rays to make sure she didn't have any broken bones, a concussion had been ruled out, and they'd cleaned all her cuts and abrasions. None were deep enough to need stitches, so she'd been sent home with pain pills and blessings.

Now night had come, but Wilson couldn't sleep. Every time he closed his eyes, he kept seeing the back end of his truck sticking out of the water and Cat floating lifelessly inside it.

Cat was restless, too. Twice she'd cried out in her sleep, and both times he'd eased her with a touch and a whisper in her ear to remind her she was safe. But when she woke just before daylight and slid her arms around his neck, his exhaustion disappeared.

"Make love to me, Wilson. My mind has been stuck on rewind all night. If I have to relive those moments when I thought I was going to die one more time, I'll scream. I need to remember what it's like to be alive."

Wilson rose up on one elbow to gaze down at her face. The room was lit by the blue glow of a full moon shining through the gap in the curtains. Even in the dimness, the scratches and bruises on her body were more pronounced than they'd been when they'd gone to sleep. But then he looked in her eyes. They were on fire. She was still the same strong, audacious woman she'd been when they'd first met, coming down a staircase in a blazing building with an unconscious man slung over her shoulder, demanding he get out of her way.

"Honestly, Cat, I'm scared to touch you. You're covered in bruises."

"They're only skin deep. The ache I have for you is bottomless."

He sighed. That was persuasion he couldn't ignore.

He kissed her then, and heard the sound of a sob—soft, barely detectable. He knew how she felt.

"I love you, Catherine. So much," he whispered, and then began a slow journey of rediscovery, making sure he acknowledged every scratch and bruise on her skin—first with his fingers, then with his lips.

She was his life.

The fear that had accompanied Cat into sleep was gone, replaced by a building fire deep in her belly. The man who'd fought so hard to win her heart was reminding her how much she was loved. She knew his tenderness, felt his passion, accepted his love. When she felt his mouth on the inside of her thigh, she moaned.

Wilson hesitated, then looked up.

"Did I hurt you?"

Cat slid her fingers through his hair and grabbed hold.

"Only if you stop."

Moonlight caught on the single earring in his ear, then on the glitter in his eyes.

"Close your eyes," he said.

Cat turned loose of his hair and grabbed hold of the headboard instead. It was none too soon. She felt his fingers, then his mouth, then the warmth of his breath as he took her where she wanted to go.

The first climax came hard and fast, rocking Cat to her bones and leaving her gasping for breath. Before she knew what was happening, he took her back to the peak, then up and over—this time shattering what was left of her.

By the time he was inside her, she was weeping.

"Are you still afraid?" he asked.

"No…God, no."

"Tell me, Catherine. I need to hear you say it."

"I love you."

He sighed.

She said it again. "I love you, Wilson."

He slid his hands beneath her hips.

She raised her arms, pulling him down until his cheek was resting in the curve of her neck.

"I don't just love you. I want to have babies with you. I want to grow old with you."

Her words humbled him. He rose up on his elbows as she added one last request.

"Make love to me again, Wilson."

"Again?"

"Yes, but this time…do it for you."

She saw his nostrils flare, and then a muscle jerked on the side of his cheek as he swept her away.

There had been a time today when he had feared he would never hear her laughter or share a moment like this with her again. Making love to her now was an affirmation of their miracle.

He wrapped his arms around her, then let himself go, rocking her world—taking them both on a collision course.

Time ceased.

Muscles burned.

Perpetual motion was a given, addictive, then explosive.

Wilson felt it building—and never wanted it to end, even though he was aching for release.

Then it came, sudden and shattering. He buried his face against her shoulder, stifling the groan that boiled up his throat as his climax exploded. He clung to Cat like a lifeline as the aftershocks rippled through him.

Jimmy Franks was sitting at the counter of a small café, nursing a cup of coffee and licking the remnants of a sugared doughnut from his fingers when another customer, a short man with red hair sitting three seats down from him, pointed to the television on the wall behind the counter.

"Hey, Angie, turn that up, will you?"

The waitress, Angie Sherman, upped the volume.

"I've already seen this twice, and it still brings tears to my eyes," she said.

Jimmy shifted his focus from having another doughnut to the news anchor who was doing a voice-over accompanying footage shot after yesterday's tornado.

"In the midst of yesterday's death and destruction, we have all witnessed a true miracle. While our chopper pilot and a news crew were filming the aftermath of the tornado that swept through the outskirts of Austin and points west yesterday, they captured this real-life drama."

Jimmy leaned forward, watching as the news crew began filming men arriving at the scene of destruction.

"Look," Angie said. "There's the man finding the truck in the pond. Now he's going into that water. Just look at his face. You can tell he thinks the driver is inside. Lord, lord, can you imagine the panic?"

The redheaded man took another bite of his biscuits and gravy as Angie continued her play-by-play.

"Look. There's where he comes up the first time. Then he goes back down. They said that older man is his father. He looks so worried. Now the man comes up out of the water, takes a big breath and goes back down for the third time."

Jimmy wished she would just shut up. They could see and hear for themselves, but Angie was too caught up in the drama to be quiet.

"Now watch! This is where he comes up out of the water and screams. Oh lordy…this just about broke my heart the first time. I thought he'd found the body and couldn't get it out or something. Then when he walked away, I didn't know what to think."

Jimmy took another sip of his coffee and thought, *So the guy was having a bad day. Well, welcome to my world.*

"He's a bounty hunter, you know," Angie said. "I heard them talking about it later. Said the woman he thought was in the pond was his fiancée. She's a bounty hunter, too."

Jimmy's eyes widened. Bounty hunter? Now that he thought about it, the man who'd been in the water looked a little like Wilson McKay.

"Uh…lady, what did you just say?"

Angie turned around, saw who was talking and almost turned her back on him. He smelled real bad; it had been all she could do to serve him. Now he wanted to start a conversation?

"I said the man is a bounty hunter. Got an office right here in Dallas."

"Did they give a name?" Jimmy asked.

"Why? You need bailing out from somewhere?"

Jimmy glared. "Do I look like I'm in jail?"

She shrugged. "I can't rightly say what you look like. I do know you need a bath."

Before Jimmy could fire back a retort, the news anchor gave him the answer.

"…McKay, a bail bondsman from right here in Dallas. The incident happened on the family ranch west of Austin, where McKay had gone to recover after being shot during an attempt on his life. Talk about a string of bad luck… Or maybe I should say, good luck. He did survive his gunshot wounds, and his fiancée, Cat Dupree, just survived a tornado. What do we have here, anyway—the Six Million Dollar Man and the Bionic Woman?"

The newscast was over. Jimmy stood up without comment and walked out of the café. Now he knew where McKay had gone. All he had to do was find a way to get there.

Luis Montoya was back in the office. He and most of the other detectives had spent the past thirty-six hours looking for the man who'd been running a meth lab in the back room of a tile factory. The explosion had turned out to be the fault of the men who'd been cooking the meth. Two had died and one was still in the hospital, suffering from third-degree burns over most of his body. They'd finally caught the head of the operation when he tried to sneak into the hospital to see his friend.

But now that was over and he was rereading his notes on the people he'd interviewed regarding Tutuola. After a long review, he decided he wasn't any closer to solving the murder of Solomon Tutuola than he had been when he'd started.

He'd interviewed the Realtor who'd sold Tutuola the property on which he'd been killed.

He'd interviewed the couple who'd been hired to cook and clean.

He'd talked to the appropriate homicide detective in the Dallas, Texas, police department regarding Tutuola's connection to convicted murderer Mark Presley.

He did know how Tutuola had come by the burn scars, but the money everyone claimed he'd had was missing, and, Luis suspected, was the reason he'd been killed.

He was at a dead end here in Chihuahua, and what happened next was up to his commander. Either he gave Luis the okay to backtrack along the path Tutuola had taken to get to their city, or the case was going to be shelved and classified as a cold case.

So he gathered up his notes and the files he'd compiled, and headed for his captain's office.

Thirty minutes later, he was on his way home to pack a bag. He didn't know whether to be glad or sorry that he'd made such a persuasive case. He did know that Conchita was not going to be happy about the fact that he was going to be gone for her birthday. Such was his life. He'd missed many family events during the years they'd been married. But it was also this job that kept them in a nice house, with money to travel now and then. His brother was nothing but a day laborer, and he and his wife and six kids were often down to nothing but tortillas and beans to put in their bellies at night.

Conchita had, as of yet, been unable to conceive. The absence of children left a huge empty spot in their lives, and the demands of his job only increased her loneliness. Still, there wasn't anything to be done about it. His job was his job, and he was fortunate to have it.

So Luis kept going over the facts in his mind as he packed, tossing in a couple of changes of clothes and reminding himself to get extra cash before he left. It wasn't going to take all that long to get from Chihuahua to Nuevo Laredo, but he didn't know what he would encounter along the way. Then he heard Conchita talking and realized she was home.

She was still on the phone when she came into the bedroom, but when she saw he was packing a suitcase, she ended her call and sat down on the side of the bed. The look on her face was one Luis had seen before.

"You're leaving again?" she asked.

"Yes."

"For how long this time?"

"Maybe two or three days."

There was an odd expression in her eyes, but he didn't want to go there, knowing it would only result in another fight.

She sighed, then looked away.

"It's my birthday tomorrow. What do I do while you're gone?" she asked.

Luis didn't know how to answer her, and because he felt frustrated, his remarks sounded short.

"Whatever you want to do," he said. "You should be glad you don't have to work."

She looked up at him then, her dark eyes swimming in tears.

"Yes, I am a very lucky woman," she said softly, and walked out of the room without looking back.

He felt like a heel, but it had been said, and he didn't know how to take it back without making things worse.

A few minutes later he was packed. He went to find her to tell her goodbye, only to find that she was nowhere to be found. When he went out to his car, he realized hers was gone.

He cursed beneath his breath, then got in and drove away. When he got back, he would make it up to her—maybe take her to Mazatlán for a quick holiday. She had family there.

Convinced that everything was fine, he never looked back.

Five

Cat put down the hair dryer, then combed her fingers through her hair before giving her face and arms the once-over. It had been three days since the storm, and while the scratches on her body were beginning to heal, the bruises were vivid hues of purple and green. There was even one bruise on her back shaped like a hoofprint. Wilson had gone through the roof when he'd seen it, and she'd understood. Thinking about how it must have gotten there gave her the creeps. She was just grateful to be alive.

She left the bathroom with slow, measured steps, paying homage to her new bruises. Today she'd chosen to wear her oldest, softest pair of jeans and a T-shirt, but since she'd lost her boots during the tornado, she was down to socks and some old moccasins.

If the tornado hadn't dumped Wilson's truck in

the pond, and if she weren't so miserably sore, she would have taken herself into Austin for a quick shopping trip. But for now she was going to have to be happy with going downstairs.

Art Ball had seen the video of her rescue and called her every day since. He wasn't just her boss, he was her friend, and she'd hated the thought of letting him down. After speaking to him last night, she'd been relieved to learn that he'd hired another bounty hunter full time. Although he'd assured her that she had a job with him any time she wanted it, they both knew her bounty hunting days were over.

The phone was ringing as she started down the hall, and she thought of Art again. Following the murmur of voices, she joined the rest of the family, who were already in the kitchen. Carter was standing outside on the porch with the phone to his ear, and when Wilson saw her, he came to meet her with a good-morning kiss.

"Morning, Tinkerbell. How are you feeling?"

"Tinkerbell?"

"She flew. You flew. The only difference between the two of you is her wings."

Cat ignored him, but Dorothy took umbrage.

"Wilson, for heaven's sake. Don't tease her about that."

"Can't help it, Mom. If I don't keep things on the

light side, I'll wind up bawling all over again," Wilson said, as he pulled a chair out from the table so Cat could sit down.

"It's okay, I'll get him back. I'm good at waiting," she said as she settled herself slowly into the seat.

Wilson thought of all the years she'd bided her time, waiting to avenge her father's murder. She was a formidable enemy, and he considered himself lucky they were on the same side.

At that moment, Carter walked back into the kitchen. "Hey, if I'd known you were up, I would have passed the phone to you."

"Why?" Cat asked.

"That was some journalist wanting to talk to you." Cat frowned. "No."

"That's pretty much what I told him," Carter said. "However, you get to tell the next one yourself."

"Next one?"

"They've been calling by the dozen ever since that video aired," Wilson said.

Cat's expression tightened. "And they've seen all of my naked butt they're going to see. All I can say is I'm really glad I was coated in muck. It covered a multitude of sins."

Dorothy chuckled. "You crack me up, honey. I love a woman with a sense of humor."

The phone rang again.

Everyone turned to Cat.

"Don't look at me," she muttered. "I'm eating breakfast."

She got up and moved to the counter to put a slice of bread in the toaster, while Dorothy poured her a cup of coffee, leaving Wilson to answer the phone.

"Hello?"

"This is Turner's Body Shop. That you, Wilson?"

"Hey, Greg. Yeah, it's me."

"Dang, man. I seen you and your girl on the TV the other day. Real glad that turned out okay."

"Me, too," Wilson said. "So…is Cat's car ready?"

"Yep. The insurance adjuster was the only thing holding us up. As soon as he came and went, we got right on it. You can pick it up anytime."

"We'll be in before noon," Wilson said.

"See you then," Greg said.

Wilson disconnected, then looked at Cat.

"Your car is fixed."

She sighed. "We'll see how long I can keep it in one piece. I sure didn't do your truck any good."

Wilson couldn't bring himself to joke about the truck, because it just reminded him of how close she'd come to dying.

"That tornado was not your fault. Besides, as long as you didn't go into the pond with it, I could care less."

Cat carried her coffee and toast to the table, and sat down. Wilson took the chair beside her, kissed the side of her cheek, then whispered against her ear, "Love you, baby."

She paused with the toast halfway to her lips, then surprised herself by turning her head and meeting his lips halfway.

"Love you, too," she said softly.

Wilson grinned, then leaned back. "I'll sit with you while you eat, then Dad and I will go get your car."

Cat thought about going, but she had too many bruises to want to face the world. Instead, she reached for the jelly and put a spoonful onto her toast. She took a bite, and as she did, her stomach rolled. Startled by the unexpected nausea, she swallowed quickly and reached for the coffee. The cup was in her hand when her stomach rolled again.

Wilson and Carter were in the middle of a conversation about where else they needed to go while they were in Austin, and Dorothy was at the sink.

"Uh…excuse me. I just remembered something. I'll be right back," Cat said, and headed for her bedroom.

The closer she got, the more certain she was that she was going to throw up. It was too long after the wreck for concussion symptoms, and it couldn't be food poisoning, because they'd all had the same thing last night and no one else was ill. She hit the door with the flat of her hand and dashed through the room, making it to the bathroom just in time.

She threw up until there was nothing left in her stomach. Finally she flushed the toilet, then staggered to the sink to wash her face and hands. She was brushing her teeth when Wilson came in.

"Honey, are you okay?"

She nodded.

"Why are you brushing your teeth? You didn't finish your breakfast."

She shrugged, then rinsed and wiped her mouth.

"I just threw up. I think I've taken too many pain pills on an empty stomach. I'll let my tummy rest a bit and then give food a try later."

Concern was in his voice and in the gentleness of his touch. "Are you sure?" He felt her forehead, thinking she might be coming down with a fever.

"I'm fine," she said. "In fact, I feel much better already. I told you, it was those pain pills."

"Maybe. Still, you should take it easy while we're gone. Mom is going over to Charlie's for a bit. One of the kids is sick, and she's going to babysit the others while they go to the doctor."

"Oh, no. Which one of them is sick?"

"I don't know. I just heard the tail end of Mom

and Dad's conversation. Are you sure you're going to be all right here while we're gone?"

"Absolutely. I'll just go back to bed. I feel a little shaky."

"Want me to tuck you in?" Wilson asked.

Cat grinned. "That is *so* not what you want to do to me, and we both know it."

A muscle jumped at the side of his jaw; then he kissed her, hard and quick, his nostrils flaring as he pulled back.

"I'm out of here before I get us both in trouble," he said softly.

Cat crawled into bed.

Wilson stood beside the bedpost, looking down at her—at the wild tangle of long dark hair, and her hollow eyes and dark bruises.

"Even beat all to hell and back, you look sexy."

"I'm going to sleep now," she said as she rolled over and tucked her hands beneath her cheek.

Wilson pulled the covers up over her shoulders, then turned off the light as he walked out of the room.

A short while later, Cat heard vehicles leaving, then nothing more as she slept.

Montoya kept one eye on the gas gauge and the other on the clock. He planned on being in Agua Caliente before sunset, to spend the night with an aunt and uncle who lived there. Although they had no phone, and he'd had no way of warning them he was coming, he knew he would be welcomed and that there would be a place for him to sleep.

As he drove, he kept going over the things he knew about Tutuola. The only thing that made sense was that someone killed him for the money, then set fire to the home to try to hide the deed.

He was a good detective and knew enough to trust his instincts. And his instincts were telling him to follow the money. All he had to do was backtrack Tutuola's trip to Chihuahua and, along the way, locate as many people as he could who'd seen him flashing cash around. Someone would tell. They always did.

The only fly in the ointment was Conchita's behavior. His absences were frequent but never long. This time his captain had given him a week to follow up on any leads he found, and after that they would either close the case or it would go cold.

Montoya didn't like unfinished business. He was hoping for a good ending. And along the way, he would find something nice to bring back to his wife as a peace offering. It wasn't perfect, but it was the way his life worked.

It was early evening when he drove into Agua Caliente. It had been at least four years since he'd been here, although he'd seen his tia Maria only last year at Christmas, when she'd come to Chihuahua to stay with his mother, her sister. It didn't surprise him to see that very little had changed. Such was the way in the small villages of Mexico. With no way of supporting a family, fewer and fewer of the young people stayed in the places where they'd been born. They usually gravitated toward the cities or tried crossing the border into the United States.

He drove up to the small adobe casa where his aunt and uncle had been living for the past forty-five years and got out. He stretched wearily, then reached inside the car to get the gifts he'd brought with him, before going to the door. Even though his uncle's house had a fairly fresh coat of whitewash and, inside, wooden floors to walk on, their existence was at poverty level.

A couple of chickens were pecking the ground a short distance away, and there was a goat tied to a stake. A blast of hot air hit him as he shut the car door and shifted his gifts more securely. He glanced around at the cluster of small adobe buildings and shook his head.

Dios Mio... Agua Caliente is a blister on the face of the earth.

Before he reached the door, it suddenly swung open. The little woman in the doorway threw up her hands in a gesture of delight, then hastened forward, talking a mile a minute.

Luis laughed as he was led inside. For the moment, his quest, Conchita's unhappiness with him and the demands of his job were forgotten. It wasn't until they'd had their evening meal and were sitting around chatting about family occurrences that his uncle finally asked him what he was doing there. Luis began to explain.

"A short time ago, a man was murdered in Chihuahua. We have few leads on the case, other than the fact that he was in possession of a large sum of money when he came to our city. We believe he was probably killed for it, and I'm backtracking his route. What we do know is that shortly before he came to Chihuahua, he was in a fire in Nuevo Laredo that nearly killed him, and that he had recently done business with a man from Dallas, Texas."

"Ah…so you will go to the United States?" his uncle asked.

"*Sì*, but not for long, I hope. Conchita is not happy with me at the moment."

His uncle frowned in understanding. "It is difficult to do your job, is it not?"

Luis nodded. "Unfortunately, crime does not wait on holidays and important family dates."

His tia Maria had been listening from the chair

in front of her hand loom, where she was working on another serape to sell to her neighbor's uncle, who came through Agua Caliente on an irregular basis and took their goods to the seaside resorts of Puerta Vallarta, Cozumel and even Mazatlan.

"This man you seek. He is very bad?"

Luis nodded. *"Es verdad…El Diablo…muy mal."*

She gasped. *"El Diablo?"*

"I will show you a picture, then you will understand for yourselves," Luis said, and ran outside to his car to get the file.

He came back with the booking photo, and then handed it to his uncle, who looked at it and frowned, then handed it to his wife.

"Dios Mio! A monster, for sure," she said. She started to hand it back to Luis, then hesitated and looked at it again. "You know…my friend, Paloma Garcia, talked of a man she once knew with such markings on his face."

Luis's eyes widened. Could it be possible that he was going to get his first lead from his own family?

"This Paloma Garcia…can I talk to her?"

His aunt nodded quickly. "She lives two houses down. Would you like me to go get her?"

Luis shook his head. "No, I will go to her, but why don't you come with me to make an introduction? I don't want this woman to be uneasy around me. You know how our people are when it comes to talking to the authorities."

Maria nodded and got up from her loom. Together, they walked the short distance to a small *casa* sitting a bit back from the street.

The air was much cooler now, and Luis glanced up as they walked.

"You know, I forget how beautiful the night sky is when the view is not marred by streetlights and noise."

Maria nodded. "*Sí*. We have been here so long now, I would not want to live anywhere else."

"That I understand," Luis said, and then moments later they were at the door.

Maria knocked. "Paloma. It's me, Maria."

There was a brief moment of silence, then the sound of a chair scooting back on a wooden floor.

"She's coming," Maria said, and smiled at her nephew, happy to be a part of his investigation, even if hers was a small, unimportant role.

Then the door opened, and Luis was face-to-face with a small woman of indeterminate age, wearing a red dress with multicolored embroidery around the neckline and matching embroidery a few inches above the hem. She had sandals on her feet and a red paper flower in her hair. Luis guessed that in her younger days, she'd been quite pretty.

At that point, Maria made the needed introductions.

"Paloma, this is my nephew Luis Montoya. He is a detective from Chihuahua. There is a question he would ask of you. Is it all right if he comes in?"

Paloma's smile had gone from welcoming to stiff so fast that Luis almost thought he'd imagined it. But the sparkle that had been in her eyes was gone, and she wouldn't look directly at him anymore. Instead of a verbal answer, she shrugged as she stepped aside for him to enter.

Maria frowned. She could tell her friend was uneasy, but Luis's smile reassured her that he knew how to deal with the chilly reception. She sighed, then hurried back up the street, anxious to get in out of the chill of a desert night.

Paloma waved toward a chair beside a small *chiminea* holding a brightly burning fire.

"Sit there," she said, and took a chair on the opposite side.

Luis had the photo of Tutuola with him, and he laid it facedown on his lap as he sat.

"Thank you for taking time to speak to me," he said.

Paloma nodded, but looked away.

Luis waited for her to relax. This behavior was typical of his people, and he knew why. They didn't have much reason to trust the police. Then he looked around at the inside of her small home and was taken aback. The amenities were surprising.

Besides the little fireplace, there was a new wood floor, and windows with real glass and curtains instead of outside shutters. There was a hand loom in the corner, not unlike the one his aunt used, but the colorful pile of hand-pulled yarns was huge. The walls smelled of fresh whitewash, and there was a lit oil lamp on a small table. He couldn't help but wonder where she'd come by the money to do all this.

"Your home is very comfortable," he said.

Paloma nodded.

"Your floor looks new."

She nodded again but still didn't meet his eyes.

Luis sighed. The conversation was going to be one-sided unless he shocked her into talking. He took the picture from his lap, then leaned forward and placed it in hers.

Paloma had no choice but to look, and when she did, she was unable to stifle a gasp.

"You know this man?" Luis asked.

Paloma shuddered, then took the picture and handed it back.

"*Sì,* I know him."

"What is his name?"

"Solomon Tutuola."

Luis resisted the urge to clap his hands. Finally, a lead.

"How do you know him?" he asked.

She hesitated only a moment, as if choosing the way she would describe their relationship.

"When I was younger, I knew many men. He was one of them."

Now Luis understood. Paloma had once had what his mother would call a bad reputation.

"When was the last time you saw him?"

She shrugged, then finally looked up. "Why do you ask?"

"I'm investigating his murder."

There was a long moment of silence; then Paloma seemed to relax.

"Bueno…El Diablo es muerte."

The devil is dead. After reading his rap sheet and remembering how the people he'd interviewed had described him, the appellation seemed even more apt than when the Realtor had used it.

"You didn't like him?" Luis asked.

Paloma shook her head. "No, no. He was bad. He was mean to everyone. Always pushing, demanding, using people for his own gain."

"So…I asked before…when was the last time you saw him?"

Paloma shrugged again. "Not so long…maybe a month. I don't know. Time doesn't mean much in Agua Caliente. One day is like the next."

"I understand," Luis said. "One more thing… when you last saw Tutuola, was he alone?"

Paloma nodded quickly. "*Sì, sì,* he was alone."

"Where did you see him?"

"He came to my *casa*…like he had a right." She frowned, then made the sign of the cross. "He was as he'd always been, mean and demanding. I sent him away."

Luis tried to imagine how this tiny woman would be able to handle a man of Tutuola's size.

"How did you manage that?" he asked.

She smiled, and for the first time Luis got a glimpse of the pretty young woman she'd once been.

"I put a curse on him. He was a superstitious man. It frightened him. He gave me much money to take the curse away. I took his money, but I did not remove the curse. I am glad he is dead."

Luis sighed. So…Tutuola already had the money when he came here.

"Did you see his money?"

"No. He went out to his car and came back with a handful. He threw it at me. I took it." Then she glared at Luis. "He gave it to me. It was mine to do with as I wished."

"Of course. I'm just trying to find out who else might have known about the money…maybe someone who followed him and killed him for it."

Paloma immediately thought of the American woman who'd been in her house, and the look of horror on her face when she realized that Paloma knew Tutuola—and that he was alive. She remembered the woman calling him the devil and almost fainting.

Paloma had seen the scar on the woman's neck. She understood that kind of fear. If the American woman had taken the money, it didn't matter to her. Solomon deserved to die.

"I saw no one," she said.

Luis nodded, then stood up.

"Thank you for taking time to speak with me. It has been very helpful."

Paloma nodded, then got up, too, and opened the door, anxious for the detective to leave. But Luis paused on the threshold.

"Oh…one last thing."

"Que?"

"When Tutuola was here, did he say where he'd been or how he came by the money?"

"No. All he wanted was food and sex. He took both without asking. I am glad he is dead."

Now Luis was the one who was ashamed—ashamed that any member of his sex would do such a thing.

"I am sorry you were mistreated," he said softly. "Thank you for your time."

"De nada," Paloma said.

Luis was on the doorstep and about to walk away when he stopped and turned around.

"I wish you a long and happy life, Paloma Garcia."

Paloma's eyes filled with tears, but she only nodded and closed the door.

Luis sighed. The world was harsh to women alone. He thought of Conchita and how many times he had left her in the same condition, then tried to assuage his own guilt by reminding himself that she was never without her comforts.

Still, as he walked back to his uncle's house, his heart was heavy. Tomorrow he would continue to head east. It remained to be seen what would happen next.

Six

Cat's bruises were fading faster than her memories of being swallowed up by the storm. She was grateful to still be here on the McKay ranch, instead of back in Dallas. Wilson had taught her that being with family was a great aid to healing, both in body and spirit. Now she was so entrenched in this world and very thankful she didn't have to return to the back alleys of Dallas to run down perps who'd skipped out on their court dates.

When she thought about it, which was often, it seemed as if Marsha's murder had been the detonator that had blown up her carefully balanced world. Before, she'd been a loner—never sharing anything of herself with anyone but Marsha and, occasionally, her old boss, Art. Before, she wouldn't trust and she wouldn't love, and she couldn't bring herself to do what was needed to change any of it. She'd been lost in a sparse and lonely routine.

But then Marsha had been murdered, and despite every intention she had of keeping Wilson out of her life, he wouldn't go away and he wouldn't give up. Now, she could only thank God for Wilson's perseverance. She couldn't imagine her life without him.

This morning, after breakfast and after everyone else had gone about their business, she had retreated to their bedroom and was now curled up on the bed with her lap full of yarn and a partially crocheted afghan. It was a skill that Dorothy had taught her on her first visit to the ranch, and one she now found soothing. It gave her great satisfaction to know that she could create beauty and warmth out of nothing more than loops and knots in a single strand of yarn.

The afghan, like Cat, was a work in progress.

Her stomach rumbled as she worked, and she paused for a moment to reach for the glass of iced cola she had on the table. Every now and then she still felt queasy, but a sip of something carbonated seemed to help, and the queasiness always went away.

Wilson was in the living room on speakerphone, talking with his secretary, LaQueen, and John Tiger, the friend he'd hired before he'd been shot. Cat knew that if it hadn't been for the two of them, Wilson's bail bond business would have gone belly-up.

From where she was sitting, she could just make out the low rumble of his voice. Although she couldn't hear what he was saying, it didn't matter. He was nearby, which was enough.

As she continued to crochet, a bird flew by the window near the bed. Cat caught the movement from the corner of her eye and paused long enough to look out. The sun was shining. The day was clear. Spring was here, but it would be a month or so before the smothering heat of summer followed.

She sighed, then leaned against the headboard of the bed, giving her eyes a rest before returning to the handwork in her lap. It probably wouldn't take her more than a couple of weeks to finish this, and then she could—

Suddenly Cat sat straight up in bed. Her heart began to pound, and her stomach turned.

"Oh. My. God."

She tossed the afghan to the side and crawled out of bed as she scrambled to reach the desk on the other side of the room. The daily calendar had been sadly neglected and was several days behind the correct date. But it wasn't the exact day she needed. It was the passage of time.

She stared at the small monthly calendar at the top of the page, then closed her eyes and made herself focus. The last time she remembered having her period was right before she'd gone to Chihuahua and gotten the life nearly beaten out of her.

She'd thought about it soon after, but had attributed being late to the trauma of the beating. And just when she'd been getting well, Wilson had been shot. After that, nothing had mattered but keeping him alive.

She sat down at the desk and began counting the days. By the time she was through, she was shaking.

Never in her life had she been late, but according to the calendar, she was two days shy of being two months overdue.

She thought of how many times lately she'd felt queasy at breakfast, and how many times she'd crawled into bed for an afternoon nap. Neither of those behaviors was normal for her.

But she'd never been pregnant before.

She got up from the chair and headed for the bathroom, then turned to stand before the full-length mirror. She still looked the same. A shade too thin, long hair in need of a cut. She touched her breasts, then shivered when they felt tender to the touch.

Her heart was hammering against her ribcage as she turned sideways and pulled up her shirt. Her belly was still flat—but at two months it would be. She dropped her shirt, then sat down on the lid of the toilet seat and started to shake.

Could this be true?

Was she having Wilson's child?

Even though they used protection, it was certainly possible. Nothing was foolproof.

Suddenly, she had to know. Thankful that her own car was back in operation, she headed out the door on the run.

Wilson was still on the phone when Cat went flying through the room. He waved a hello, but she didn't even look his way.

Curious, he quickly ended his conversation and ran to catch up.

She was already on her way out the back door with her wallet and car keys in her hand.

"Hey! Where's the fire?" he asked, as he caught up with her on the porch.

Cat felt like a kid with her hand caught in the cookie jar.

"Uh…I'm just going to make a quick trip into town. I'll be right back."

"Wait. I'll go with you," Wilson said.

"No, it's okay. I won't be long."

Wilson frowned. "What's going on?" he asked.

She hesitated. She didn't want to hurt his feelings, but this wasn't exactly how she would have planned on telling the man she loved that he was about to become a father. Besides, she didn't know that for sure.

"Nothing. I just need to pick up some stuff at the pharmacy."

"Why can't I go with you?"

Now she felt cornered. "Maybe I just want to shop on my own."

Wilson knew something was up, but he'd come too close to losing her too many times to let her stubbornness stand in the way of needing help.

"I'll stay in the car," he said.

"Fine. But I'm driving."

"Do you know where the nearest pharmacy is?"

She glared. "No."

"Then wouldn't it be better if I drove while you sulked?"

Cat handed him the keys and got into her newly repaired SUV. He was still on the porch by the time she'd buckled up. The look she gave him was enough to get him moving.

He got behind the wheel, then started the engine.

"If you dawdle, I'm going to be pissed," she muttered.

He grinned. "That's all right. My favorite kittens in the litter were always the ones that were all hissy-pissy."

Cat tried to be mad, but it was the grin on his face,

and that little gold loop in his ear glittering in the sunlight just like the gleam in his eyes, that told her she wasn't going to win this round.

She threw up her hands and leaned back.

"I'm ready when you are," she muttered.

Just for the sake of aggravation, Wilson stayed five miles under the speed limit all the way into Austin.

"Will this one do?" he asked, as he pointed to a large chain pharmacy at the end of the block.

"Yes. It'll be fine," Cat said.

Wilson nodded, then pulled into a parking space.

Cat's hand was on the handle when she paused, then turned to Wilson.

"I won't be long."

He sighed. "I'll wait in the car like I promised."

She knew she was behaving just like she had before, keeping secrets, not willing to share the personal side of her life with him, even after they'd been sleeping together. Regretting her earlier snub, she put a hand on his arm.

"Thank you. I'm not shutting you out. I just need you to trust me for a bit." Then she leaned over and kissed him square on the lips, lingering just long enough to start an ache in his belly. "Be right back," she said, and was out the door and into the pharmacy before his blood pressure settled.

A muscle jerked at the side of his jaw; then he made himself relax and dropped his hands into his lap. So what if she was making him crazy? He wouldn't have it any other way.

Inside, Cat was scanning the aisles, looking for feminine hygiene products and guessing that pregnancy test kits would be nearby.

They weren't.

She wasted so much time looking that she began to fear Wilson would get tired of waiting and come inside, and that wasn't how she wanted him to find out, either. Finally she gave up and went to the pharmacy counter to ask for help.

A helpful clerk stepped out from behind the counter and led her to a nearby display. The neat metal tag on her smock had the name Vicki Ostrowski on it.

Cat tried to imagine going through life with that last name, wondering how many times Vicki Ostrowski had to spell it over the phone to be understood.

"What kind do you prefer?" Vicki asked.

Cat's pulse accelerated. The last thing she needed was pressure.

"Kind? There are kinds? I don't know. All I need to know is if I'm pregnant."

The tension in her voice was telling. Vicki took pity on her and chose one for her.

"This one is the simplest. Follow the instructions, and if a cross shows up on the tester, then you are. If there's a minus sign, then you're not. How's that for easy?"

"A lot easier than it was to get this way," Cat muttered, and took the box Vicki gave her.

Vicki stifled a grin as Cat headed to the checkout counter. A couple of minutes later, she was on her way to the car with her sack in hand.

Wilson saw her come out and wisely refused to comment on the bag she was carrying as she got inside and buckled up. He couldn't imagine her suddenly going all shy on him about buying feminine products, but he wasn't going to be an ass a second time and insist she tell him what she'd bought when he'd already insisted on coming with her. Just because the bruises were fading and Cat was moving normally, that didn't mean she felt all right. If he'd been blown six ways to Sunday by a tornado, he might be acting a little strange, too.

"Need to do any more shopping, baby?"

It was the tenderness in his voice that was Cat's undoing.

She shook her head and then, to her horror, started to cry.

Wilson was stunned. It took more than kind words to make Catherine Dupree cry. He couldn't imagine what was wrong, but now he was scared.

"Honey…baby…I'm sorry. I'm sorry I pushed you into letting me come with you."

Cat swiped at her cheeks, irked that she seemed to be coming undone. "And I'm sorry I reacted the way I did."

Wilson's heart skidded to a stop. Had the twister done something awful to her that she was just now realizing? Had she been hurt in some way from the beating she'd suffered and now was afraid to tell him? A thousand scenarios ran through his mind in the space of seconds, and none of them were good.

"If there's something you want to tell me, we can deal with this together. Whatever it is…know that you don't have to do this alone."

"I know," she said. "Just get me home and then we'll talk. I don't want to go into it yet."

Wilson tried to put on a brave face, but he was past scared and getting down to terrified. He couldn't imagine what was wrong, but this was Catherine's call. She'd asked him to wait until they were home, so wait he would.

The drive home was silent. The sack Cat had carried out of the pharmacy was in her lap, beneath her hands. Every so often the plastic would crackle a little, like a rattlesnake shaking its rattles, a warning for all to remember it was there and steer clear.

Wilson kept glancing at Cat, trying to read her mood, but it was impossible. He finally gave up and just drove.

Cat knew she'd handled this badly. She'd led him to believe something was wrong, but that wasn't true. She wasn't worried, just anxious. She wanted it to be true, but all of this was taking some getting used to.

She'd never even thought about her future until she'd met Wilson McKay, and she'd never really thought about having babies until she'd found baby Maria Elena and her dead mother in the desert on her way to Agua Caliente. There'd been something so natural about cuddling the little girl to her breast—and surprisingly painful about giving her up.

Now, here she was, trying to come to terms with the thought of having a baby of her own. If only…

"We're home," Wilson said.

Cat looked up in surprise. She'd been so lost in thought, she'd missed them turning off the highway, then driving down the long road to the ranch. But then what he said finally registered.

Home. He'd said they were home.

She looked at the sprawling ranch house with the gray roof and white siding, and its deep shady porches, and thought of all the children and laughter this house had held. In the short time she'd been here, it had become more of a home to her than her Dallas apartment had felt like all the years she'd been there.

Wilson killed the engine, gave Cat a long look, and then quietly got out of the car and went into the house.

She took a deep breath and followed him in.

The kitchen was rich with the scent of chicken frying. A large red plate was piled high with homemade cookies. Carter was opening a jar of peaches, and Wilson was at the sink, washing his hands.

"Hey, there you are," Dorothy said. "I was wondering if you two would come back for dinner."

Cat glanced at Wilson, then managed a slight smile. "Give me a few minutes. I'll be back to help."

"You just take your time," Dorothy said. "Carter is all the help I need."

Cat nodded, then left the room. The closer she got to the bedroom, the faster she went. By the time she was inside, she was running. She went straight to the bathroom and closed the door, took the test kit out of the bag, tore into it and began reading. After following the directions, she took the test stick, went back into the bedroom, sat down on the side of the bed and began to stare at the clock.

It was turning into the longest three minutes of her life.

She began remembering bits and pieces from her childhood that she hadn't thought of in years—times when her mother had slept with her when she was sick. Times when her mother had taught her to say her ABCs while she brushed the tangles from her hair. Memories of baking cookies and picking flowers and holding her mother's hand when they crossed a street. Then she'd been killed in the car wreck and Cat had lived, and now memories were all she had left.

She glanced out the window, watching the old tomcat stalking a meadowlark in the backyard. Her vision blurred. She wiped away tears, then looked toward the clock. Only a minute? It seemed like a lifetime.

She glanced at the afghan lying in a heap on the bed and pictured it wrapped around her own shoulders while she sat in the chair nursing her child. She shivered and looked at the clock, watching as the numbers blinked, indicating yet another minute had passed.

Two down. One to go.

Her hands were shaking. It was hard to breathe. If this test was positive, then she'd been pregnant when Solomon Tutuola had beaten her senseless, and she'd been pregnant when she'd been sucked out of Wilson's pickup truck and tossed into the tornado funnel like so much garbage. If she *was* having a baby, would it be okay, or would the things she'd endured be the cause of it coming into this world less than healthy and whole?

She gave the digital clock one more look just as the numbers changed again.

Three minutes were up.

The test stick was in her hand.

All she had to do was open her fingers and look down.

It wasn't much. Just the simple act of opening a thumb and four fingers, and bending her head, but—*dear God*—so much was riding on this. She whispered a prayer then looked down.

Her legs were shaking as she stood up, but all she could think about was getting to Wilson.

She headed for the door, only to meet him striding down the hall.

"I was coming to look for you," she said.

Wilson stopped at the threshold, waiting for an invitation. "Here I am," he said.

Cat took his hand and tugged.

"Come inside with me."

Wilson couldn't read her mood, but her eyes were glassy, proof she was on the verge of tears. In his mind, that didn't bode well. He didn't know what to think, but he was scared. When she turned to face him, it was the jut of her chin that startled him. He hadn't seen that in months. Mutiny had been an active part of her past, and he didn't want it back. Even scarier, when she began to speak, he couldn't read the tone of her voice.

"Do you remember when you came over to my apartment with beer and pizza right before I took off for Mexico?"

Wilson began to get nervous. "Yes?"

"And do you remember those five twenty dollar bills you tossed on my bed when you left?"

He felt like he'd been kicked in the gut. His eyes narrowed. "Is this what you've been stewing about all day? If it is, then please tell me what I've done now that resurrected the attitude."

"I'm not stewing, and I don't have an attitude," Cat said.

"Then why are you bringing it up if you're not still pissed?"

Cat handed him the test stick.

"This is what you bought for your money."

Wilson looked down. For a few seconds the implication didn't register; then he began reading the company name on the plastic stick, and suddenly, he got it.

He looked up at Cat and could tell she was nervous—even a little anxious.

"Oh my God, Catherine. Did we just go into Austin to buy a pregnancy test kit?"

She nodded.

His heart skipped a beat.

"Does this cross mean you are—or you aren't?"

"Are."

He started to smile. "You're pregnant?"

"Yes. Are you okay with this?"

He couldn't speak. He just picked her up in his arms, swung her off her feet and kissed her. Softly, at first, and then with as much passion as he could muster in the face of overwhelming joy.

The warmth of his lips was a mirror to the warmth in her heart. Right now, her world couldn't be any better. Then he turned her loose with a soft, achy groan and hit her with the same question.

"From my side of the fence, this is the best news I've had in years, but how do *you* feel about being pregnant?"

"Oh, Wilson, I want this baby so much, but... I'm scared."

He frowned. "Scared of having a baby...or becoming a parent?"

"No. None of that. But if the test is correct, then I was pregnant when Tutuola beat me to within an inch of my life, and pregnant during the tornado that chewed me up and spit me out somewhere in the middle of one of your dad's pastures. What if the baby's been harmed?"

Wilson kissed the side of her cheek, then laid the flat of his hand on her belly.

"Right now that little baby is in the safest place it could ever be. And if you *had* been going to lose it, I think it would already have happened. Still, I'll call my sister and find out the name of her obstetrician."

Cat grabbed his hand. "Wait. If you do that, then they'll all know."

He grinned. "So? I want the world to know."

"Look, it's no big deal to me, but I have a feeling that it will matter to your folks that we're not married."

"Oh, hell no," he said. "Mom's been trying to get me married off for so many years, she'll just look at this as the perfect incentive. Besides, you and I have already talked about getting married. We just haven't done anything about it."

"I know, but there's the matter of Jimmy Franks still being at large."

Wilson frowned. "And they may never catch the bastard. I'm not going to let someone like him ruin the rest of our lives just because he's hiding out in the sewers of Dallas."

Cat sighed. "So what do we do?"

Wilson cupped her cheek, then brushed a kiss across her lips.

"Go eat Mom's fried chicken before she comes looking for us."

"Just like nothing is wrong?"

Wilson put his arms around her and pulled her close.

"Baby…nothing *is* wrong. In fact, for the first time in years, everything is right."

"Okay, lead the way, but remember, no telling anyone yet. I want to get a doctor to verify this before we drop the bomb."

Wilson nodded as he led her out of the room.

"Just remember, when they do find out, they're going to be very, very happy."

It began to rain in Dallas just before nightfall. Jimmy Franks was on the streets and heading for a homeless shelter he knew about when the first drops fell on his face. He shivered, then pulled the collar of his jacket up and hunched his shoulders as he headed for the awning over a bakery shop a couple of doors away.

He got beneath it just as the rain began to fall in earnest, then looked around to make sure he was alone before he pulled a cell phone out of his pocket. He'd lifted it from the old woman he'd met at the other homeless shelter, along with the twenty-four dollars she'd had in her purse.

He didn't care that he'd taken all her money. Someone would take care of her. But he couldn't ask for help for himself, because the cops were looking for him. However, with this phone, he could try to find his brother, Houston. The only place he knew to start looking for him was to call home. And he also knew that if he did, his mother was going to give him hell for the mess he was in. She might be seventy-nine and walking with a cane, but she was as tough as they came, and even now, after all the years of trouble he'd been in, she was the one person who could bring him up short. Still, he had business to tend to, and he could use Houston's help—even if the bastard had abandoned him before.

He dialed the number to his family home in Abilene, shivering from the blowing rain against his pant legs as he waited for someone to answer. Just when he thought there was no one home, he heard his mother's voice.

"Hello?"

She sounded breathless, as if she'd been hurrying

to get the phone, and Jimmy knew how red her cheeks would be, and how her long, graying hair would be straggling down from the ponytail she always wore.

"Hey, Mom, it's me, Jimmy."

Silence.

Jimmy was immediately on edge. She must have already talked to Houston, or she wouldn't be this pissed.

"Mom? Are you there?"

"I'm not giving you any money."

Jimmy stifled a curse. "Did I ask you for anything? Did I? Did I? No! I just called to talk to my mother, like a good son should."

He heard what sounded like a snort, then Momma lit into him.

"Good son? You don't know the meaning of the word 'good.' And before you start spinning one of your big lies, I'm going to tell you now that Houston was here. He told me what you went and did. He told me that you shot and killed your bondsman. I didn't raise you to be a druggie. I didn't raise you to be a killer. I'm done with you, do you hear me?"

Before he thought, he blurted, "Well, you're wrong. The bondsman isn't dead." Then he groaned, realizing he'd just admitted to shooting Wilson but not finishing the job.

The line went dead in his ear.

He stared down at the cell phone, then, in a fit of anger, threw it to the ground and stomped it until it was in pieces. Despite the rain, he left the shelter of the awning and started walking, with his head down and his mind on revenge. He would get to Austin and finish what he'd started, if he had to walk the whole way and choke the man with his bare hands.

But the stolen twenty-four dollars were burning a hole in his pocket, and before he'd gone three blocks, he found a dealer who'd taken shelter in an abandoned car in the alley between two apartment buildings and bought himself a fix.

For the moment, revenge had taken a back burner to riding his high.

Seven

It had taken Luis longer than he'd planned to leave Agua Caliente. Part of it had to do with the fact that he kept trying, without success, to get Conchita on the phone, and part of it had to do with his aunt and uncle.

He knew that, with their advancing age and the amount of time that passed between his visits, the chances of seeing one or the other alive again were always lessening. It was almost noon before he finally said goodbye, and he still hadn't talked to Conchita. After checking his map, he headed for the next village east, Casa Rojo.

Lieutenant Dominguez had been the chief of police in Casa Rojo for years. It didn't pay much, but it was easy, and jobs were hard to come by in this part of Mexico. At noon, his wife had brought him a large meal of frijoles and tortillas. By the time she left, he was engorged and sleepy. Within a few minutes, he'd gone back into one of the cells and lain down on the bunk inside. Soon he was sound asleep. Sometime later, he was awakened by the sound of someone calling out.

"Here. I am here," he said, and quickly rose to a sitting position, before getting to his feet.

He smoothed down the front of his shirt, then tucked the tail into his pants before moving to the outer office. Unfortunately, he'd forgotten to smooth down his hair, and the left side of it was slightly flat and pushed upward, like the broken wing of a bird.

He caught a glimpse of his reflection in a hall window just as he saw his visitor. Embarrassed, he combed his fingers through his hair several times to put it back in order.

The man waiting for him on the other side of his desk was of average height and appeared to be somewhere in his forties. His hair was straight and black as night. He wore it tied at the back of his neck in a short ponytail, giving him a slightly rebellious look, although his skin was the same warm brown as Dominguez's own. He was wearing a pair of dark pants and a light-colored, short-sleeved shirt. When their gazes met, the stranger flashed a badge.

Dominguez drew himself up a little straighter.

"Good afternoon. I am Lieutenant Dominguez. How can I help you?"

Luis Montoya stifled a grin. He'd caught the other policeman sleeping in one of the cells. He couldn't blame him. It was time for a siesta. He would have liked to do the same, but he had too many miles still to cover. He reached across the desk and offered his hand.

"Detective Luis Montoya, Chihuahua Homicide."

Dominguez straightened his shoulders even more. A real detective from the city. He waved toward the chair on the opposite side of his desk. As soon as the visitor sat, Dominguez did, too.

"What can I do for you?" he asked.

Montoya took a picture of Tutuola out of a file folder and slid it across the desk.

"Have you ever seen this man?"

Dominguez's eyes widened in shock at the man's appearance.

"Definitely not. I would have remembered him for sure."

Montoya sighed. That wasn't what he'd wanted to hear.

"So why are you looking for this man?" Dominguez asked.

"I'm not looking for him. He's dead. I *am* looking for the person who killed him," Luis replied. "We know that he was most likely in Nuevo Laredo before he came to Chihuahua, and that he had a large sum of money on him when he arrived in our city. We're hoping to find his killer by finding out how many people knew of the money as he traveled through the country."

Dominguez nodded firmly, indicating that he, too, understood the process.

Montoya stifled a grin. The lieutenant was a bit full of himself. He suspected the worst things to happen in this small village probably involved sleeping with someone else's wife and stealing a few chickens. However, this man's lack of knowledge did not exclude the possibility others had seen Tutuola.

"Have there been *any* strangers through your village in the past month or so? Say, someone out of the ordinary?"

Dominguez started to say no, then suddenly remembered the American woman.

"There was a woman—an American. But that was a while back, and she was alone."

"How did you come to know her?" Montoya asked.

"It's quite a story," Dominguez said, then leaned back and got comfortable before he began to talk.

"She was a tall woman, with an exotic face. Quite beautiful, but too skinny for my tastes. Her hair was dark and long, and her eyes were hard. Oh…and she had a most terrible scar at her throat, as if someone had slashed it with a knife."

Montoya frowned. Even though Tutuola had been a monster of a man, a strong woman with street smarts could have done him in.

"She came to you?"

Dominguez nodded. "It was quite a sight. She drove up just as you did, only she came into my office carrying a baby girl. The woman was dusty and weary, but she was holding the baby with much care. She said she'd found the child in the desert, and that the mother's body was in the back of her vehicle."

Montoya's opinion of the woman began to shift. Murderers weren't usually Good Samaritans, too. He listened as Dominguez continued.

"We ascertained that the mother and baby had probably been abandoned by a coyote…smuggling illegals across the border. The woman found them just in time to save the baby's life and the mother's body from being eaten by animals. Then she did something quite out of the ordinary. We found identification papers in the mother's belongings stating that she was from Adobe Blanco. The crazy

American woman made me promise not to call the authorities to come get the baby until she went there to see if she could find any family members. In fact, she came close to threatening me. She seemed angry that we might let the baby become lost in the government system."

Montoya was hooked on the story. This was like something from a movie. "What happened?" he asked.

"So this crazy woman drove away like the hounds of hell were after her and found Adobe Blanco, although it is hardly more than a pile of donkey dung. She returned with the baby's grandparents and a priest, as well, and all before sunset."

"Where did she go after that?" Montoya asked.

"I don't know. She just headed west. That's all I saw."

Montoya frowned. West. Chihuahua was west.

"By chance, do you remember this American woman's name?"

Dominguez nodded. "Oh yes…I remember it well. Her name was like *el gato*…the cat. She called herself Cat Dupree."

Montoya's pulse kicked. He knew that name. But from where?

He opened his files and began going through his notes. Then he saw it.

Cat Dupree was the woman who'd trailed Mark Presley across the border into Nuevo Laredo for killing her friend. And Mark Presley was the name on the card he'd found in Tutuola's possessions. But Presley had been arrested just after Christmas. That was months ago. She would have gone back to Dallas with him when he was taken into custody. So why would she have come back to Mexico so much later? Unless she'd known about the money and decided to go after it?

Questions and more questions, and all without answers. It was all about the timing. The American had admittedly been in Mexico. Dominguez could be off on the dates.

"Tell me, Lieutenant. How sure are you about the timing of Miss Dupree's visit to Casa Rojo?"

"Positive," Dominguez said. "I know, because the day after she left was my wedding anniversary, which was April 29."

Montoya added that to his notes. Proof that she'd come back. But why?

"One more thing…where is Adobe Blanco from here?"

Dominguez frowned. "It is a long trip back west and then south. A little place in the middle of nowhere."

"Can you tell me how to get there?" Montoya asked.

Dominguez shrugged and then nodded.

Montoya wrote down the directions, then asked where he could buy fuel and took his leave.

A short while later he'd filled both his car and the two extra gas cans in the trunk of his car with fuel. Now he was on his way to see what the people of Adobe Blanco had to say about a woman called *el gato*.

Padre Francisco was repairing a crack in the outer wall of his church when he heard the sound of an approaching engine. Many came to the little church, but almost always on foot. Few drove.

Curious, he turned to see who was coming. When he saw the stranger get out of his car and come toward him with a badge in his hand, the first thing he thought of was the American woman who'd rescued baby Maria Elena from death. When she'd given her fine American car to his church, the whole village had rejoiced.

She'd been responsible for returning the baby to her grandparents and bringing the body of her mother home to bury. Then only a week or so later, he'd received a letter from her, along with the proper papers donating her car to the church. All he'd had to do was go to the airport in Chihuahua to get it and say a prayer for her when he had the time. Also, she'd asked that he not speak of the details.

He'd known then that she'd been in trouble. But he knew an angel on earth when he saw one, and she was such an angel. So nothing that came out of this stranger's mouth was going to change his mind about keeping what he knew to himself. The American woman had asked him to pray for her. In his mind, it was as close to a confession as she'd been able to come, and in confession, what was told to a priest was sacrosanct.

Luis Montoya saw the priest's gaze move from the badge in his hand to his face and was surprised to see his expression shut down, rather than turn welcoming. Adobe Blanco was one of the poorest places he'd seen in his country, and he doubted many strangers came their way, so maybe the priest was just naturally suspicious..

"Padre…I am Detective Luis Montoya of the Chihuahua Police Department."

The priest smiled and offered his hand. "Padre Francisco at your service. Please come inside. I have a little wine. Some beans and tortillas. You will eat and drink with me."

Montoya relaxed, deciding that his earlier opinion of the man had been wrong. This old man wasn't hiding anything but his age.

"*Gracias,* Padre."

"*De nada.* Come, come."

Montoya followed him inside, through the narrow, shadowed entry, past ten dusty pews, into a tiny room that obviously served as the man's living quarters. At the priest's urging, he sat, then watched as the old man prepared the food, then carried it to the small table. When he pulled an old decanter from a small cupboard and filled their glasses with wine, Montoya couldn't help but notice the raised veins and gnarled knuckles on the priest's hands.

Padre Francisco sat down then, blessed the food, and pushed the plate of cold tortillas and beans toward the detective.

"Please serve yourself," the priest said, and then pointed to a small bowl of salsa. "One of the women of the village makes this for me. It is good and hot to my liking. I hope you agree."

Montoya smiled. "Hot is perfect. I thank you for this, Padre. It's been a while since I've eaten. My stomach was complaining of neglect."

The priest laughed, helped himself to a tortilla, added a spoonful of beans and a generous helping of the hot salsa, and dug in.

They passed the meal in near silence, talking only to ask that something be passed, or to offer a second glass of wine. But Montoya was very aware of the other man's meager existence, and limited himself to only two tortillas and one glass of wine.

When they had finished, the priest brought out a dented tin. Inside were a few small cookies covered with a light dusting of powdered sugar. Montoya took one, the priest another, and then the meal was finished. It was the priest who started the conversation.

"So, tell me, Detective…why is it that you have come so far from Chihuahua to our little village? There isn't much here but mountains and scrub brush and a few hardy people."

Montoya nodded. "You speak the truth, Padre Francisco. But it is information I seek."

The priest nodded, awaiting the questions to come.

Montoya took out his file and slid the picture of Solomon Tutuola in front of the old man. Within seconds, the old man's nostrils flared, and he quickly made the sign of the cross before shoving the photo back across the table.

"El Diablo."

It wasn't the first time Montoya had heard that, and he wondered if Padre Francisco had met Tutuola.

"Have you ever seen this man?" he asked.

The priest frowned. "No. And I have no wish to meet him. Look into his eyes. They are evil. Who is he? Why do you look for him?"

"I'm not looking for him. I'm looking for whoever killed him."

The priest gasped, then leaned back in his chair. His gaze shifted to a small painting of Christ on the wall above the detective's head, and he thought of the scar on Cat Dupree's neck as he absorbed the full impact of the detective's words.

"So you are looking for this man's murderer. What led you here?"

"I'm just following up on leads as they come," Montoya said, then shifted gears. "I have another question to ask you."

"Of course."

"Do you know a woman named Cat Dupree?"

Padre Francisco exhaled on a sigh. So. It had finally come to this.

"Yes, but of course. She is viewed as something of a heroine around here."

Montoya nodded. "Lieutenant Dominguez from Casa Rojo said as much."

The padre frowned. "If you already knew this, why did you bother to come all this way to ask about her?"

"What was your impression of the woman?" Montoya asked.

"That she had courage and a tender heart. She kept a little baby from being lost in the government's welfare system, and went out of her way to make sure that the body of the baby's mother could be laid to rest in a proper manner."

"So you admire this woman?"

"Very much," Padre Francisco said.

"After she left here, did you ever see her again?"

"Yes. In fact, we followed her back to Casa Rojo. I brought the grandparents of the baby with me. We parted company in Casa Rojo, after the baby and her grandparents were reunited. Then we brought the baby's mother back for burial. I never saw her again, but I will not soon forget her."

Montoya frowned. "Did the American woman ever say what she was doing in Mexico, or where she was going?"

The priest shrugged. "Not that I remember. But we were so wrapped up in the sadness of the situation, we didn't really talk."

Montoya nodded. "I understand."

Padre Francisco stood up and began clearing the small table. Then he returned the decanter to the cupboard.

Montoya knew he'd been dismissed, and truth was, he was of the opinion that this had been a wild-goose chase. But it was his job to follow the leads, even the ones that went nowhere.

"I thank you for the food and wine and conversation," he said, as he gathered up his papers and returned them to the file. Almost as an afterthought, he took a handful of bills from his pocket and laid them on the table.

"An offering for your church, Padre."

The priest nodded. "Appreciated and accepted, Detective. As you can see, we are a very poor community."

"I'll be going now. It was a pleasure to meet you," Montoya said, and before the priest could stop him, he moved toward the back door. "I'll just go out this way. A little walk back to my car will be welcome. I have far to go before I sleep tonight."

Padre Francisco started to call out, but it was too late. Montoya was outside and already staring at the obviously opulent SUV parked at the back of the church.

Montoya stared for a few moments, then turned around.

"Considering the poverty of your church and community, I have to say that's a surprisingly nice car you have, Padre."

"It was a donation, of course," Padre Francisco said, silently asking forgiveness for failing to keep Cat Dupree's secret.

"Ah. From whom?"

"Why, from the American woman. When she realized we were in need, she made it her business to help. A very Christian thing to do."

Montoya circled the vehicle. He peered inside, then frowned. There was a dark stain in the back and a couple of small ones on the front seat.

"There are some stains on the seat."

The padre frowned. The detective's questions were beginning to sound like accusations.

"Yes. I know. Bloodstains don't come out easily."

Montoya was surprised by the admission. He'd expected the old man to skirt the truth as far as he could.

"Why were there bloodstains?" he asked.

The priest arched an eyebrow, then gestured grandly, as if the detective must surely be senile for not coming to the understanding on his own.

"The little mother, of course. She was dead when Señorita Dupree found her, remember? I don't know if Dominguez gave you the details, but the coyotes—the animals, not the human animals," he said in disgust, "had been at her. She scared them off, rescued the baby, and also carried the body to the vehicle all on her own. There was blood on her and on the baby, as well as on the body."

Montoya felt like a fool. Of course there would have been blood.

"I'm sorry. I forgot about—"

Padre Francisco shrugged. "If you'd seen it— and her—you would not have forgotten any of it. It was terrible. If she hadn't come along when she did, the baby would have been food for the animals, as well."

"But if she drove away in this car, how did you come by it later?"

Padre Francisco mentally sifted through the facts and decided that the detective from Chihuahua didn't need to know that this very vehicle had been parked at the Chihuahuan airport when he'd gone to claim it.

"It was a miracle. One day it was here, complete with title, keys and money for the gas to drive it. She is a saint, that woman. There should be more like her in this world."

Montoya eyed the car one last time, then nodded and waved goodbye. He circled the church in haste, suddenly anxious to be gone. It was a long way to Nuevo Laredo.

Padre Francisco watched until the dust had settled, and then he went back into the church, walked to the front of the altar and dropped to his knees. He made the sign of the cross, bowed his head and began to pray for Cat Dupree, who was unaware that the Mexican police were on her trail.

Then, when he was through, he prayed yet again, but this time for the sins of his omissions.

* * *

A couple of days had passed since Cat's revelation and there were things to be done toward ending one way of life before another could begin.

It had been simple for Wilson and Cat to convince Carter and Dorothy that they needed to drive back to Dallas to check on their apartments, pay some bills and go by Wilson's bail bond business.

Wilson knew he wasn't strong enough yet to run down bail jumpers, and being on the streets while Jimmy Franks was still on the loose wasn't smart, either. Franks could lie in wait in any alley and take Wilson out from almost any direction without Wilson being able to see it coming. And after finding out he was going to be a father, dying wasn't an option.

As for Cat, she'd been anxious to confirm her test results with a doctor's opinion, and to reassure herself that the baby was still okay.

A few days later, they'd left Austin before daybreak, arriving in Dallas in plenty of time for her doctor's appointment. Wilson had gone as far as the waiting room with her, then stayed behind as the doctor examined her. Half an hour later, the nurse came out and ushered him back to the room where Cat was waiting for the results.

Wilson followed the nurse to find Cat sitting on the side of the examining table, chewing on a hangnail. As the nurse closed the door behind him, he pulled her thumb out from between her teeth and kissed her.

The moment their lips met, all the tension she was feeling disappeared. She sighed, then wrapped her arms around his neck and leaned into the kiss.

"You okay?" Wilson asked, as he scooted her over and sat down on the examining table beside her.

Cat nodded.

"What did he say about the bruises? Did he think there was any need for concern?"

"He told me he'd seen the footage on the news and didn't even realize who I was until a couple of days later, when he happened to catch my name as they were airing it again. He said I was one lucky woman."

"What did you say?"

"I reminded him that cats have nine lives."

Wilson grinned, then gave her another quick kiss just as the doorknob turned. By the time the door opened, they were sitting politely side by side, smiling at the doctor who entered.

"So this is the lucky fellow," the doctor said.

Wilson's smile widened. "Do we have a due date?" he asked.

Cat blinked. That was something she hadn't even thought of.

The doctor nodded. "It's a calculated guess, but I'm pretty good at stuff like this, and I think you're going to like it."

"Like what?" Cat asked.

"The due date. How do you feel about February fourteenth?"

Wilson's eyes widened. "Valentine's Day! Man. That's a birthday you can't forget."

Cat grinned in spite of herself. A Valentine baby.

"Am I all right?" she asked.

The doctor nodded. "Considering what you've gone through, I'd say you're amazingly all right. Are you still living in Dallas?"

Cat looked at Wilson, who squeezed her hand and answered for her.

"We're going to be moving to Austin," he said. "I think the bounty hunting business has become a little risky for the both of us, since we're going to be parents. I'm going to work the family ranch with my dad, so we'll be living there."

"I know a good ob-gyn in Austin. I'd be happy to refer you."

Cat nodded. "Please."

"I'll have my nurse make your first appointment

for you. Then the rest is up to you. You can pick up the information before you leave today."

"Thank you," Cat said. "In the meantime, is there anything I should be doing?"

"And shouldn't be doing?" Wilson added.

Cat ignored him.

"I'm going to give you a prescription for prenatal vitamins. Other than that, eat healthy, get exercise and no more riding tornadoes. That should do it."

"That, I can promise," Cat said. "The next time I even see a dark cloud, I'll be the first one in the cellar."

Both men laughed, and a short while later, they were on their way to Cat's apartment.

"I need to talk to the manager, pick up a change of address to mail to the post office, and find a mover who'll pack up my stuff and put it in storage until we have a place of our own," she said. "Also, there are some summer clothes I want to take with us."

"Same here," Wilson said. "And I want to go by the office and talk to LaQueen and John Tiger. It seems like forever since I've been there."

"Are you going to be sorry you're not doing this anymore?" Cat asked.

"No," Wilson said, absently rubbing at the bullet scar on his chest as they waited for a red light to change. "I don't want our children to ever be in danger from something I do for a living, even if the chance is remote. Before, I never gave the danger much thought, but I'm proof it can happen."

"Are you going to sell the business?"

The light changed, and they drove through the intersection. It was a few moments before he answered.

"I'm still not sure. Keeping it would bring in extra income for us, and the ranch can always use that. However, I'd still be connected, if only long distance, and I'm not really comfortable with that anymore. Between the two of us, we've racked up some enemies, and I'd rather not have them come looking for us."

"I feel the same way," Cat said. "I've known all along that I didn't want to chase bail jumpers for Art anymore, but once I found out I was pregnant, there was no way."

"Have you told Art?"

"Yeah, more or less. I'll call him while we're here and make it official."

Then Wilson changed the subject with a grin.

"Are you still okay with getting married in a judge's chambers instead of having a big whoop-de-doo at a church? I had to pull in a favor to get the seventy-two-hour waiting period waived, but it's done."

Cat sighed. "Wilson, the last time I was in a church was in Adobe Blanco, and I was looking for a dead woman's family to come claim a baby. Before that, not in years. It seems a bit hypocritical to get married in one when I've been boycotting God for all these years for taking my parents away from me."

A wave of empathy for what she'd endured during her lifetime swept through him so quickly his vision blurred.

"Oh, honey, it wasn't a boycott. You were just lost and didn't know how to find your way back."

"Until you found me," Cat said.

Now Wilson really was in tears. He braked again for another red light, then looked at her.

Cat was stunned that someone could weep for her in a way she'd been unable to weep for herself. She squeezed his hand, then gave him a shaky grin.

"You do know I love you madly, right?"

"It took you long enough," he said softly.

She laughed, and then they were moving again. A short while later, they arrived at Wilson's office.

His secretary, LaQueen, saw them from the window before they could get out of the car, and came out squealing and waving her arms in delight. Her dark brown eyes and café au lait skin were a perfect accompaniment to the gold-and-brown print dress she was wearing. Her thick dark curls were loose about her face and bounced when she walked. Before Wilson knew it, she had her arms locked around his neck and was kissing him soundly on the cheek.

"Lord have mercy, I didn't think I was going to see you two again," she said, as she turned him loose and gave Cat a similar greeting.

Wilson blushed. Cat grinned. Then John Tiger came out. He hadn't changed since the last time Cat had seen him. He was still the tall, solemn Indian with short, spiky hair, just like Wilson's. John started to shake Wilson's hand, then hugged him instead.

"I'm glad to see you up and walking, my brother."

"So am I," Wilson said, then poked John lightly in the belly. "Are you getting fat?"

John grinned and pointed to LaQueen. "She's too good a cook."

LaQueen beamed. "I like my men with a little meat on them."

Cat's smile widened. "So you two are officially a couple?"

LaQueen lifted her chin, her dark eyes flashing. "We aren't officially anything…yet."

John put his arm around her and gave her a quick hug.

"Oh, yes we are, woman. So stop fussing."

"Until there's a ring on my finger, there's nothing official," she muttered.

Wilson knew when to change the subject, and he knew how to do it.

"Is there anything crucial pending this afternoon?"

"No," John said.

"Just paperwork," LaQueen answered. "Why?"

"We need a couple of witnesses."

"To what?" John asked.

"To our wedding," Cat said.

LaQueen's mouth dropped, and then she squealed again.

"You're getting married! Oh lordy! I am so happy for the both of you. Wait! You need—"

Wilson held up his hand. "I know what's needed. I've been on the phone for the past three days calling in every favor owed. It's okay. Trust me."

John shook his hand and then clapped him on the shoulder. "We would be honored," he said, then added, "You do know that you've gone and set the bar pretty high for me, here. I'll never hear the end of it now."

LaQueen held up her hand to stop the conversation.

"I don't know about the rest of you, but Cat and I are going shopping."

Cat's mouth dropped, but it was Wilson who asked, "For what?"

LaQueen drew herself up to her near-six-foot height and got that stubborn look that always made Wilson nervous.

"For a wedding dress, mister. That's what for. What time you gonna be at the judge's chambers?"

Wilson looked a little nervous. "I told him we'd be there by four."

LaQueen glanced at the clock. "Fine. That leaves us about three hours. We'll see you there." Then she pointed at John.

"Make sure he wears something besides a pair of jeans and that darned black leather jacket, will you?"

"I have suits," Wilson muttered.

Cat grinned. She'd never seen Wilson cowed. She thought it was funny, and then her smile faded.

"Now that I think about it, I don't have any dresses."

LaQueen's eyes widened in disbelief. "Not even one?"

Cat shrugged. "Where would I have worn it? Kind of hard to run down a perp in high heels."

LaQueen was shaking her head and muttering to herself as she took her purse from the desk drawer.

"Good thing we're going shopping, then." She turned to the two men. "We'll see you at the courthouse. Cat, you're coming with me."

Cat shrugged, then waved at Wilson. "See you later."

He frowned. "This isn't going exactly like I'd planned."

"Then you shouldn't have included me in your ceremony, because I'm not having this pretty woman married in blue jeans, and that's a fact," LaQueen said.

The door slammed shut behind them.

Eight

Cat and LaQueen were in a small room off the judge's chambers, waiting for court to end so he could perform the wedding.

But the past three hours had not been wasted. Once they'd left Wilson's office, LaQueen had made one call to John, warned him to get Wilson to the courthouse on time and not to expect to see Cat again before the ceremony, and then they'd headed for the Galleria.

The Galleria was a huge, multi-storied mall that Cat generally tried not to frequent, but this time it felt different. Once they'd gotten into the rhythm of the place, she'd alternated between feeling silly and having a growing sense of excitement as she'd tried on dress after dress. She'd never had much use for them, so she was surprised by how feminine she felt every time she put one on.

The one she finally settled on wasn't traditional, but then neither was she. It was, however, definitely in keeping with the pink butterfly tattoo on her hip. The dress was a pale rose-colored fabric, mid-calf length, with a plunging neckline bordered with a soft flounce of the same fabric. It didn't hide her fading bruises, but it made her feel pretty. The silver high-heeled sandals she picked out added almost three inches to her height, but that wouldn't matter. Wilson would still tower over her.

Once the shopping was behind them, LaQueen swept Cat off to a beauty shop and coerced one of the stylists into taking her on the spot. Under LaQueen's guidance, the stylist turned Cat's no-nonsense hair into a sexy do to suit the pink dress. She gathered the long dark strands at the crown of Cat's head, curled the loose ends, then let them fall in loose abandon.

"I look like I stuck my finger in a light socket," Cat muttered.

"You look amazing," LaQueen countered.

She looked and felt like a stranger, Cat thought, but in a way, it seemed fitting. The old Cat Dupree would never have stood for any of this, but that Cat was gone. This Cat was a woman who had learned how to trust and how to love, and she was marrying the man who'd taught her.

Now here she was, waiting for a judge to change the rest of her life—and so sorry Marsha wasn't here to stand beside her. But as saddened as she was by the loss of her best friend, she was ready to move on.

Before sunset today, she would no longer be Catherine Dupree. Tomorrow morning she would wake up and for the rest of her life be known as Catherine McKay. It wasn't the loss of her last name that was sad as much as the fact that her father's bloodline ended with her. Yes, her children would share his DNA, but there would never be another of her people with the same last name.

As a child, her father had told her how special she was—that she was the first daughter to ever be born to a Dupree. He'd told her often how Antoine Dupree had been the first of her ancestors to set foot in this land. That he'd come from France to the New World during the early seventeen hundreds, landing in the area now known as New Orleans.

From there, he'd told her, Antoine's heirs had ridden west into territory known only as part of the Louisiana Purchase. One had fought in the Revolutionary War, and later, two others had fought on opposite sides in the War Between the States.

He'd had one great-great-great-grandson who'd fought in the Great War, the war that was supposed to have been the last—World War I—and he'd had a grandson who had flown Spitfires during World War II.

Three of his sons went to Vietnam, too young to be parents, but not too young to die. Only one of the three had come home—whole in body, but not in mind. He'd fathered just one son before he'd hanged himself from the rafters in his garage with a length of clothesline. That son was Justin Dupree, Cat's father, whose untimely death ended what had been a remarkable—and long—line of courageous, adventurous men.

In the entire line—from Antoine to Justin—Cat was the only female to have been born a Dupree. It explained her valiance, as well as her sense of duty and determination, but it didn't change the truth.

Antoine had been the alpha. Cat was the omega.

But while Cat was giving up a name today, she was also gaining something she thought she'd lost forever: a family. Marrying Wilson and belonging to that wonderful, noisy clan of McKays was, for Cat, life altering. Knowing the child she carried would become one of them and be loved without question meant everything to her.

While waiting for the tardy judge, she glanced

out the window, and as she did, she saw her reflection. For a moment it was like looking at a stranger; then she recognized herself and smoothed her hand down the front of her dress, lingering a little longer on her belly.

I know you're in there, my baby. I promise, if I never do another thing in my life, I will keep you safe.

LaQueen touched her shoulder.

"Honey, you have a visitor."

Cat frowned. "But you said Wilson wasn't allowed—"

"It's not Wilson. Someone has to give you away. I figured Art Ball would stand up for you just fine."

Cat felt as if she'd been sucker punched. Her eyes widened as she looked toward the old man standing in the doorway. He was wearing a grin and a royal-blue polyester suit straight out of the seventies. His sparse gray hair was slicked back from his face with hair oil as old-fashioned as the suit.

"Hey, missy. You didn't think you were gonna sneak out and do this without me, did you?"

Cat was too moved to speak. She just shook her head and walked into his arms.

A little embarrassed by her show of affection, he patted her awkwardly on the back, then handed her a handkerchief.

"Wipe your eyes and blow your nose. If Wilson McKay sees you with me and you look like you've been crying, he's likely to whip my ass before he finds out why."

Cat laughed through tears as she did what he said.

"Thank you for doing this…and if you don't mind, this will be my something borrowed."

"Absolutely," Art said, as she tucked the handkerchief into her bra. "You got the rest of that hoopla?" Art asked.

"She sure does," LaQueen said with a smile. "The something old is that necklace with the little cat charm. Said her father gave it to her years ago. Something new is her dress and shoes. You gave her something borrowed, and I gave her something blue."

"What's that?" Art asked.

"Undies."

Art blushed. "Oh…well…I didn't mean to…"

Cat laughed. "I know exactly how you feel. This is all weird for me, too."

"It don't matter," Art said. "You look real pretty."

Cat laid a hand on his forearm. "And you look very handsome."

Art preened. "I cut a fine figure in this suit in my day."

"You still do," Cat said. "And I will be forever grateful that you wanted to do this for me."

"Can't think of anywhere I'd rather be right now," he said.

There was a knock at the door. LaQueen answered it, then came back.

"That was John. He said the judge is in his chambers now. It's time to get this party started." She looked at Cat. "Are you ready?"

A calm washed over Cat. Was she ready? She'd been waiting for this day her whole life. She just hadn't known it.

"Yes."

"Then off we go. Art, you're escorting the bride."

"What are you doing?" Art asked.

LaQueen grinned. "Running the show."

Wilson was in over his head. What had started out being a simple trip to the courthouse to get married was turning into a three-ring circus with LaQueen as the ring-mistress. She'd sent John home with him to wait while he dressed. Then John had asked him twice on the way to the jewelry store if he knew Cat's ring size.

"I will know it when I see it" had been Wilson's answer both times.

He knew everything that mattered about the

woman who held his heart. Whatever else there was to learn would come through the years.

And now he stood beside the judge's desk, waiting for Cat to come through the door. He thought he was ready, but then the door opened. Not once in the time he'd known her had he ever seen her in a dress. He exhaled as if he'd been punched in the gut.

She was stunning.

The moment Cat stepped into the room, she looked for him. When their gazes met, he saw her blink back tears and lift that stubborn, beautiful chin, and he thought he might die from the joy of this moment as she moved to stand beside him.

"Are we all here?" the judge asked.

"We are, your honor," LaQueen stated.

"Then we begin," he said.

In the back of his mind, Wilson could hear the judge speaking, then Art stating he was standing in for her father. But it was the look on Cat's face and the fierce grip she had on his fingers that told him she was as moved as he was by what was happening.

Sometime during the service, he thought he heard Cat say "I do," but his heart was hammering so loudly, he might have imagined it. When John Tiger elbowed him, he jumped, confused as to what he'd missed.

The judge repeated the question.

"Do you, Wilson, take Catherine to be your lawfully wedded wife? And do you promise to love her and honor her, in sickness and in health and forsaking all others…until death do you part?"

"Yes."

"Please place the ring on her finger."

He felt Cat shiver as he took her hand, then slid the ring down the length of her finger.

The judge was still talking, but Wilson didn't focus in on it until he heard him say, "Wilson and Catherine, it is my honor to pronounce you husband and wife. What God has brought together, let no man put asunder. Wilson, I suggest you seal the deal and kiss your bride."

Cat's lips were trembling. Wilson was shaking all the way to the bone. Then their lips met and the world settled.

Someone was taking pictures, because Cat heard the clicks and saw the flashes from the corner of her eye. She suspected LaQueen, but before she could confirm her suspicions, Wilson wrapped his arms around her and very softly whispered close to her ear, so that only she could hear, "You will never be alone on this earth again."

Cat swallowed back tears as she looked up into his face. Leave it to Wilson to know and assuage her greatest fear.

Then everyone started talking.

Art and John congratulated Wilson and kissed Cat. LaQueen continued to snap pictures. She didn't quit until the camera did.

By the time it was over, Cat was thoroughly rattled by the rush of emotions. When Wilson took her by the hand and started toward the elevator, she was grateful.

"Art, thank you for coming, and LaQueen and John, thank you for being our witnesses," Cat said, as they all piled into the elevator.

"Oh, believe me, honey, the pleasure was all ours. So…what's next?" LaQueen asked.

"The honeymoon, to which you are not invited," Wilson said.

"I could get another camera," LaQueen offered.

"You might find yourself arrested when you try getting the pictures developed," John teased.

Laughter followed, and when they got to the parking lot, they all parted company, leaving Cat and Wilson alone beside their vehicle.

The sun was warm against his face—the breeze just strong enough to shift the curls on Cat's head and set the flounce of fabric around her neck aflutter. He was so moved by the moment that he struggled to find the right words to speak. Finally he just cupped her face with his hands and said what mattered most.

"Wife."

Cat's hands were on his chest, feeling the rhythm of his heartbeat against her palms. At that moment the staggering losses she'd endured during her lifetime had just been rendered null and void.

"Wilson…I love you more than I know how to express…and I love the baby that we made. Thank you for not giving up on me."

He brushed his mouth across her lips, then gave her hand a soft squeeze.

"Sweetheart, you were always worth the wait. You just didn't know it. However, that's all in the past. Today is a new beginning for the both of us…and our baby. We'll call Mom and Dad so they won't worry that we're not coming back tonight, and then get something to eat before we go back to your apartment. I'm not telling them about the ceremony over the phone. Are you okay with that?"

She nodded, suddenly weary.

Wilson saw it. "Are you okay?"

"Just a little tired."

"What sounds good to you?" he asked.

Cat looked up at him. "You."

Wilson's heart stuttered before it settled back into a regular rhythm.

"We can always order in."

"Great," Cat said.

They made the phone call to Austin on the way home, and less than thirty minutes later, were inside her apartment and naked as the day they'd been born.

Cat was lying with her hand on his heart and her head pillowed on his shoulder. The steady rhythm of his heartbeat was a poignant reminder of the day she'd watched it stop. She'd been afraid plenty of times in her life, but that moment was the first time that she'd felt helpless to change what was happening. The fact that he'd been given back to her was something she would never take for granted.

"Love you, Cat," he whispered.

"Show me."

So he did.

Jimmy Franks woke up in the alley behind Lowry's Gas and Guzzle, only to realize another day had come and gone while he'd been unaware. He'd been stoned for days, and he'd been dog bit and rained on. Every stitch of his clothing was wet and reeked with filth. Now, with the rising sun, it was also steaming. Figuring that he was about as low as he'd ever been in his life, he relieved himself behind a Dumpster, then checked his pockets to see if he had any change left for a cup of the coffee he could smell emanating from beneath the back door of the convenience store. When he came up empty, he wandered around to the front of the store.

The parking lot was empty.

He looked inside.

There was a middle-aged woman behind the counter nursing a cigarette and a cup of coffee. He wanted that coffee and some food. And he needed some cash and a way out of town. Time to go shopping.

Wilson woke up to the scent of fresh-brewed coffee. He opened his eyes just as Cat entered the bedroom with two steaming cups. But it wasn't the coffee that got his attention. The only things she was wearing were her necklace with the cat charm and her pink butterfly tattoo.

"Lord have mercy," he groaned, as he rolled over to the side of the bed and then sat up. "To think that I'll be waking up to you and this for the rest of my life. Lord, if I just died and went to heaven, then no resurrections, please."

Cat smiled like the proverbial feline with the dish of cream, handed him his coffee cup, then sat down beside him. She blew on her coffee, then took a slow sip.

"I've made all my calls," Cat said. "I talked to the apartment manager. I have two months left on my lease, but I was such a good renter for so many years, he's letting me out without issue. Plus, he saw the footage of me coming through the weeds in all my natural glory."

Wilson frowned. "Did he make a pass?"

Cat laughed out loud. "I was on the phone with him, not in a bar."

"Oh yeah, right," Wilson said.

"And…just because I married you, that doesn't mean I've gone all helpless on you. I'm still me, and don't you forget it."

He set his cup down, then set hers aside, too.

"Hey, I wasn't through with that," she said.

He wrapped his arms around her neck and pulled her backward onto the bed.

"Yeah…and I wasn't through with you."

It was an hour later and Wilson was still in the shower when Cat came out wrapped in a towel, picked up the remote and turned on the TV as she began to dress.

The news anchor was in the middle of a story regarding a robbery and murder that had taken place on the west side of Dallas. She sat on the foot of the bed, watching as they played a short clip from the store's security camera.

It was grainy black-and-white footage of the robbery. Unfortunately, the robber never looked up, so the camera only caught a downward view of his face. It could have been anyone. But she knew that if he was in the system, the police would likely be making an ID soon. The perp was leaving his fingerprints all over the place.

As she watched, the man suddenly vaulted over the counter and hit the woman in the jaw with his fist. She went down hard and didn't get up. The perp began rifling through the shelf beneath the counter. When he suddenly pulled out a gun and shot toward the floor, Cat jerked as if the bullets had hit her and not the victim.

Then the robber opened the register, pocketed the money in it and momentarily ducked out of camera range. When he came back up again, he was carrying something in his hand. As she tuned back in to the broadcast, she realized he must have been going through the woman's pockets for her keys.

"...then stole her car. The clerk, a woman named Debi Moore, had been an employee of the station for eleven years, and during that time, it had been robbed five times. According to her grief-stricken husband, she'd turned in her resignation a month ago. This would have been her last night on the job."

"Man. Talk about a bum deal," Cat muttered.

"What's happening?" Wilson asked.

Cat didn't even know he'd come out of the bathroom, but when she looked up, he was already half-dressed.

"Some creep robbed Lowry's Gas and Guzzle over on the west side. Killed the clerk in cold blood and stole her car. They've got footage from a security camera, but the quality was so poor, you couldn't see his face. However, if he's in the system, they'll ID him soon. He left prints all over the place."

Wilson frowned. "I've been in there before. It wasn't Debi Moore, was it?"

"Me, too," Cat said. "And, yes. Poor Debi. She was always so friendly. It was her last night on the job."

Wilson shook his head as he put on his shirt. "The sorry bastard. I hope they get him off the streets, and soon."

Cat nodded.

By noon, they were on their way home.

Louis Montoya woke up in his Nuevo Laredo hotel room, rolled over and looked at the time. It was already past noon. He pushed back the covers, then sat up on the side of the bed and reached for his cell phone. He didn't know why, but he sensed something was terribly wrong at home.

He'd dreamed about Conchita last night, and it was still painfully fresh in his mind. In the dream, he'd been standing on the front steps of his house, but the door key no longer worked. He kept ringing the doorbell and calling out her name, but the person inside just kept saying, "She doesn't live here anymore."

In his head, he knew it was just a dream, but he needed to hear her voice, to make sure she was okay and that they were still on the same page.

He punched in the numbers, then counted the rings. When the answering machine clicked on, he left a brief message, stating that he would try her cell, and that he loved her.

But when he dialed her cell next, there was no answer there, either. This constituted three days straight during which he'd been unable to speak to her. He told himself it didn't mean anything, but on the heels of the nightmare, it was unsettling.

He headed for the shower, hoping to wash away the memory of the dream along with the road grime he'd been too tired to deal with when he'd checked in last night.

The plan was to talk to the local authorities, visit the site where Presley had been caught and where Tutuola supposedly suffered the burns that had scarred him, and see what turned up. If nothing broke, then he would go to Dallas. He wanted to get the facts about Cat Dupree's involvement in that fire firsthand—if in fact she'd had any involvement at all.

What he did know was that in the business of crime, coincidence was as rare as honesty, and hers was the only name that kept turning up. Just like a bad penny.

Jimmy Franks felt like a million dollars. He'd bought himself a change of clothes at Wal-Mart, a burger, fries and a six-pack of beer to enjoy on the road, and he was heading west in his new ride with a smile on his face. As much as he would have liked a hit of the good stuff, the bigger high was knowing that he was finally on the road to finishing what he'd started all those weeks ago.

He tipped his last can of beer to his mouth, emptied it, then tossed it out the window as he drove.

"Say your prayers, McKay. I'm on the way."

Cat and Wilson had continued the discussion all the way to Austin about when or how they would tell his parents they were married, and whether they would mention the pregnancy now or wait until it became obvious. But it was Cat who finally summed everything up.

"I do not want to start this marriage with secrets."

Wilson nodded. "I agree, but I wanted it to be your call."

"Then I say we tell them as soon as we get back."

Wilson glanced down at what John Tiger had

called "a hefty rock" and grinned. "Glad you like it," he said.

Cat splayed her fingers, then tilted her hand toward the light. The facets of the stone in her wedding ring caught fire as the sunlight spilled through it.

"What's not to like? It's embarrassingly large, and I love the square cut. It matches your jaw."

Wilson laughed. "Great. I'm right up there with the jewelry, but that's all right. It's always good to know where you stand."

Cat grinned, then reached for the can of pop he'd bought for her at their last stop and took a sip, although it wasn't her usual Pepsi. She'd opted for ginger ale in the hopes it would settle her stomach. She was still experiencing infrequent bouts of nausea and hoped the symptoms would dissipate as her pregnancy progressed.

"Feeling any better?" he asked.

"Yes," she said, and took one more sip before putting the can back into the cup holder.

Wilson glanced at his watch. "We're about half an hour from the ranch. It will be good to get home."

Cat leaned back and stretched her long legs as best she could beneath the dash as she thought about what he'd just said.

"You know, once we move out, your parents will

probably be glad to get their house back to themselves."

"I know. The old home place is about three quarters of a mile north of where the house sits now. It's pretty run-down, but it could be fixed up. Or, if you don't like it, we can pull it down and build a new one."

Cat frowned. "Let's take a good look at it first. I'm partial to stuff with character."

"Ah…that would explain why you fell for me."

Cat rolled her eyes and laughed.

She'd never thought life could be this good.

Nine

Dorothy McKay was standing watch at the front windows as Carter came in from the kitchen with a handful of still-warm peanut butter cookies she'd made earlier.

"Hey, honey, what are you looking at?"

"I'm watching for Wilson and Cat."

Carter handed her a cookie. "They'll be along soon. Why? What's the deal?"

"Something's up," she said, then took a bite, chewing thoughtfully.

Carter stuffed a cookie in his own mouth as he continued to talk. "Like what?"

"Don't talk with your mouth full, honey," Dorothy said absently, then took another bite of her own cookie.

Carter grinned. He'd loved this woman for the

better part of his life and was still going to be loving her with his last breath. But she had a tendency toward mothering him, and he didn't need a mother. He preferred his wife. Still, it was a good idea now and then to agree.

"Yes, ma'am," he said. "But these sure are good." Then he stuffed another cookie into his mouth, chewed and swallowed without missing a beat.

Dorothy turned and smiled, then wiped a cookie crumb from the corner of his lips before giving him the last bite of her cookie, too.

Never one to turn down sweets, Carter took it, but fussed at her for brushing away the crumbs. He growled playfully, then snapped at her fingers like a puppy who was in danger of losing its bone.

"Hey. I was saving those crumbs for later," he said, and then grinned.

Although she'd heard that phrase at least a thousand times over the years they'd been married, she still laughed. Partly because he expected her to, and partly because he was serious.

She threw her arms around his neck, and gave him a quick hug and kiss. He would have followed through with something more, but when he spied the familiar sight of Catherine's SUV coming over the hill, he settled for giving her backside a soft pat instead.

"Here they come," he said.

Dorothy spun out of his arms and headed for the door.

"Dang, honey, give them time to get parked."

Dorothy frowned. "Oh, all right. But mark my words…I'm telling you, something's up with them."

"Why do you think that?" he asked.

Dorothy's tone was firm. "I always knew when my kids were keeping something from me, and I could hear it in Wilson's voice when he called earlier. Just because they all outgrew me and started shaving and having babies doesn't change a thing."

Carter grinned. Yep. He loved this woman pretty much to distraction and back.

"Okay…consider your words marked."

Wilson pulled up to the front yard and then parked.

"Well, here we are. Home at last." Then he laughed. "I always wanted to say that."

Cat gave him a nervous look. "You can quit trying to cheer me up. I'm going to be a little uneasy until everything gets said."

He hated that she was afraid, even a little bit, of his folks.

"I swear, they're going to be happy for the both of us."

"Then let's go spill the beans, okay?"

He leaned over and gave her a quick kiss. "Okay."

They got out in unison, then met at the back of the SUV to get the suitcases of extra clothes they'd packed in Dallas. The rest of their belongings would be shipped to the ranch, along with the contents of their respective apartments, but not for some time. They'd made arrangements for the stuff to go into storage until they had a permanent place to live.

As they started toward the house, the door opened.

Wilson watched Cat's jaw clench as Dorothy came flying out.

"You're back! My goodness, we've gotten so used to the both of you being here that it was lonely without you."

"Thanks a lot," Carter said dryly, as he followed her out.

Wilson grinned. His parents were a hoot.

"We missed you, too," Cat said, and was only mildly surprised to realize that she really meant it.

"Then come in, come in," Dorothy said, and reached for Cat's hand. As she did, she saw the ring on her finger and froze. She looked at Cat, then down at the ring again, then back up at Cat, before throwing her hands up in the air. "I knew it! I knew it!" she said, and then started laughing and hugging them both.

"Knew what?" Carter asked, completely confused.

Wilson rolled his eyes, then looked at Cat. "What did I tell you?"

Cat couldn't help but laugh. Dorothy was so funny, and Carter looked so confused.

"Will somebody please tell me what's going on around here?" Carter said.

"We're married," Cat said.

Carter's eyes widened. He looked at Wilson, then at Cat, grinned and shook his head.

"It's about time."

Wilson saw all the tension fading from Cat's posture, but it was the light in her eyes he loved best.

Dorothy took Cat by the hand. "Let's get inside. You must be starving. You can tell us all about it while we eat."

"You don't mind that we did this without the family?" Cat asked.

Dorothy paused on the threshold and turned around. Her eyes were dancing.

"Of course not. It's your lives, but, honey, you better mark it down in your memory book, because it will probably be the *last* thing they'll let you do alone."

Wilson slid his arm across Cat's shoulders as his mother moved into the house ahead of them.

"I'll be carrying you across the threshold when we get our own place, okay?" he said.

Cat's heart skipped a beat. "Absolutely, okay," she whispered back. "But when do we tell them about the baby?"

Dorothy squealed. "Baby? Oh my lord…there's a baby, too? I am in *heaven!*"

Wilson frowned. "For Pete's sake, Mom, do you have microphones hidden around here that we don't know about?"

Dorothy was laughing and crying simultaneously as she hugged them all over again. "It's not microphones…it's just a mother's ears. One of these days Cat will know what I'm talking about."

"Do you think so?" Cat asked.

Dorothy hugged her. "I know so. So now we really have something to celebrate. I'm calling the family."

Cat looked at Wilson over Dorothy's shoulder, grinning as she went from her arms to Carter's.

Carter gave her a hug and then patted her on the shoulder.

"Do you know that of all the grandkids Dorothy and I have, not one of them is named for me?"

A little startled, Cat still managed to smile. "I'll keep that in mind."

Dorothy frowned. "Carter, are you still harping about a namesake? For goodness sake, Catherine, don't pay him any attention. He's been making the same complaint for years."

Wilson took Cat by the hand as they went inside.

"Wilson, why haven't any of your brothers or sisters named one of their children after your dad?" Cat asked.

"Because his name isn't really Carter. It's Rupert."

Cat's eyes widened, then she started to laugh. She was still laughing when they walked into the kitchen.

"What's so funny?" Dorothy asked, as she set a bowl of fruit salad on the table beside a platter of tuna salad sandwiches.

"I am so going to love being a part of this family," Cat answered.

Dorothy beamed. "Well, that's great, honey, because we love that you're part of it, too. Now sit, sit. I want to hear all about the wedding. Where did you have it? What did you wear? Where are you going to live? You know we would love for you both to be here. There's plenty of room. Wilson, your father is glad you've decided to help run the ranch. It's about time. He's getting up in years, and you're the only one of our sons who cared a fig about ranching. Did you—"

"Mom!"

Dorothy blinked, a little startled by the tone of Wilson's voice.

"What?"

"Take a breath."

Carter grinned. "I've been giving her that advice for years. You can see how good it took."

"Oh, never mind," Dorothy said. "I'm going to call everyone now. Tomorrow's Saturday. We're having a party. The girls can bring cakes. I won't have time to bake, because I'll be using the oven to do the ribs."

Cat watched Wilson's mother in rapt fascination, wondering if this was what her mother would have been like. Would she have been this excited about seeing Cat married?

She reached for half a sandwich, scooped some of the fruit salad onto her plate, as well, then picked up a grape with her fingers and elbowed Wilson.

"What?"

"Open your mouth."

He complied. She popped the grape into his mouth, then handed him a sandwich.

"I suggest we eat while your mom and dad are otherwise occupied."

"We are definitely getting a place of our own—and soon," he muttered.

Carter overheard Wilson's comment, then added one of his own.

"The old home place needs some work, but it's yours if you want to live there."

Cat was overwhelmed by how fast everything was happening, but at the same time, excited. This wasn't just the day she got married. It was the first day of the rest of her life.

"I'd love to see it," she said.

"If you're up to it, we'll drive over after lunch," Carter said.

"Why wouldn't I be up to it?" Cat asked.

Carter blushed. "Well, you being…I mean, you're gonna have a…"

Dorothy snorted indignantly. "Oh, for the love of God, Carter. She's pregnant. I can't believe, after all the children we raised and all the grandchildren they've given you, you still struggle with that word."

Cat took a big bite of her sandwich, then rolled her eyes as she chewed and swallowed.

"Carter, you never mind what to call my…condition. This is delicious, and if it's still down in half an hour, I'm good to go," she said.

Happy for his reprieve, Carter grinned, then dug into his own lunch.

Dorothy ate in between phone calls, chewing and talking and laughing with her daughters and daughters-in-law without Cat being able to tell from her end which was which. It was obvious that Dorothy loved them all equally.

Cat finished her meal, then excused herself to go to the bathroom. On the way down the hall, she couldn't help but feel a bit like Alice, when she'd fallen down the rabbit hole. What on earth could happen next?

Luis Montoya was more than a little angry. He was tired and wished he were anywhere but in a hotel in Nuevo Laredo. Conchita was still AWOL, and his focus wasn't what it should be for worrying about her. Tomorrow he would visit with the local authorities and see what, if anything, they knew about Solomon Tutuola, and what kind of reaction he got when he mentioned the name Cat Dupree.

His stomach grumbled—a complaint that he had not fed it enough today. But dinner wasn't happening until he knew what was wrong with his wife, and the one person who kept her finger on the pulse of the entire family was his mother, Amalia. The only problem was, if he called and asked her where Conchita was, she would think something was wrong with their marriage.

Then he sighed. Hell. Something *was* wrong with their marriage. He'd spent a lot of time away this past year, and now it might be about to bite him in the ass. And if something had happened to Conchita, his family would have called him. Still, he couldn't rest until he made sure she was okay.

So he sat on the corner of the bed, punching in the numbers to his mother's home phone and trying to figure out a way to get the information he needed without letting on that he was concerned.

The phone rang twice; then he heard his mother's voice.

"Hello, Mama, it's me, Luis."

Amalia Montoya giggled. "I know it is you. Do you think I don't know my own son's voice?"

He smiled. Her infectious giggle was something the whole family teased her about.

"So how are you? Is Papi feeling better?"

His father was recovering from a broken leg and had been whining for weeks.

"Your father is a big baby," Amalia said. "I told him so. He only has a little cast on his leg. I gave birth to eight of his children. He doesn't know the meaning of the word pain."

Luis's smile widened. This was a familiar chant that his mother pulled out whenever she wanted to end a conversation in her favor.

"I know, I know," he said. "And speaking as child number two, I am forever grateful."

She giggled, which lifted Luis's anxiety just enough to put him a little more at ease. Then she added, "Conchita told me you were gone again and that maybe you will be traveling into the United States?"

His heart skipped a beat. At least Conchita was alive and still speaking to his family, or his mother would not have known this much.

"Yes. I didn't want to go, but I had my orders."

"I know, I know," Amalia said. "You are a good son."

"Thank you, Mama." Then he voiced his concerns. "I haven't been able to get Conchita on the phone for several days. I know she can take care of herself, but I worry. Do you know if anything is wrong?"

There was an uneasy moment of silence, which only raised Luis's concerns.

"Mama?"

"It is not for me to tell," she finally said.

Luis felt all the blood running from his face. He leaned forward, bracing his elbows on his knees, and found himself staring at the toes of his shoes while his heart tried to crawl out of his throat.

"Is she ill? Has something happened to her?

Damn it, Mama, I have a right to know if my own wife is in trouble."

He heard his mother sigh, then muffled conversation between her and his father.

"Your father tells me to mind my own business, but I told him you are my son and you have asked your mother a question. It is my duty to answer it, no?"

"Yes. It is your duty. Now what the hell is going on?"

"She has gone to Mexico City."

"So?... That's no big deal. She and her sisters often go there, especially when I am gone. Why doesn't she just answer her cell phone? She always did before."

"Maybe it is because she isn't awake yet."

Luis frowned. This was getting stranger and stranger.

"She's gone to Mexico City to sleep?"

"Not exactly."

"Mama. Please."

"She went to have a boob job."

Luis felt as if someone had slapped him in the face. It was the last thing he'd ever expected to come out of his mother's mouth.

"Why on earth would she want to do something like that? She is beautiful the way she is."

Amalia sighed. "It was her birthday. You couldn't be bothered to stay around for it. She is at loose ends, my son. She has no children. Shopping is no longer enough to entertain her when you're not around. So, as your mother, I am giving you some advice. When you get home this time, you need to make time for your family. And you need to see about adopting a baby for Conchita. If you don't, your wife is liable to turn out looking like that crazy American rock star who keeps having doctors cut on his face."

"Who?"

Amalia sighed. "You know…Mickey Jackson."

"Do you mean Michael Jackson?"

"Mickey…Michael, whatever," Amalia said. "But you don't tell her that I'm the one who told. When you come back, you pretend to be surprised. Do you hear me?"

"Yes, Mama. I hear you. And believe me, it will not be difficult to be surprised."

He could tell that his mother had missed the point of his sarcasm when she giggled. "Good, good. It is always best to not hurt someone's feelings and ruin a surprise."

Luis sighed. "Yes, I completely agree." Then he glanced at his watch. "Anyway, Mama, it's getting late and I haven't had any dinner yet. Tell Papi I said hello, and I'll talk to the both of you when I get back."

"Be careful, and don't shoot anyone."

He pinched the bridge of his nose to keep from cursing. "Yes, Mama, I'll try my best."

He disconnected, then looked up, unaware there were tears running down his face. All he knew was that, while he was chasing after some bastard who probably deserved to die, his wife was so lost that she was letting doctors operate on her to change her looks. If he did what he wanted to do, he would call in, tell his boss the trail had gone cold and get home where he belonged.

He tossed his suitcase on the bed, changed into a clean shirt and left to go find some food. Tomorrow was another day. Maybe then, Conchita would answer her phone. Maybe by then he would know what to say to her that would make her world all right.

Jimmy Franks had already run out of money before he ran out of gas, which happened in the middle of traffic on the Austin city bypass. He managed to get the old car onto the shoulder of the road, then waited for a break in the traffic and abandoned it, telling himself it was just as well. The cops were sure to be looking for it by now.

He walked until he was deep into the inner city, then found himself a place to sleep. The weather was balmy, and it sure wasn't the first time he'd slept on the streets. This time, he found a big cardboard box and pulled it out of the Dumpster where it had been discarded. The hunger cramps in his belly and his need for a fix were distracting, but he knew enough not to try to find a dealer right away in a strange city, so he crawled into the box and pulled the flaps shut behind him.

The box smelled faintly of barbecue and urine. He didn't want to think how that combination of scents had come to be there, so he closed his eyes, fidgeted around until he found a fairly comfortable place to lie and fell asleep, only to be awakened a couple of hours later by a city garbage truck making the rounds.

He heard the *beep, beep, beep* of the truck's backup signal and rolled out of the box just before it was crushed beneath the wheels.

Still shaking from his near miss, he watched as the Dumpster was emptied. He didn't make a move until the truck had left the alley; then he looked at his box. It was ruined, as was his ability to sleep.

Withdrawal symptoms were setting in—muscle tics, a sensation of bugs crawling under the skin, and the gnawing need for a fix that only another junkie could understand. He swiped away the snot running from his nose and then ran his fingers through his hair. His new clothes were still holding up; there were only a couple of small stains. He would just have to start walking and see what turned up. Just because he'd hit another roadblock, that didn't mean he was quitting. He was in Austin—and that much closer to Wilson McKay. He would have to find another way to get what he needed, and that was all there was to it. No one messed with Jimmy Franks and got away with it.

No one.

Ten

Dorothy was still making phone calls when Carter took Wilson and Cat to the old homestead where he'd grown up. Cat could hear the excitement in Carter's voice as he drove. She knew he was happy that Wilson was coming home to work the ranch with him, and after what she and Wilson had been through, they were both ready for a change of pace.

She couldn't imagine a better place to raise a family than this. She watched with interest as they drove, listening to Carter point out the special places on the ranch. But it was her first glimpse of the old home place that caught her attention. By the time they'd parked beneath a pair of tall oak trees, she was in love.

The house was two-story with a wraparound

porch. Some of the shutters were off, others were hanging by one hinge, and it was sadly in need of a paint job, but she saw beyond the age to the structure beneath.

"Oh, Wilson. This is beautiful."

"Yeah, it is, isn't it?"

She got out quickly, anxious to look inside. "Why on earth isn't someone living here now?"

"I don't know…I guess they all wanted something new. When we were growing up, this was just Grandma and Grandpa's house. They died just after my youngest sister was married. Their deaths were fresh in our minds, and no one wanted to be here. It seemed like it was still their place. Now…"

"It's lonely," Cat said.

Carter eyed her sharply. "That's what my mother used to say about old houses. She would always choose character over flash and style."

"Smart woman," Cat said. "Can we go inside?"

"Sure," Carter said, and took the key out of his pocket. He started to go with them, then hesitated, handed Wilson the key and said, "You two go on in by yourselves. You don't need me along."

Wilson smiled his thanks, and off they went, while Carter settled onto the tailgate of his truck to wait.

Wilson took Cat by the hand, and together, they walked up the steps.

"Here we go," Wilson said, as he unlocked the door.

The hinges squeaked as the door swung inward.

Cat stood on the threshold, taking in the entry and the big staircase sweeping up to the left.

"Oh, Wilson. Just look at this place."

All he saw was peeling wallpaper and dusty floors.

"Yeah, I'm sorry it's in such bad shape, but we can—"

She turned, her eyes wide with excitement. "Bad shape? Are you nuts? This place is amazing."

She took off through the foyer, aiming for the great room beyond. A large fireplace made of natural rock centered the wall at the far end. The mantel was huge—a single beam of timber over fifteen feet long and two feet thick. Cat walked toward the bay window and looked out to the prairie beyond.

"The view goes on forever."

Wilson walked up behind her, then gathered her into his arms and kissed the back of her ear.

"So can you see yourself living here?" he asked.

"Oh, Wilson…yes."

"The kitchen and dining room are through here, and needless to say, in serious need of updating."

Cat eyed the exposed beams in the ceilings, as well as the size of the rooms.

"It's really big," she said.

"Lots of room for kids," he said.

Her hand automatically went to her belly. "One at a time, please."

Wilson suddenly shivered, then took her in his arms.

"What?" Cat asked.

He buried his face against the curve of her neck as he pulled her close.

"I don't know. I just had a sudden need to hold you."

Cat frowned. She was a believer in instinct. It had saved her life more than once over the years.

"Are you worried about Jimmy Franks?"

He thought about it for a moment. "I don't know. Maybe. I certainly should be."

Cat's frown deepened. "You know, I promised myself that if the Dallas police didn't get him, I would."

Wilson tightened his grip on her arms. "Oh no you don't, especially not now. I will not risk losing you again. Besides, you have to remember that it's not just what you feel like doing on your own anymore. You're carrying precious cargo."

"I know. I'm not crazy, okay?"

"Okay," Wilson said, and then tugged her hand. "There's still more to see. A couple of bedrooms downstairs and four up."

"Bathrooms?"

"One down. One up."

"Show me."

They made the rounds together, talking, planning, seeing themselves living under this roof as his grandparents had done before them.

The floors of the old house creaked and popped as they walked through the rooms, as if announcing their presence. By the time they were through, Cat was sold.

"So what's the verdict?" Wilson asked. "And remember, we can always build a new—"

"No. This is where we belong," she said.

He smiled. He'd felt it, too, but hadn't wanted to influence her decision.

"Let's go tell Dad. We'll need to hire a contractor to bring it up to code electrically and do the needed repairs. You can pick out colors and flooring, and tell the contractor what you think we'll need in the kitchen."

"I'm going to ask your mom to help me with that," Cat said.

"She'll love that," Wilson said. "And now we'd

better get back to the house. Someone needs to rein Mom in before she invites the whole of Austin to dinner tomorrow."

It was just after two o'clock the next day, when LaQueen came back to the office from a late lunch. She'd left John manning the phones and had promised to bring him a burger and fries, but what she'd seen during lunch had changed everything. The TV at the sports bar had been showing a replay of a soccer game between Italy and England when the broadcast was interrupted by a bulletin.

She'd watched long enough to realize that her boss's troubles weren't as far behind him as he might have liked. She'd grabbed John's order, tossed some money down on the table and headed for the exit.

When she got to the office, she hit the door running, startling John to the point that he got up from the desk and went to meet her.

He grabbed her by the arms. "What's wrong?"

"Here's your lunch," she said, and thrust the sack into his hands. "I've got to call Wilson."

"Why?"

"Were you watching the television?"

"No. There were too many calls."

"Remember Debi Moore, that woman who was murdered over at that gas station on the west side?"

"Yes."

"The police have identified her killer by his fingerprints."

"So?"

"It was Jimmy Franks."

John's eyes narrowed angrily. "The man who shot Wilson."

"Yes. And they just found the car that he stole abandoned on the side of the highway in Austin."

"Oh no."

"Exactly," LaQueen said. "Wilson needs to know the sorry rat is pretty much in his backyard."

"Do you think he's going after Wilson?"

"It's hard to say, but I'm not much of a believer in coincidence."

"You'd better let him know," John said.

"Right. You eat. I'll talk."

John smiled. "Gladly, woman. I have no intention of trying to outtalk you."

LaQueen swatted at him, but she was smiling. She loved this man. All she needed was for him to make a move and she was his for life. But—they both knew Wilson needed to be brought up-to-date on what was happening. No way were they going to let that crazy meth-head Jimmy Franks get close to him again.

She dialed Wilson's cell phone, then waited for the familiar sound of his voice.

The party was on. While Cat and Wilson were the center of attention, they were also on the receiving end of a goodly amount of teasing. At the moment, they were short of seating, and Wilson had pulled Cat down to sit on his lap, while his brother Charlie had gone after extra folding chairs from the storage room.

Charlie's wife, Delia, was putting plates and silverware on the long table in the dining room, while another brother, Lee, was setting up a folding table. Carter was in his easy chair with a lapful of grandchildren, which was exactly where he wanted to be.

Cat kept watching the family as they interacted with each other, listening to them repeat family stories and hearing the outbursts of laughter that came with each one. The joy of knowing she was now a part of all this was more than she could put into words.

Wilson's hand was splayed across her belly as he held her on his lap, and she quietly put her hand on his, thinking of the tiny life that lay beneath. Even now, they were protecting it together.

She watched the children running in and out of the house, and the ones playing outside. This time next year, their baby would be learning to sit up and maybe beginning to crawl. It was difficult to picture herself as a parent, and yet thinking of it seemed natural.

It wasn't until Wilson said her name and gave her a quick squeeze that she realized someone had asked her a question.

"What? I'm sorry. What did you say?" she asked.

"Yeah, she's gonna fit in to this family just fine," someone said. "She's already learned how to tune us out."

Cat grinned. "I didn't tune you out. It's just that my ears have gone numb."

The laughter that followed was loud and long.

"Way to go, baby," Wilson said, and quickly kissed the backside of her ear.

"What's so funny?" Dorothy asked, as she came into the living room.

Carter pointed at Cat. "Your newest daughter just put this wild bunch in their place."

Dorothy giggled. "That's our girl." Then she pulled Cat out of Wilson's lap. "Come with me, honey. I have something to show you."

Cat went willingly, glad to be out of the line of fire, if only for a short time. She followed Dorothy down the hall, then into a small storage room below the stairs.

"I put this up after my youngest started school. Told Carter I wasn't having any more babies and he'd better get used to it."

Cat grinned. She could readily understand why Dorothy had called a halt. They'd raised a houseful and then some. Then she saw what Dorothy was uncovering and gasped.

"Oh, Dorothy…"

Dorothy tossed back the old quilt that had been covering an old wooden rocking chair, then stepped back so Cat could get a better view.

"My father made it for me when I was pregnant with Wilson. I've rocked every one of my babies in this. None of the other kids wanted it. They either wanted something with cushions or claimed it didn't fit their decor. But since you like Grandpa and Grandma's house, I guessed you might like this, as well."

Cat immediately sat down, then ran her fingers along the arms and the seat, feeling the patina born of years and years of wear. She pushed off with the toe of her shoe, and as she began to rock, she was hit with a sudden sense of sadness. It wasn't often that she thought of her parents with such despair, but she could only imagine the delight they would be feeling, too, knowing they were about to become grandparents.

Suddenly overwhelmed, she looked down at her lap to hide her tears, but Dorothy somehow understood. She put a hand on Cat's head, gently soothing her.

"Your momma would be proud of you, honey."

Cat looked up, her eyes brimming with unshed tears.

"Thank you," she said.

Dorothy smiled. "You're welcome, and just so you know, we're all so proud you've joined the family. Wilson is my oldest, and I think I worried more about him than all the others, because he never seemed able to settle down. Meeting you was the best thing that ever happened to him."

Cat tried to laugh. "There were plenty of days when he would have argued that with you."

Dorothy giggled. "Well, shoot, honey. That's what we women have to do to keep them guessing. Now, we'd better get back before they come looking for us. There's a houseful of hungry people here."

Cat nodded, but when she got up, she covered the old rocker protectively with the quilt again before following Dorothy.

"Hey, where did you two go?" Wilson asked, as she came back into the living room.

"We just got our first baby gift," Cat said.

His eyes widened, and a look of delight spread across his face.

"What was it?"

"Your mother's rocking chair."

"Oh, man," Wilson said softly. "That's great. Grandpa made it for her when she was pregnant with me. We've all heard the story a hundred times."

"She said none of the other kids wanted it."

"But you do?"

Cat nodded. "It has character…just like our house."

"I love you," Wilson whispered.

"Love you, too," Cat said.

"Hey, you two! Can the cuddling until after we eat, would you? I'm starved," Charlie yelled. "Besides, Mom says dinner is ready."

"We're coming. We're coming," Wilson said, then took Cat by the hand. "Are you feeling okay?"

"I'm starved, too."

Wilson laughed. "So, morning sickness is fading?"

"It's not morning," Cat pointed out. "And those ribs smell fabulous."

"Then let's eat," he said, and they headed for the dining room to join the rest of the family.

* * *

Wilson was carrying a tray of dirty glasses into the kitchen when his cell phone began vibrating. The house was still full of family and friends, and Cat was lost somewhere in the living room in the middle of the melee. He'd promised to rescue her, but first things first. He set down the tray and, because of the noise level, headed for the back porch to answer.

The old tomcat wrapped himself around Wilson's legs as he sat down on the porch swing to talk. He scratched the cat's head as he answered.

"Hello."

"Wilson, it's me."

"Hey, LaQueen. What's up?"

"When you and Cat were here the other day, did you happen to hear about the robbery and murder at Lowry's Gas and Guzzle on the west side?"

"Yes, we did. We were watching the video at her apartment after the wedding. We both knew Debi, the woman who got killed. It was pretty gruesome. Why?"

"It was Jimmy Franks."

Wilson's heart dropped. "No."

"Yes. And that's not the worst of it."

Wilson took a slow breath, bracing himself.

"Talk to me."

"In addition to the robbery and murder, he also stole the clerk's car. They found it abandoned on the side of a highway in Austin."

Wilson felt as if he'd just been sucker punched.

"Shit," he whispered. "Is that it?"

"Isn't that enough?" LaQueen muttered.

"He knows where I am, doesn't he? That tornado footage told him right where we are."

"What do you want me to do?" she asked.

He sighed. "There's nothing you *can* do. I'll give the Austin police a call and tell them what's going on, and hope they find him before he gets this far."

"I'm sorry," LaQueen said.

"It's not your fault. Thanks for the heads up."

"Wilson…wait."

"Yeah?"

"Be careful."

"Absolutely," he said, and hung up.

A cow lowed somewhere out in the pasture, calling her calf. A jet plane flying overhead was leaving a contrail to mark its passing.

Wilson noted it absently, but his head was spinning. This changed a lot of things. He needed to talk to Cat and fill her in. And, while he was at it, he needed some luck, a gun and a pair of handcuffs.

The squeak of the hinges on the screen door behind him alerted him that he was no longer alone. He turned.

"Hey. I wondered where you'd gone," Cat said, and slid onto the seat beside him.

Wilson took her hands as he looked straight into her eyes. There was no hesitation in his decision to tell her. She was his equal in every way, and now that they were married, what affected him affected her. She had to be told.

"I just got a call from LaQueen."

Cat frowned. The tone of his voice was telling. "What's wrong?"

"Remember when we were in Dallas, how we saw that film clip of the robbery at Lowry's Gas and Guzzle?"

"Yes. Why?"

"It was Jimmy Franks."

A chill of foreboding swept through her. And she could tell by the look on his face that that wasn't all.

"And?"

"And they found the car he stole abandoned on the side of the highway in Austin."

Cat stood abruptly. The anger in her eyes was instantaneous.

"He's coming after you, isn't he? He said he would. We have to—"

He grabbed her hands, then tugged her down onto his lap.

"Stop it. We don't have to do anything but pay attention."

"Someone needs to go after him. I could—"

"What did we talk about yesterday?"

She knew what he was talking about, but it still didn't set well with her. She couldn't just stand by and let a killer waltz back into their lives without doing something.

Wilson could see the thoughts going through her mind. "You are not hunting a killer with a baby in your belly, do you hear me?"

Her eyes narrowed angrily. "I know that. I wouldn't put the baby in danger, but you aren't going, either. So what do you suggest?"

He sighed. "We have to tell Mom and Dad. This puts them in danger, too. Damn it. I hate this. I never meant for my job to put my family in danger."

"You're not at fault. The world is full of losers. He's one of them."

"I'll wait until the others leave before I bring this up with Mom and Dad."

Cat nodded. But even after they'd joined the rest of the crowd, her thoughts were flying, trying to figure out how to take down Jimmy Franks. She knew she was going to have to have some faith in the Austin police department, but if that sorry little bastard came looking for them, she would have no qualms about putting him under six feet of Texas dirt.

* * *

Luis Montoya was not having a good day. Although he was no longer worried about his wife's whereabouts, he was now concerned because she still wasn't returning any of his calls. He'd put off going to the Nuevo Laredo police department until well after ten in the morning, but he could delay no longer.

He'd had no trouble finding it, and after introducing himself, he was now following an officer who was taking him to one of the policemen who'd participated in the arrest of Mark Presley. He needed to find out what they knew, if anything, about his murder victim.

As they passed the booking area, he saw a prostitute trying to talk her way out of an arrest, while a junkie in need of a fix was crying and apologizing for killing his best friend. He kept saying that all he'd wanted was the dope his friend had scored. If he'd shared, his friend would still be alive.

Luis frowned, then looked away. Drugs were at the core of more than half the crimes committed in his country. He hated them and everything they represented.

Finally the officer stopped, then knocked on a door before opening it.

A short, stocky man with a bald head and a neatly trimmed goatee looked up.

"Yes?"

"Detective Mesa, this is Detective Luis Montoya from Chihuahua Homicide. He needs to talk to you about a case you worked."

Mesa stood up and waved toward a chair on the other side of his desk. "I am Alejandro Mesa. Please sit."

Luis sat while taking in the neat stacks of paper on the detective's desk, as well as a family picture hanging on the wall. He wondered if this man's wife was as unhappy as his, then noted the four children in the picture and decided she wasn't.

"How can I help you?" Mesa asked.

Luis pulled a photo out of the folder he was carrying and laid it on the desk.

"Have you ever seen this man?"

Mesa frowned. "No, and believe me, if I had, I would have remembered him. What is his name?"

"Solomon Tutuola. Does it sound familiar?"

Mesa shook his head. "Again, I am sorry, but no. You know, this information could have been ascertained by phone or fax. Why do you come so far?"

"The man was murdered in our city. Judging from his rap sheet, he was a very bad man. But still, murder is against the law, and someone pumped a lot of lead into him before setting him and his house on fire."

Mesa whistled softly below his breath. "That is an ugly way to die."

"Dead is dead, no matter how one comes to be there," Montoya said.

Mesa shrugged. "This is true. But why do you think we would have knowledge of this man?"

"A few months ago an American came through Nuevo Laredo, then was tracked to an abandoned house outside this very city. His name was Mark Presley."

Mesa's eyes widened, then he began to nod. "Yes, yes. I remember it well. It was actually a tricky situation. As you know, bounty hunting is not legal in our country, and yet this Presley was trailed south through Texas and then over the border by two American bounty hunters. Murder charges had not yet been filed against him, nor had he been brought to court, so there was no bounty to claim. Yet he was on the run. One of the bounty hunters was a woman. She is the one who came for him. As I remember, she believed him guilty of murdering her best friend, who was pregnant with his child. As it turns out, she was right. And since there was no price on his head and he hadn't jumped bail, technically, they weren't hunting bounty, you see."

"This woman…what was your impression of her?" Montoya asked.

Mesa arched an eyebrow, then smiled. "She was the kind of woman you dream about taking to bed…until you look into her eyes. She was a very beautiful woman, but I think if you were her enemy… she would be a very dangerous one. And there was a terrible scar across her throat." Then he asked a question of his own. "If you are looking for this man's killer, why are you asking about Mark Presley? He's in a Texas prison."

"We found his business card with the belongings of my murder victim," Montoya said. "I've been trying to piece together the last few weeks of Tutuola's life, and I was thinking that maybe, at one time, the two men had been together."

Mesa was leaning back in his chair, fiddling with the end of his pen, clicking it in and out, in and out, as he thought. Then he suddenly sat up.

"There is a thing about Presley's capture that I just remembered."

"What is that?" Montoya asked.

"The bounty hunters claimed that Mark Presley wasn't alone when they found him. That there was another man with whom they exchanged gunfire, but they said he died when the house caught on fire and then exploded, although when we checked a day later, we found no body."

Once again, Montoya remembered the Realtor

Chouie Garza's description of the man he'd sold the estate to and the raw wounds that looked like newly healing burns. "To your knowledge," he asked the other detective, "did either of the bounty hunters come back into Mexico afterwards?"

Mesa shrugged. "I did not see them, but that means nothing."

"Do you remember the bounty hunters' names?"

"The man was named Wilson McKay, and he called the woman Cat. Cat Dupree."

Montoya slid the photo back into his file and stood up.

"Is there someone who could take me out to where the fire and capture took place?"

Mesa nodded. "I will get one of our officers to take you, although I don't know what you expect to find. Very little is left of the building, and after all these months, if there was anything of value left to find, it will be gone."

"I know. Still, I would like to see for myself."

"Of course. Come with me. And if there's anything else we can do for you, please don't hesitate to let me know."

"I appreciate it," Montoya said, and he did. The sooner he got this over with and got home to Conchita, the happier he would be.

Eleven

The police car that sped past the alley was running hot. The lights were flashing, the siren a mind-shattering scream echoing through the darkened streets. Jimmy Franks flattened himself up against the wall behind a Dumpster, holding his breath until they had passed.

Less than an hour ago, he'd left the shift clerk at Bob's Liquor Store dead behind the counter. The money that had been in the till was now in his pocket, making him six hundred dollars to the good. To celebrate the take, he'd also helped himself to a fifth of their best bourbon.

Once he was certain the cops were long gone, he took a slug of the liquor, then continued on his way, slipping through the back alleys of Austin until he was more than a mile from the scene of his latest crime. As he walked, he experienced a revelation.

It was getting easier to kill.

By the time he met up with Wilson McKay again, the man wouldn't know what hit him. But for now, he needed to lay low. He didn't think that the liquor store had a security camera, but even if it did, he was feeling smug. He'd done this twice now without so much as a hitch. The gun he'd killed the clerk with in Dallas was heavy against his thigh, even though it was a slug lighter than it had been before he'd gone into the liquor store here in Austin.

And so he walked, feeling high on crime. A short while later, he came upon a seedy motel. The vacancy sign was on, but only the V and the Y were working. All the other letters were dark. Jimmy glanced up and down the street before coming out of the alley. It was perfect for what he needed. The clientele at a no-tell motel wouldn't be concerned with the identities of their neighbors.

He slipped into the office with his head down, walking with a shuffle and a limp, and paid cash for a couple of nights. He needed a place to hide out until he figured what his next steps would be.

The clerk didn't even look up. He just took Jimmy's cash and slid a key toward him.

"Room 120," the clerk mumbled. "Bottom floor, all the way in the back."

Jimmy grabbed the key and limped out, clutching the bottle close to his chest. As soon as he cleared the office, he resumed his normal jerky stride and didn't relax until he was in the room with the door locked behind him.

Once inside, he barely gave the room a glance. It was a dive, but to a man who'd been spending most of his days and nights on the street, it was a luxury. And, since he was flush with money, he was ready to indulge his hunger.

He sat down on the side of the bed and flipped through the yellow pages until he found listings of restaurants that delivered. Several of them had been circled, most likely by past customers who knew the area. He opted for Chinese, called in his order, and then kicked back on the bed to wait for its arrival.

There was a water stain in the corner of the ceiling, and a poorly patched hole in the Sheetrock wall where someone had put a foot—or a fist. The bedspread was brown, as was the indoor-outdoor carpeting, obviously chosen to hide the stains left by the guests. He had a couple of hits of meth, money in his pockets and a roof over his head. Living the life of Riley, as Houston used to call it.

As he thought of his brother, he frowned. He had

a right to be pissed at Houston. If he hadn't gone off and abandoned him back in Dallas, then Jimmy wouldn't have had to rob that quick stop or kill that woman. Not that he was losing any sleep over it, but it did increase his visibility, which did not suit his purposes.

His belly grumbled. He glanced at the clock. It would be at least another twenty minutes before his food arrived. He might as well watch a little TV—catch the local news and see what was up. He flipped channels until he found a station he recognized, then crossed his feet at the ankles, bunched a pillow behind his head and upped the volume.

It wasn't until the second commercial break was over that the news anchor switched from national to local news. When he did, Jimmy was shocked to see a booking shot of himself on a split screen along with the clip of him robbing Lowry's Gas and Guzzle in Dallas.

"Crap," he muttered, and sat up, leaning forward to catch what was being said.

"The police here in Austin have also identified an abandoned car on the freeway as the same one that was stolen from the murder victim in the Dallas robbery. Authorities have issued a BOLO—a be-on-the-lookout order—for James Dale Franks in this city, as well."

Jimmy came up off the bed, cursing. Now what? If Wilson McKay was watching the news, he'd just been forewarned. And even if he wasn't, there were plenty of people who would be letting him know.

This screwed up everything.

His mind was racing as he began to pace. Should he leave? Had the clerk gotten a good look at his face? Or was it riskier to be out on the streets than to just stay put?

"Damn, damn, damn," Jimmy muttered.

He was still trying to figure out what to do when someone knocked on the door. He jumped and grabbed his gun, then remembered he'd ordered dinner. He dug money from his pocket as he went to the door, opening it only a few inches.

The delivery man was waiting with a sack and a ticket.

"Delivery for Room 120."

"How much?" Jimmy asked.

"Fifteen seventy-five."

Jimmy handed him a twenty, took the sack and shut the door in his face. The scent of food made his belly growl, but he waited until he could no longer hear the delivery man's footsteps before he opened the door and peeked out again. Satisfied that he was as anonymous as he needed to be, he began unpacking all the little boxes, sampling each dish as he opened it. For a man raised on corn bread and beans, chopsticks were useless. He began eating voraciously, using both his fingers and the white plastic fork he found in the bag.

He was down to the fortune cookies when the news ended and the movie of the week began to play. It was a suspense movie about two men switching identities, and halfway through, he got an idea. And the more he thought about it, the more certain he became that he knew what he needed to do to get the cops off his back. All he needed was to find someone with his hair color and general age and build, and he would be good to go.

But first he needed to be able to move about freely, which meant he needed to change his appearance. There was a small pharmacy across the street from the motel. It should have everything he needed. He patted his pocket to make sure his money was in place, then opened the door. Once he was certain no one was watching his room, he slipped out.

Dust rose in small clouds, coating Luis Montoya's pant legs as he walked through the remnants of the burned-out hacienda. He wasn't an expert at investigating fires, but it was obvious this one had started with an explosion. The indentation in which he was standing was a good five or six feet in diameter and at least six inches deeper than the surrounding area.

The blast site.

What had ensued must have been true hell on earth. The fire had burned Tutuola badly. And yet it had not killed him.

That had happened in Chihuahua.

He knew how many bullets had been pumped into Tutuola's body before someone set him on fire again, this time turning him to charcoal. It was a brutal death, but he still didn't have a suspect, and it was obvious there were no answers to be had here. What he did know was that two other people had been here when *this* place burned. Two bounty hunters from Texas.

At least one of them had come back into Mexico again. He needed to find out if the man with Cat Dupree had come, too.

The officer who'd shown him the way out here was long gone. Luis was alone with his thoughts as he moved toward his car. Then his cell phone rang, and when he glanced at the caller ID, his hands began to shake.

Finally.

"Conchita…sweetheart, I have been waiting for your call. Are you all right?"

She was talking and crying. He couldn't tell what she was saying, but he knew she was upset.

"Slow down. Slow down. I can't understand what you're saying."

He heard a sob, then a deep, shuddering breath.

"Good," he said gently. "Now talk to me, *querida.* Are you home yet?"

"*Sì, sì.* I am home. I talked to your mother. She said she told you where I'd gone."

He sighed. At least he didn't have to worry about letting that piece of information slip. "I was worried when you didn't answer or call me back. I was afraid something had happened to you."

There was a long moment of silence, then a question that broke his heart.

"Would you have cared?"

He reacted in anger. "How can you ask such a thing? Haven't I always cared for you? Provided for you?"

"You have given me nice *things,* Luis. What I need is *you.*"

"My job is what provides you with those nice things."

"Your job is what takes you away from me," she countered.

He leaned against the fender of his car and closed his eyes. He'd never heard such despair in her voice.

"Are you all right?" he finally asked. "From the surgery, I mean."

"I didn't do it," she said. "I meant to, but at the last minute, I knew that it would not make me happy, either."

He didn't bother to hide his sigh of relief. "What can I do? You are my world. What can I do to make you happy?"

"I want a baby."

"Yes. Yes. When I get home, we will talk to an adoption agency."

"When are you coming home?" she asked.

"Soon."

"Where are you?"

"Nuevo Laredo. But I must travel to Dallas, Texas, before I can come home."

"You are going into the United States?"

"Yes."

"Will you bring me something special for my birthday?"

He struggled with the urge to weep.

"Yes. I will bring you something special. I promise."

"Okay."

"And will *you* do something for *me?*" he asked.

"Yes. What is it you want of me?"

"Please. Take care of yourself."

"I will."

"I will be home soon," he promised. "I love you very much."

"I love you, too," she said.

Then she hung up.

Luis knew he was in trouble. He just wasn't sure how to make things right.

He dropped his cell phone in his pocket and got into the car, but instead of starting the engine, he leaned his head on the steering wheel, then closed his eyes.

And he prayed.

He prayed for a miracle, because that was what it was going to take to put his world back together again.

Finally he drove back to his hotel. He needed to check in with his lieutenant, tell him what he'd learned so far, and make sure he was going to be permitted to continue his investigation before he crossed the border.

It was after midnight when Luis heard a gunshot in the hotel. At first he thought he was dreaming, until he heard the second one, then a third. They sounded close by. He rolled out of bed, pulled on his pants, and then grabbed his room key and gun. Someone ran down the hallway past his door as he was stepping into his shoes. By the time he went into the hallway, people were coming out of their rooms.

"Did you hear that?" someone said.

"Was that gunshots?" another asked.

"Did you see anyone come running down the hall?" Luis asked, as he held up his badge.

Voices rose in unison, but no one knew any more than he did. He knew the footsteps had gone south past his door, so it stood to reason that they'd come from the north.

"Get back in your rooms," he said, and then pointed at a young woman who was standing in her doorway. "You…call the police. Tell them there was a shooting on the fourth floor and that there's a policeman already on the scene."

She nodded and disappeared back into her room as Luis started down the hall in the direction of the shots, his gun drawn.

"Get inside. Get back inside," he kept saying as he passed people standing in their doorways.

One by one the doors closed behind him until he was alone in the hall. He was almost to the end of the hallway when he saw a door partially ajar. As he moved closer, he looked down to the floor and saw that a bloody hand and arm were keeping it from closing. He gritted his teeth and then shouted out, "Police! Come out with your hands up!"

No one answered. The door didn't move.

"This is the police," he repeated. "I'm coming in."

He pushed on the door. It swung part of the way inward, then stopped. He looked inside. The body of a woman was blocking it from opening all the way.

"Hello! Is anyone there?" he asked, knowing the shooter was undoubtedly long gone, as he knelt and felt for a pulse.

There was none.

He started to back out and leave the crime scene to the local authorities when he heard something that stopped his heart.

A small voice cried out. "Mama? Mama?"

"Madre de Dios," he muttered, and pushed his way into the room just as a tiny girl crawled off the bed and started toward him.

She had a small stuffed toy in one hand and her blanket in the other, and as she walked, Luis caught glimpses of tiny toes peeking out from the hem of her nightgown.

"Mama," the little girl said, and pointed to the woman on the floor.

"Poor little *niña,*" Luis muttered, as he picked her up and carried her out into the hall.

She handed him the stuffed toy. It was a much chewed on doll that appeared to have been handmade. He wondered if the dead woman had made it.

In the distance, he could hear the sound of sirens approaching.

"Help is on the way," he said softly.

To his surprise, the little girl laid her head down on his shoulder, pulled her blanket up beneath her chin and closed her eyes.

He was still holding her when the police stepped off the elevator and rushed down the hall toward him.

He was holding up his badge as he walked to meet them.

"My name is Detective Luis Montoya, from Chihuahua. There is a dead woman in room 418. She's been shot twice in the chest, although I heard three shots."

The door across the hall opened, then another and another, until, one by one, the people emerged, confirming his story.

One of the officers pointed to the child.

"Is she yours?"

Luis looked down at the sleeping baby and then regretfully shook his head.

"No. She was in the bed when I went in. She called the woman Mama."

The officer nodded. "I'll call the authorities. Someone will come get her."

"I'll take care of her until they get here," Luis said. "I'm in room 410. I'll leave my door ajar."

The officer watched as Luis carried the toddler into his room, then hurried away. Luis had no desire to get mixed up in another murder investigation when he was already up to his eyeballs in one of his own. But he might not have a choice. Like the other people on the floor, he was as close as the cops had to a witness.

He started to lay the little girl down, but as he did, she stirred. Not wanting her to wake up and cry, he sat down on the side of the bed and just held her.

An hour and fifteen minutes later, she was still asleep in his arms when someone knocked on his door. He opened it to find a woman in uniform. She flashed a badge. She was carrying a blanket and a bottle of milk.

She looked at the child, then held out her arms.

"Here, give her to me," she said briskly.

"What's going to happen to her?" Luis asked.

The woman shrugged. "Her mother will be identified, then we'll search for relatives."

"What if she has none?" Luis asked.

"She will be cared for," the woman said, and deftly wrapped the baby in the blanket she'd brought. When the little girl stirred, the woman poked the bottle in her mouth and started out the door.

"Wait!" Luis said, and handed her the toy. "She

was carrying this. It might help…later…when she wakes up."

The woman took the doll and stuffed it into her tote bag, then left as abruptly as she'd come in.

Luis was sick to his stomach, but sleep was impossible. He decided to go talk to the detectives in charge and see what, if anything, they'd discovered.

Cat was sitting in the outer office of the ob-gyn her doctor had recommended. Other than the occasional bout of nausea, which seemed prompted by certain scents, rather than foods, she was feeling pretty good. Still, she knew this was proper procedure, and she intended to do everything the right way. No more winging it. This baby was unplanned, but not unwelcome.

"Mrs. McKay, the doctor will see you now."

It took a few seconds for the name to register, and when it did, Cat caught herself smiling.

"Right this way, please," the nurse said, and led her down the hall to a cluster of exam rooms. "My name is Allison. I'll need you to take off all your clothes, put on this gown and have a seat up on the table. The doctor will be with you shortly."

"All my clothes?" Cat asked.

Allison nodded. "Yes. Sorry."

Cat shrugged. "No big deal. Naked is not the

worst thing that's happened to me in the past few months."

"Excuse me?"

"Oh nothing," Cat said. "I was just being a smart-ass."

Allison laughed. "My kind of woman."

As soon as the door closed, Cat stripped down, put on the gown and climbed up on the table. As she waited for the doctor to come in, she began thinking of her friend Marsha. Not too many months ago, Marsha had been in a similar situation, and her refusal to end her pregnancy had gotten her killed.

She couldn't help but wonder how scared Marsha must have been, sitting in a room like this by herself, waiting to find out if her world was about to crumble beneath her feet. Then she shook off the thought and leaned back. This was not a time for sorrow.

As she was waiting, her cell phone began to ring. She reached for her jacket pocket.

"Hello."

"Hey, baby, it's me. I parked the car. If you need me, I'm here now."

"Okay, but I'm good, I think. Just waiting for the doctor to come in. If there's any kind of consultation, I'll have them come get you, but I think it's just an exam and making an appointment for the next visit."

"Whatever…just know if you need me, I'm here for you."

I'll always need you. But before she could say what she was thinking, the door opened, so she said goodbye and dropped the phone back in her jacket pocket.

Luis couldn't get that little girl out of his head. Even though he'd planned to cross the border into Texas today, he knew he wouldn't be any good to himself or to the case until he found out how the child was faring.

He had a call in to the local authorities and was waiting for a call back as he finished his breakfast. He added another spoonful of spicy salsa to his scrambled eggs and then ate them with gusto. When the waitress came by, she topped off his coffee as she took away his dirty plates.

He was waiting for the coffee to cool when his cell phone rang. A quick glance at caller ID told him it was the captain he'd dealt with earlier.

"Hello."

"Detective Montoya, I have the information you requested."

"Captain Garcia, thank you for calling," Luis said. "What can you tell me about the little girl?"

"The mother was a prostitute. Why she had her

child with her is a mystery, but the girl *was* hers. We found the doctor who delivered her eighteen months ago. According to a man who claimed to be her pimp, she didn't know who the father was."

"What's going to happen to the child?" Luis asked.

"It is sad, but she is legally an orphan."

"What would someone have to do to begin the adoption process?"

"Are you serious?" Garcia asked.

"Yes."

"There are procedures that must be followed."

"Of course, of course," Luis said.

"What if she isn't well? She could have been born addicted—or worse. She could have HIV. You should have a doctor check her out before you consider such a thing."

"You don't understand," Luis said softly. "My wife cannot have children, which makes her very sad. Only yesterday, I prayed for a baby. It seems to me that God heard and answered my prayer. I cannot turn my back on this child…not when she needs us as much as we need her."

"Your wife might not share your desires, especially if she learns the child's mother made her living on her back."

"No child should suffer for the sins of its parents."

"Yes, yes, that is so," Garcia said.

"So who do I call?" Luis asked.

Garcia gave him the name and wished him well before hanging up.

Even though this was a drastic step that would change their lives, Luis didn't hesitate. He'd promised to bring Conchita a surprise, and this definitely constituted a big one.

He made the second call, and by the time he was through, he knew that his trip into the United States was going to be delayed. He didn't intend to leave and lose the child—his child.

Twelve

Luis Montoya had been working with the welfare system for the better part of two days, meeting with the director, interviewing with whomever they sent him to, and then finally talking to a judge, who'd granted him and his wife temporary custody of the baby, but only in the capacity of foster parents.

He knew his position as a law officer had made it easier for him to pull strings. His lieutenant had vouched for him, as had his priest. After all was said and done, it had been enough. Actual adoption procedures would take months and a lot more investigating, making sure there were no relatives to stake a claim, but this was the first step in the right direction.

Luis wasn't concerned. He knew the little girl was meant to be theirs, because he'd prayed to God, and God had answered.

He glanced at his watch. It was time to get to the airport to pick up his wife. She was due at any time, and he didn't intend to leave her waiting. As soon as they picked up the baby, they were flying home. He would fly back within a day or so, pick up his car and resume the investigation. But for now, his job was going to have to take a backseat to his life. Solomon Tutuola wouldn't be any deader a few days from now than he was today, and whoever had killed him already believed they'd gotten away with it, so they weren't running any farther than they'd already gone. He wasn't quitting the investigation. He was just taking a detour.

He hurried outside, remembering the joy in his wife's voice when he'd told her what had happened. He'd reminded her to say prayers for the mother who'd died, because were it not for her death, Conchita would still be childless, but nothing could truly dilute her joy—or his.

In a way, it didn't seem right that they should be so happy when a little girl's mother was dead. But at least they could give thanks that they were able to care for the child instead of leaving her to the courts. Still it was, for them, a most fortunate turn of events. It remained to be seen how everything would play out, but it was making Conchita happy and, for now, that was enough.

Cat and Dorothy had driven into Austin right after breakfast, heading to Hardware Heaven with a long list of supplies to pick up for the contractor, who planned to start work on the house within days.

Cat had to choose colors for the walls, as well as order flooring and appliances. She started out excited, wound up overwhelmed, and was thankful Dorothy was along.

"Thank you so much for helping," Cat said, as they sorted through tile samples for the kitchen backsplash and the shower walls.

Dorothy grinned. "No, thank you for letting me. I love stuff like this. Oh, look! This would be perfect in the master bath you're going to add. The walls are going to be that really pale turquoise, remember? So think how pretty this tile would be on the inside of the shower."

Cat picked up a tile, running her fingers over the pearled surface of the squares and admired the swirl of turquoise and gold threads.

"You're right. They'd be great."

Dorothy beamed. "I'll make a note," she said,

then wrote down the pattern number in the little notebook she was carrying.

"What's left to choose today?" Cat asked.

"Nothing. That's it," Dorothy said, then gave Cat a closer look. "Why? Aren't you feeling well?"

"I'm fine. Just a little tired, which is weird. I never used to be tired."

"Honey, this is just the beginning. All I'm saying is, sleep every chance you get now, because once you become a parent, rest will become a precious commodity."

"Oh, great. Thanks for the warning," Cat said.

Dorothy patted her on the shoulder. "You'll adjust—basically because you have no other choice."

Cat grinned. "You're just full of good news today, aren't you?"

Dorothy giggled as they neared the checkout. "Well, someone had to tell you."

Cat was still smiling when she heard a commotion at one of the registers and turned around.

"What on earth?" Dorothy said.

A heavyset man in a red plaid shirt and blue jeans was running toward the register where they were waiting. When he started to shout, Cat saw the gun in his hand and knew there was going to be trouble.

"Damn you, Mandi... I told you what I'd do if you left me. If I don't get you, no one does."

"No, Clyde! Don't!" the woman begged.

Without thinking, Cat took a step forward, putting herself between Dorothy and the ensuing drama as the woman called Mandi started screaming.

"Call 911. Call 911. That's my ex. He's going to kill me."

Cat spun and grabbed Dorothy's arm. "Get down! Get down now!"

Dorothy stared. "What on—"

"Just do it!" Cat snapped.

They were less than six feet from the woman, and Cat could tell by the look on the man's face that he was seconds from shooting. No matter what else happened, they were going to wind up in the line of fire. It was gut instinct that made her react.

She grabbed a shovel from a floor display with one hand as she shoved Dorothy to the floor with the other. She knew she was in the man's peripheral vision, but was counting on him being too focused on his ex to see her until it was too late.

She swung the shovel as she ran, hitting him in the back of the head with the spade about a half second before the gun went off.

Mandi took a dive behind the counter as the bullet went into a wall near the ceiling. When she began to hear people clapping, she peered out from behind the counter. When she saw her ex on the floor, she jumped up.

"What happened?" she cried.

"That woman knocked him out with a shovel," someone said, and then laughed.

"Oh lord, oh lord!" Mandi cried, as she ran to Cat. "You saved my life."

"I called 911," someone said.

When they heard the man stirring, Mandi jumped back and screamed again. "He's coming to."

"No he's not," Cat said, and swung the shovel again, aiming for the crown of his head like a golfer putting against a strong wind. The blade hit Clyde's head with a solid clang. Blood began to ooze from a cut on his head, but he was no longer moving.

Dorothy was still on the floor on her belly, staring up at Cat as if she'd never seen her before.

"I can't believe you just did that," she whispered, then slowly got to her feet.

Cat frowned. "Sorry, but I couldn't just stand there and let him pull the trigger, now could I?"

Dorothy eyed the grip Cat had on the shovel handle and the fire in her eyes, and shook her head quickly.

"Absolutely not," she said.

"Are you all right?" Cat asked. "I didn't mean to push you so hard, but I was afraid he'd start shooting up the place, and I didn't want you to get hit."

"Right," Dorothy mumbled, and then put her fingers to her lips, wondering if they were as numb as they felt.

"Look, the police are here," Mandi said.

A half dozen police cruisers had pulled up to the front of the building. Cat counted at least eight uniformed officers coming through the door with guns drawn.

"Here we go," she murmured, as they began to shout.

"Hands up! Everyone on the floor!"

Dorothy shook her head in disgust. "Oh, for the good lord's sake. The only one who had a gun is already on the floor."

She pointed at the gunman and the gun Cat had kicked loose from his fingers.

One of officers grabbed the gun, while another turned the guy over.

"There are no bullet wounds," he said, as he handed the gun off to his partner, then rolled the unconscious man back over on his belly, yanked his hands behind his back and cuffed him.

Clyde, still unconscious, was as limp as a rag doll.

Dorothy put her arm protectively around Cat's

shoulders. "That's because my girl downed him with a shovel."

"She's a hero," Mandi said, as she pointed to the man on the floor. "That's my ex-husband, Clyde Bridges. I have an order of protection against him, but a fat lot of good it would have done if it hadn't been for her. He came into the store with that gun in his hand and was ready to shoot me dead. She stopped him. She hit him with that shovel just as he pulled the trigger. I hit the floor, and the bullet hit the wall up by the ceiling."

Cat's chin jutted in a defensive gesture. "Well, I couldn't just—"

Then one of the bystanders suddenly spoke up. "Hey, I know who you are! You're the woman they found out in that pasture after the tornado, aren't you? You're that bounty hunter, Cat Dupree."

The policemen stepped back, eyeing Cat with more than a little curiosity.

"Is this true, ma'am? Are you Cat Dupree?" one of them asked.

Cat shrugged. "My name is Cat McKay now, and there's nothing I can tell you about this man other than that he came in the door with a gun, threatening to kill her. I hit him with this."

She handed the officer the shovel. "If you need to talk to us again, call my cell." She rattled off the number. "I just want to go home." She looked at Dorothy for support. "I think we've had enough of shopping for one day."

"Amen to that, honey," Dorothy said, and took her by the hand. They walked away from their full shopping cart without a backward glance.

"Thank you again," Mandi said, as Cat walked past her.

Cat nodded and kept on walking. They got to the car, but when Cat hit the remote to unlock the doors, she realized her hands were shaking. She shuddered, then took a slow breath and handed the keys to Dorothy.

"I think you'd better drive."

"Are you all right?" Dorothy asked, eyeing her nervously.

"I will be," Cat said.

Dorothy slid behind the wheel, and they were soon on their way home.

"That was weird," Cat said.

Dorothy glanced at the strained expression on her daughter-in-law's face, then started to giggle.

"Honey, that's the understatement of the day."

Her giggle broke the ice.

Cat started to relax. Then she remembered Wilson. "I don't even want to think about what

Wilson is going to say," she muttered, then looked at Dorothy. "Maybe we just won't tell him?"

Dorothy rolled her eyes. "All I'm saying is, it will be better coming from you than him hearing about it on the evening news."

"The news? Oh, no. Do you think they'll mention it?"

"Are you serious? I saw half a dozen people with their cell phones out, getting the whole thing on video. You put down a would-be killer in Hardware Heaven with a shovel. You'll be on one of those crazy Web sites by tomorrow, you mark my words."

Cat sighed. "Wilson is going to blow a fuse. Not that it matters, because I don't intend to explain myself every time I leave the house."

Dorothy shook her head in quiet amazement. "Maybe. Maybe not. I'm just beginning to understand what you two faced just trying to do your jobs. It's not as simple as I first believed, is it? I mean…you don't exactly knock on doors and pick up people who don't show up for court, do you?"

Cat stifled a laugh. Obviously Wilson had been feeding his mother quite a line.

"It's not always that simple, no."

"It's dangerous, isn't it? I remember how beat up you were when you first came to us. Did one of your bail jumpers do that to you?"

Solomon Tutuola's burned and tattooed face slithered through her mind, then out again.

"In a manner of speaking," she said.

"Lord, lord, and all these years Wilson assured me it was no big deal."

"Well, we're out of the business now, so don't worry, okay?"

Dorothy's frown deepened. "When I think of all those years I slept in peaceful bliss, thinking my children were just fine in their chosen professions with this Jimmy Franks mess and now this, Wilson just flat-out lied to me. I may have to wring his neck on general principle. In fact…you just leave him to me. If he gives you trouble about all this, he's mine."

Cat laughed out loud. "It's a deal."

A delivery truck from Blaine's Lumber Yard had just delivered a load of two-by-fours to the old home place and was on the way back to the highway when Wilson's cell phone rang. He glanced at the caller ID, then frowned. Channel Four was calling, which begged the question: Why?

"Hello?"

"Hello, may I speak to Wilson McKay?"

"I'm Wilson McKay. How can I help you?"

"Mr. McKay, I'm Joanie Eckert from Channel Four. Is your wife the former Cat Dupree, from Dallas?"

Wilson's stomach knotted. "Yes. Why?"

"Is she home yet?"

"No, and why, may I ask, do you even know she's gone? What's going on?"

"We'd like to send out a film crew to get some footage to run with the sound bite we'll be running on the evening news."

Wilson was immediately defensive. Just thinking of seeing Cat back on the news was like sending up flares, letting Jimmy Franks know exactly where to look to finish the job.

"What the hell for?"

"For the shooting at Hardware Heaven of course."

"There was a shooting at Hardware Heaven?"

Ms. Eckert should have been alerted by the odd tone of Wilson's voice. "Yes, only a short while ago. If—"

Wilson disconnected the call, then immediately dialed Cat's number.

She answered on the second ring.

"Hi, honey," she said.

"Don't 'hi, honey' me," Wilson muttered, then he heard Cat say, "He already knows."

"No thanks to you. I had to hear about it from

some damn reporter from Channel Four. The first thing I want to know is, are you and Mom all right?"

He thought he was still talking to Cat when he heard his mother's voice answer instead.

"It's only thanks to Catherine that we're fine, so you take that tone right out of your voice, mister. She not only saved our lives, but she saved the life of a woman at Hardware Heaven, as well."

"God, Mom…what happened?"

"I will let you talk to Catherine, but you do not raise your voice to her. Do you hear me?"

"Yes, ma'am."

Dorothy obviously handed the phone back to Cat, because the next voice he heard belonged to his wife.

"It's me."

"Cat…honey? What happened?"

"So it's honey now?"

He sighed. "Yes. Talk to me… Please."

"Your mom and I were ready to check out when this crazy man comes running in waving a gun. He was screaming at a woman, who turned out to be his ex. She had an order of protection against him, but you know what they're worth."

"Yeah, less than the paper they're printed on."

"Right. So, anyway, we were all bunched up together, and I figured once he shot her, he was probably going to empty his gun into the crowd. I grabbed a shovel from a floor display and whacked him with it. Dropped him like a sack of potatoes."

There was a long moment of silence.

"Wilson? Are you still there?"

He just managed to say, "Uh-huh."

"We're almost home. We'll tell you all about it when we get there, and your mom says don't scare Carter when you tell him."

"Fine. I won't scare Dad any more than that journalist just scared me."

"I'm sorry," Cat said. "But I didn't want to tell you over the phone. For God's sake, how was I to know those vultures would already be after their bit of fresh meat for the six o'clock news?"

"Okay, I get it," Wilson said. "I wouldn't have wanted to tell you over the phone, either."

"Thank you."

"You're welcome. I'm sorry. I love you."

Cat sighed. "Love you, too. See you soon."

Jimmy Franks was sitting in the back of the dining hall at the downtown Salvation Army shelter, waiting for the free meal of the day to be served. He'd undergone a transformation so drastic that neither Houston nor his mother would have recognized him. He'd shaved his face smooth, pushed his hair back with a pink plastic headband, and was wearing eye makeup and lipstick of a shade that would have staggered a whore. Instead of his usual clothes, he'd gotten a pair of women's slacks and a loose silky blouse from a secondhand store, and was decked out like a trannie. The cops would never spot him in drag. Now, if he could just find a patsy to use for a body double before some homophobe decided to beat the hell out of him on general principles, he would be good to go.

Several men walked past him, eyeing him nervously, as if what he had might be catching. A pair of teenage boys pointed at him and laughed. But when another man sidled up to him and actually started to flirt, Jimmy pitched a fit.

"Get away, you fuckin' pervert," he snarled.

Confused by the mixed messages, the man ducked and quickly slunk away.

Someone rang the bell that meant dinner was served.

Jimmy stood up. He waited until the chaplain blessed the food and then took his place in line, all the while scanning the crowd for another small, skinny man with sharp features and dishwater-blond hair.

He got through the line, carried his plate to a nearby table and quickly began to eat, while continuing to watch the people coming and going.

Thinking this was going to be a bust, he dumped

his empty plate and cup into the trash and walked out. He was standing on the curb, waiting for the light to change, when he sensed someone behind him. He glanced over his shoulder, and his heart skipped a beat.

Holy crap! Talk about an "Ask, and ye shall receive" moment... Jimmy looked more like the guy behind him than he did his real brother, and even better, the guy was a stoner. He could tell by the way he was acting that he was in bad need of a fix.

"Hey," Jimmy whispered. "I've got something you want."

The guy blinked twice before he managed to focus on Jimmy's face.

"Naw, I don't swing that way," he mumbled, and started across the street as the light changed.

Jimmy jumped off the curb and hurried after him.

"No, no. I wasn't talking about sex. I've got prime smack. Let's talk price and then we can party."

By the time they reached the other side of the street, the stoner was all but holding Jimmy's hand to get what was in his pocket.

"So what's your name?" Jimmy asked.

"James Martin."

Jimmy laughed out loud.

"What's so funny?" James asked.

"My name is Jimmy."

"Oh. Yeah. Right. That's a real coincidence. So where's the party?"

Jimmy put his hand on James Martin's shoulder.

"Just follow me. I've got a room over at a motel that's nice and cozy."

"Whatever," James mumbled, and stumbled along beside Jimmy, unaware he'd taken up with a killer.

James Martin was dead.

Jimmy stepped back to eye his handiwork. It was pretty much finished, and it had been easier than he'd imagined.

First, he'd gotten him high, then he'd made him strip down.

James Martin had been too wasted to argue and figured the hit was worth whatever came next. He'd figured wrong. As soon as he'd gotten naked, Jimmy had told him to get dressed again, only this time in clothes other than his own.

He didn't give a fuck what he was wearing. He just wanted to lie down and ride out the high. As soon as he'd dressed, he passed out on the bed.

Jimmy had been planning this for the better part of two days and was well prepared for the next step.

He took off his costume and laid it on a chair on the far side of the room, then put his wallet in James

Martin's pocket. He scattered some drug paraphernalia and a handful of girlie magazines around the bed, making sure that his fingerprints were on everything.

The next step was erasing this man's identity and substituting his own.

Yesterday, as Jimmy had been passing a construction site, he'd picked up a discarded piece of rebar about four feet long and brought it back to the motel. Now he pulled it out from beneath the bed, hefted it firmly, then raised it over his head, bringing it down squarely in the middle of James Martin's face.

Martin's body bucked from the impact as his face split like a ripe melon. He never knew what hit him.

Now that the first blow had been struck, Jimmy got down to business. He hammered the dead man's face so many times that it no longer looked human, and when he was through with that, he started on James Martin's hands. He didn't intend to leave anything to chance. No facial recognition. No fingerprints.

It was a brutal execution, and when he was done, he was covered in blood and brain matter.

He wiped the rebar clean of prints and tossed it on the bed beside the dead man, then calmly walked into the bathroom and showered off every drop of blood and gore from his body.

Afterward, he redonned his transvestite gear, pocketed all his cash and James's, and left without a backward glance, well aware that the maid would discover the body sometime tomorrow.

It would be soon enough.

Now he had all the time he needed to put the last part of his plan into action. He needed another ride, some ammunition for his recently acquired gun and directions to the McKay property.

There was no need to rush. Not once the police discovered poor Jimmy Franks beaten to death, at least.

His fingerprints were all over the room. They would assume they belonged to the body as well. If they felt the need to run a DNA test, he knew it would take weeks, if not months, to get back a report. By then he would be long gone and Wilson McKay would finally be right where he belonged: six feet under.

Thirteen

It was nearing sunset, and Cat and Wilson had been at the old homestead all day, working with the contractors as the remodeling continued. The workers had gone home a few minutes ago, and Cat had wandered through the rooms in progress, then out onto the back porch.

As she sat on the steps, she became caught up in an unfolding drama taking place in the sky. She was watching a bevy of small birds dive-bombing a red-tailed hawk that had made the mistake of flying through their airspace. The hawk was flying fast and low, trying to escape the smaller birds' beaks and claws. Cat watched until they flew into the sun and she lost sight of the chase.

"Hey, what are you doing?" Wilson asked, as he came outside, wiping the paint off his hands with an old rag. He tossed it aside, then sat down on the steps beside her.

"I think I was watching the ferocity of parenthood in action."

"There's plenty of it in nature," Wilson said. "Dad always said that Mom was meaner than an old mama bear when someone messed with her kids."

"I think I'll be like that," Cat said.

"Oh, honey, I *know* what you'll be like," he said, and then kissed the backside of her ear as he wrapped his arms around her.

She sighed, then moaned as she leaned into his embrace.

"What will I be like?" she asked.

"An absolute angel until crossed. After that, it's shovel time."

She laughed.

She was still being teased by the family for taking out the gunman with a shovel. Charlie and Delia had come over the night after it had happened, bearing Cat and Wilson's first housewarming gift.

When Cat saw the shovel with the big red bow, she knew she was in. Teasing was a major part of this family's dynamic, and she'd just been roasted.

"I admit I'm not the shy, retiring type," Cat said. "So what?"

Wilson laid his hand on her belly, then rubbed it gently.

"So I say this baby is going to be real lucky. That's what I say."

She sighed, then turned in Wilson's embrace and put her arms around his neck, then whispered in his ear, "Don't you think it's time you carried me across the threshold?"

Wilson's breath caught; then he tightened his arms around her and stood, taking her with him into the house.

Once inside, he put her back on her feet, then proceeded to kiss her senseless.

"Sweet lord…there's no bed in this place," he muttered.

Cat cupped her hands on his cheeks, then ran a finger around the single gold hoop in his ear.

"Since when does a pirate need a bed in which to ravish?"

When she began to undo her pants, his eyes glittered.

She watched a muscle jerk at the side of his jaw and knew this man was never going to give her a moment of regret.

When he knelt at her feet and pulled her pants down around her ankles, then off, she began to shake.

She wanted him.

Now.

"Wilson…"

He shed his shirt, then his belt, and got as far as unbuttoning his jeans before she put her arms around his neck and her legs around his waist.

After that, it was all a blur.

The wall was at Cat's back, while the last rays of the setting sun were in her eyes. She felt the waning heat on her face, then a blast of heat within her belly as Wilson took her hard and fast.

She hung on all the way to the end of the ride, but when he suddenly hit the brakes and came to a shuddering stop—still inside her—she groaned. Both of them were shaking.

Cat was past the edge of reason—all the way gone with love for this man. Her fingers curled, her nails digging into his shoulders as she struggled to hold on.

"Wilson…Wilson…"

His eyes glittered, his nostrils flaring as he struggled to breathe. One last thrust was all he had left. He closed his eyes and gave it up.

Cat screamed as the climax rocked her, shot through and through by the heat of his spilling seed.

Luis and Conchita Montoya had become parents overnight. Today marked the second day of their new life. The only name the authorities had come up with for the orphaned child was the one the pimp knew her by, which was Boo. While that was a sweet baby name, it wouldn't get her far in the real world. So they named her Amalita, after Luis's mother, Amalia, who Conchita credited with helping to save their marriage.

Amalita took to Conchita and Luis as if she'd known them all her life. Luis suspected that the little girl had been exposed to far too many people in her brief life, and was used to new faces coming and going.

She'd only said the word "Mama" once since they'd arrived back in Chihuahua, and Luis had been holding her at the time. He'd just calmly turned around and put her into Conchita's arms and said, "This is your mama now. Give Mama a kiss."

The little girl had complied.

The crisis that might have been had passed without incident.

Now Luis was standing in their extra bedroom, which had been turned into a nursery overnight, watching his wife rock Amalita to sleep.

When Conchita looked up and saw him watching, she smiled. Luis swallowed past the lump in his throat. He'd never seen her this happy and felt shame that he'd been unaware of how empty her life had been.

"Is everything all right?" he asked softly.

Conchita nodded, then went back to the business of mothering, so Luis left her to it.

Tomorrow, he was flying back to Nuevo Laredo to retrieve his car and finish what he'd started. This time, when he left, he doubted he would be missed.

He'd called the Dallas Police Department earlier and made an appointment to meet with Detective Bradley, the man who'd closed the case on Mark Presley. After that, there would be one more interview—this time with a bounty hunter named Cat Dupree. Where things went from there would be anybody's guess.

Cat's morning had taken a turn for the worse when she woke up nauseated. She'd made it to the bathroom in time to throw up and was now sitting in bed, sipping a cup of hot tea and nibbling on a piece of dry toast, hoping it would settle her stomach. Wilson had gone into the kitchen to eat breakfast with his parents, so when Cat heard him running down the hall, she quickly set her food aside.

"What's wrong?" she asked, as he entered the bedroom and quickly turned on the TV.

"Listen to this," he said, and then sat down on the side of the bed with her.

"What is it?" she asked.

"Just watch," he urged, and upped the volume as the morning newscast came back from commercial.

"As we said before the break, the body found yesterday in a local motel has been identified as that of Jimmy Dale Franks, of Dallas, Texas. An arrest warrant had been issued for Franks last week, after he was identified as the man who robbed Lowry's Gas and Guzzle in Dallas, killing the clerk and stealing her car, which was later found abandoned here in Austin.

"According to authorities, Franks' death was the result of a brutal beating. If anyone has any information regarding this crime, they are asked to call Crime Stoppers. The number is at the bottom of the screen."

Cat leaned back with a sigh.

"I can't believe it. After everything he did, it's over. Just like that."

Wilson hugged her. "It's about time things started falling our way. Now we can concentrate on the important things in life, like bathtubs and babies."

Cat grinned. "Bathtubs?"

"Yeah, they're supposed to deliver them this afternoon."

"Oh. For our house."

"That has a nice ring to it," Wilson said, and then gave her a quick kiss before he slid off the bed. "I'm going to leave you alone. Maybe you can get a little more sleep."

"I'm not sleepy. Just sick to my stomach," Cat said.

"Don't rock the boat, then. Take your time, okay?"

Cat nodded. "Tell your mom that I'll help her snap beans as soon as I can get dressed."

"Okay, but don't stress about it. There are enough beans in that garden to feed an army. Before it's over, we'll *all* be snapping beans."

"I know this is old hat to you, but it's pretty exciting to me," Cat said. "I need to learn how to do this so I can—"

"Good lord, no," Wilson said. "Mom does this because she likes to. Unless you happen to fall in love with growing stuff, we'll be buying our food at the supermarket."

Cat laughed. "I have to admit, that's something of a relief. I'm not sure how green my thumb is."

Wilson shook his head. "You don't need a green thumb, just the patience to live with me. I come with a lot of baggage."

Cat's smile died. "Revenge is baggage. I'm the one who still has things to learn."

Wilson watched her face run the gamut of expressions and knew she was remembering her showdown with Tutuola. She'd still never talked about it. He wasn't sure he wanted to hear it.

"You're doing just fine, baby," he said softly, and gave her a quick kiss before tucking her back into bed.

She made it up in time to help peel potatoes for the noon meal and felt fine the rest of the day. Just knowing that Jimmy Franks was no longer a threat had changed the tone of their lives.

The next morning began with a promise of rain, which meant Wilson wouldn't be tearing off the old roof on the home place as planned. And since it was Saturday, that meant the contractor and his crew were off, too.

That just left Dorothy and her beans.

Green beans—the first produce of the season— were coming to fruition in Dorothy's garden. Every time someone sat down, she put a big bowl of beans in their lap to be snapped. This morning she was hauling empty canning jars from the storm cellar to wash and sterilize before filling them with a new crop of green beans.

And every time she started back to the cellar, she paused at the old doghouse to play with the kittens, who were just beginning to venture out to play on their own.

Carter had suggested they move the cat and her

babies back to the barn before she started bringing them all onto the back porch, but Dorothy had said no. She told Carter that the momma cat had a reason for moving them to begin with, so they needed to butt out of her business.

Since his suggestions were being met with resistance and he was sick and tired of snapping beans, Carter volunteered to drive over to the home place to make sure the contractors had shut all the windows before they'd left last night. After all their hard work, they didn't want their remodeling to get rained on.

Cat knew the windows were fine—she and Wilson had checked them all themselves—but if his dad wanted a little while on his own, she wasn't going to argue.

So she sat on the back porch with a lapful of beans, watching as Carter drove out of the yard.

Wilson was in Austin, picking up feed.

It was business as usual.

Life was finally calm and orderly.

For the first time in more years than she could remember, her troubles were finally behind her.

Luis Montoya's flight from Chihuahua to Nuevo Laredo was rough. He got out of the small commuter plane with his legs shaking and his stomach still in knots. Once or twice he'd feared that they were actually going to crash, though the little plane had only been bouncing in and out of air pockets. Even so, he was glad to be on the ground.

He reclaimed his luggage and headed for airport parking, where he'd left his car. Within the hour, he was on his way to the border.

He had a mental list of questions that needed answering from either the Dallas PD or the American bounty hunters—or both. And before he left, he would have his answer as to why Cat Dupree made a second trip into Mexico.

Last night Jimmy Franks had been forced to make a decision about his transvestite look. Either he found a new way to disguise himself or he had to get out of Austin altogether. While he was heading through the back streets on his way to find a new ride, he'd come close to getting beat all to hell by a pair of good old boys who'd taken offense at his lipstick, his eyeshadow and his pink silk blouse.

So he'd taken himself to another secondhand shop this morning and come out with two sacks full of gear. He caught a cab and, a short while later, checked into another no-tell motel on the other side of town. Within the hour, the makeup was off his face and he was in the process of cutting his hair. But the scissors he was using were dull, and every time he grabbed up a hank of hair to cut, it pulled like hell and made his eyes water. He'd managed to cut himself once, but it had to be done. His new look called for bald. When he'd finally finished hours later, he dressed in his new garb and gave himself one last look. He was ready to move.

Bald head.

Fake black leather jacket and pants—which, now that he had them on, were making him itch.

Old army boots that were run down at the heels.

Fake swastika tattoo on the back of his neck, and an oversize chain with one end hooked to his belt buckle and the other to the wallet in his back pocket.

Skinhead.

Who would have thought?

Houston would have a fit if he saw him dressed like this.

Then Jimmy shoved his chest forward and lifted his chin, glaring himself down in the mirror.

Damn it, he needed to remember that Houston's opinion of him didn't matter anymore.

His older brother should never have abandoned him like he had. It was all Wilson McKay's fault. If he'd died like he was supposed to the first time, they would both have been long gone. Houston had tried to talk him out of finishing the job, but Jimmy didn't like being told what to do. Now he'd gone too far to turn back.

With one last look at his new persona, he tossed the room key on the bed and strode off down the street. All he needed now was a ride.

Medical examiner Marge Asher was in the middle of an autopsy on a white male, approximate age thirty-three years old. Even though the victim's cause of death looked to be a savage beating, in a homicide, an autopsy was standard procedure.

The blood and tissue samples had been sent to the lab. Identification through facial reconstruction or dental records was, in this case, impossible. The man's face was basically a gelatinous mass, and his extremities looked like they'd been put through a meat grinder, which meant no fingerprints were going to be available, either.

But she had an ace in the hole. A few minutes earlier, she'd pulled a serial number off the dead man's hip replacement. The ID on the artificial joint was specific to one person only. She made note of the number, including it in her report, and soon after she was done, so she closed him up, posted her findings and sent them through the proper channels, then moved on to the next body waiting for her attention.

Her report wound up on Detective Andy Parker's desk, but he'd caught two new homicide cases and was in hot pursuit of a man who'd killed his wife of thirty-two years, and disappeared with three million dollars of company money and his best friend's wife.

Parker came in late the next morning and was nursing a cup of coffee as he went through the papers on his desk. When he got to the coroner's report on the body tentatively identified as Jimmy Franks, he expected it to be a confirmation. But when he began to read, he realized their murder case had taken an unexpected twist. Yes, someone had been murdered in Jimmy Dale Franks's motel room, but it wasn't Jimmy Dale Franks.

"Crap," he said, and headed for his lieutenant's office with the paperwork in his hands. He knocked once, then went in without waiting for permission. "We've got ourselves a hitch in the Franks murder."

Lieutenant Jakowski, a twenty-seven-year veteran of the force, had dealt with plenty of hitches in his career, so his response was less than concerned.

"Yeah, like what?" he asked.

Parker laid the report in front of Jakowski.

"We've still got a killer on the loose—probably Franks. The vic from the motel was not Jimmy

Franks. According to the doctor who put an artificial hip in him five years ago, he was James Martin of Waxahatchee, Texas."

"I thought we had fingerprints."

"We did…do. I'm thinking Franks is a lot smarter than we've given him credit for. He took that room, left his prints all over the place, then killed himself off, which took the heat off the search. He's still a loose cannon. Do we notify the press? Should we let that bail bondsman know?"

"What bail bondsman?"

"A few months ago Franks tried to kill a bail bondsman named Wilson McKay in Dallas. He got away and has been on the run ever since. He robbed a Dallas convenience store last week. Killed the clerk and stole her car, the one—"

"Oh yeah…that was found abandoned on the Austin bypass."

"Right. And since Wilson is at his family home outside Austin, still recovering from the gunshots, there's a possibility Franks is stalking him."

"I know who you're talking about now. Isn't he the guy that went into the stock pond after his fiancée? The woman who got caught in the tornado?"

"Yeah, that's him."

"Crap," Jakowski muttered. "We got ourselves a

local hero who's under the belief that his shooter is dead. Hell yes, let him know. Don't notify the press, though. If you do, it will just alert Franks that we're on to him again."

"Yes, sir," Parker said, and started to leave.

"Wait!"

"Yes, sir?"

"Double-check the findings before you make that call. We've already fucked up once. I don't want it happening again."

"Are you telling me to doubt Marge Asher's report?"

"I'm just telling you to make sure of your facts before you call McKay."

"Fine, but I'm not calling Marge. If you want her to recheck anything, *you* call her. I don't have the balls to stand up to that woman."

Jakowski sighed. "I'm not sure I do, either."

"Well it's your call."

Jakowski frowned. "Just check what you can on your own. You don't have to go through the M.E.'s office to verify stuff, damn it. Do I have to tell you everything?"

"No, sir. I'm on it."

"Good. Let me know when you've finished. I'll make the call to McKay myself."

"Thanks, boss."

"Yeah. It's why I make the big bucks, right?"

Parker laughed. They both knew that people who went into law enforcement sure didn't do it for the money.

"Yes, sir," he said.

"Shut the door on your way out," Jakowski added.

Parker made sure not to slam it; then he was off to check what he could before the story got changed.

Fourteen

Jimmy Franks was strutting like a bad boy. He had bad-boy clothes. Bad-boy attitude. Badass gun in his jacket. But he still needed a car, and now he had the perfect plan to get one.

For the better part of the morning he'd been watching the north side of a mall parking lot, noticing that most of the employees parked at the back edge, either at the request of the bosses, who probably wanted the closer parking spaces left for paying customers, or because they didn't want their own vehicles exposed to constant dings by parking too close to someone else. All he had to do was wait until someone drove up alone. If the car looked presentable, it was his.

By the time he'd decided on how he would do it, he didn't have long to wait.

About thirty minutes later a young woman wheeled off the access road into the parking lot in her small gray Honda and headed right toward where he was standing. He stepped farther behind the shrubs bordering the lot and waited for her to park.

When she got out of the car and went to the rear of the vehicle to pop the trunk, he made his move.

"Hey, honey, need some help?" he asked.

Surprised by his unexpected appearance, she jumped.

"Oh, my goodness…you scared me to—"

Jimmy knocked her cold, then stuffed her inside the trunk. He gave the parking lot a quick glance, making sure he'd been unobserved, then got in the car and drove away.

He'd thought about killing her outright; then, for no reason, after he'd seen her up close, he'd changed his mind. Maybe it was because she'd been smiling at him when he decked her.

Whatever the reason, he decided to just dump her in some isolated place on his way out of town. He'd seen an old junkyard earlier, so he when he reached the area, he drove around to the back and pulled up to where a piece of the picket fence was missing. He sat for a moment, making sure no one was around, then popped the trunk and felt for her pulse. She was still alive. Whether she stayed that way was going to be up to her. Within moments, he dragged her through the hole in the fence and rolled her beneath the stripped and rusted body of a '56 Chevy.

"1956…I hear that was a good year," he said, laughing at his own joke as he jumped back into the car and drove away.

He had a general idea of where the McKay ranch was located. Now all he had to do was find it.

When the contractor began applying varnish to the woodwork, Cat was evicted from the house.

"Sorry, Mrs. McKay, but these fumes aren't healthy for someone in your condition," he said.

"But the windows are open, and I was going to—"

Wilson stuck his head around the corner. "Out. Now."

Cat thought about arguing, then decided it wasn't worth it. Besides, she'd never been pregnant before. For all she knew, they were right.

"Okay, okay. I'm going back to the house now, then."

"Good idea," Wilson said. "I'll be along later.

They're setting the countertops, and I told the guys I'd help carry them inside. They're heavy as hell."

"You're the one who decided on granite," Cat said.

"I know, I know. But you're gonna love it."

Cat grinned. "Oh, I already love it. The stuff is gorgeous. Just don't drop it on your foot."

He made a face at her, then disappeared, leaving her to make her way back to the house alone. She never would have admitted it, but on a scale of one to ten, her energy level was barely a four.

When she got back to the house, Dorothy came out to meet her.

"Hi, honey. How's it going?"

"Super. Everything is going to be so pretty. I still can't believe all this is happening."

"Like what?" Dorothy asked.

Cat shrugged. "You know…everything. I've gone from the biggest loner in Dallas to listening for the sound of one man's footsteps. That house is just amazing. Truthfully, I'm so psyched about living there, I can hardly wait. I haven't had a real home in so long that I'd just about forgotten what the word even meant. Add a baby to all that, and I'm still pinching myself."

Dorothy laughed. "I see what you mean. Well,

just so you know, Carter and I consider you a real jewel and the smartest thing Wilson Lee has ever done."

Cat laughed.

Dorothy patted Cat's cheek, then frowned. "You look pale. Why don't you try to get in a nap before lunch?"

"I was going to help you," Cat said.

"You can help later."

"You talked me into it," Cat said, and headed for the bedroom, unaware that Dorothy was right behind her.

"Hey, I promise I was going to mind. You don't have to check up on me," she said.

Dorothy frowned. "I'm not checking up on you. I'm fussing. I always fussed when my kids were sick. You don't get to cheat me out of another chance. Now kick off those boots and get comfy."

Cat did as she was told, then sighed with relief as she stretched out on the bed.

"Oh man, this feels good," she said, and had started to pull the afghan up over her legs when Dorothy took it out of her hands and did it for her, then went so far as to tuck her in.

Cat was touched by her kindness. "You don't have to do that. I'm pretty tough, you know."

Dorothy's eyes welled. "I know all too well how capable you are, my dear. But it's the why of it that breaks my heart. You missed out on too many years of tender loving care to suit me, so let me do my thing, then we'll both feel better."

Those simple words had Cat in tears.

"Oh, for pity's sake, don't cry," Dorothy said. "You'll have me bawling, and then Carter will get in a tizzy. He can't bear to see a woman cry."

Cat put her arms around Dorothy's neck.

"Then I thank you for showing me what a mother's love is all about."

Dorothy hugged her fiercely, then kissed her cheek before moving away.

"I'm off to the garden," she said.

"Happy picking," Cat said.

Dorothy giggled as she left.

Cat closed her eyes. The last thing she remembered thinking of were the rows and rows of green beans that continued to reproduce faster than anyone could pick them, despite Dorothy's diligence.

With the countertops finally in place, Wilson was anxious to get back to the house and check on Cat. Despite her arguments to the contrary, he was well aware of how much she was struggling with nausea. His mother had assured him that usually passed after the first three months. He hoped she was right.

When he drove into the yard, he saw his mother

in the garden and shook his head. She was at it again. Lord, they were going to be eating green beans every day for the next year.

He stopped and got out at the garden, then took the bushel basket of fresh produce out of her hands.

"You plant a garden just like all us kids were still at home," he said.

"I know. Old habits are hard to break. One of these days I'll quit altogether, then get fat and sassy just sitting around doing my crochet and rocking my grandbabies."

Wilson grinned. His mother's body shape had been ample for years, but she wouldn't be Mom otherwise.

"Dad won't care how fat you get, and you're already sassy."

Dorothy punched him on the arm, but she was smiling. She knew he was right. She and Carter loved each other to distraction, which had often been a cause of embarrassment for their children as they were growing up. Now they just teased them about it, but with love and no small amount of envy.

"Where's Cat?" Wilson asked, as he set the basket of beans in the shade on the back porch.

"She's taking a nap, I hope. Go see if she's awake. If she is, I'll make lunch. It's about time."

"Where's Dad?" Wilson asked.

Dorothy shrugged. "He said something about going up to the north pasture to check on the momma cows and calves. Now that I think about it, he's been gone a long time."

"Give me a few minutes to look in on Cat, and then I'll go check on him."

Dorothy hesitated. "He's been operating on his own for a long time. I'm not sure he'd appreciate being 'looked after.'"

"Whatever you think," Wilson said. "We sure don't want to put a burr in his britches."

"Exactly," Dorothy said, as they went into the house together.

Jimmy Franks saw the name McKay on the mailbox just as he drove past it. He slammed on the brakes and drove onto the shoulder of the road to let the semi behind him pass, then backed up to make sure.

He was right. The mailbox was clearly marked "Carter McKay."

So this was the right location. Now what? He thought about just driving down the driveway and getting it over with in a burst of firepower. He could picture how it would go down. Whoever he saw first would be the first to go down.

Then he frowned. This was Texas. Every rancher

in the state kept weapons. If there were very many people at the ranch, he could get himself shot before he ever even saw Wilson McKay.

Better to take it slow.

Do it right this time, then maybe head for Mexico—or better yet, he might check out New York City. The farthest he'd ever been was Arizona. He could hire out as a mechanic and get lost in America. People did it all the time.

Yeah. That was a better plan.

He put the Honda into gear and began to drive, this time looking for a side road that would take him in on the back side of the McKay place. He had no idea how big the property was, but he figured he would be okay if he just took the next left and saw where it took him. After that, he would play it by ear.

Henry Ralphs was looking for a part for a 1975 Buick and cursing beneath his breath. He was sick and tired of trying to keep his dad's old car running. Even though his old man could afford to buy two new Buicks, he refused to part with a cent other than what it took to keep the old one running.

Henry was of a mind to quit right now, and go back and tell his dad that it was time; parts were no longer available. But he'd never been a good liar and knew his dad would see right through him.

"Son of a squeaky bitch," he mumbled, then almost fell on his face as he stepped sideways on an empty beer can. It rolled as it went flat, almost taking him with it. "That's all I need," he said, and kicked at the empty can as hard as he could.

It ricocheted against the rusted-out body of an old Chevrolet, then hit the ground a few yards away. He'd started to walk away when he heard what sounded like the faint mewing of a cat.

As cranky as Henry was about working on his daddy's car, he was a softy when it came to animals. He thought about some small abandoned kitten starving to death out here, and stopped and went back, calling as he walked.

"Here…kitty, kitty, kitty. Come here, kitty."

The sound came again, but this time it stopped him cold. He was no longer hearing kittens. Someone was calling for help.

He began running, looking under car bodies and around piles of rubble.

"Keep yelling," he called out. "I'm trying to find you."

"Help…help…I'm here."

He saw movement beneath another rusty car body and rushed forward.

"Oh, dear God," he whispered, as he saw a young girl trying to crawl out from beneath the old wreck.

Her head and face were bloody, and she was covered in dirt and grass.

He dropped to his knees and helped her the rest of the way out. "Come here, sweetheart…I got you. I got you. My name is Henry. What's your name?"

"Tita Little." Then her face crumpled, and she began to cry. "I want my momma."

"I know, honey, I know. We'll get you to your momma real soon. Just sit still and let me get you some help."

He yanked his cell phone out of his pocket and quickly dialed 911. Within six minutes, the old junk-yard was crawling with police and a pair of EMTs.

A policeman was walking beside the gurney as they wheeled the young woman toward an ambulance.

"Who did this to you?" he asked.

"I don't know. A man…a biker guy. You know. Bald. I'd never seen him before."

"Did he touch you? Sexually?"

Near hysterics, she covered her face. "I don't know. I can't remember. My car…I think he stole my car."

"What make and model?" the policeman asked.

"A gray 2001 Honda. It has a vanity tag. My daddy gave it to me."

At the word "daddy," her tears began to fall faster.

"The tag…what's on the tag?" the policeman asked.

"It says HER TOY, only it's written like one word." She sobbed again.

"Did you call Momma and Daddy? Did someone call my momma and daddy?"

The policeman felt sorry for the kid and patted her arm as they loaded her into the ambulance. "Yes, miss. They'll be waiting for you at the hospital. You're going to be okay. You're a lucky little lady, okay?"

"Okay," Tita said, and then the doors closed and she was whisked away.

Henry Ralphs went home with good news and bad to give his dad. He'd just saved a young woman's life, and like it or not, his dad was going shopping for a new car.

Carter was tightening the barbed wire on a loose section of fencing when he saw a small calf suddenly stop playing and stare off into the distance.

He knew cattle well enough to know how curious they were, but he thought nothing of it until he realized he was hearing a car engine. He looked up just as a small gray car topped the rise on Mel Tupper's side of the fence and started down the hill toward where he was working.

His first instinct to be wary. Mel had been dead

for three years, and his place was for sale. It was probably a Realtor showing the property to a potential buyer. But as the car got closer, he realized that there was only one person inside. By the time he could see the driver's face, he was at his truck.

This man didn't look like the kind of fellow who was looking for a working ranch. Not with all that black leather and chains.

Carter opened the truck door, then stood behind it, making a show of pulling out a water jug, while he slid out a rifle from behind the seat. He knew the rifle was loaded. He kept it that way for shooting at the occasional coyote or feral dog that showed up to mess with the new calves.

With the door as a shield, he took a drink of water while keeping an eye on the driver, who was now walking toward him.

Carter put down the water jug and stepped out from behind the door with the rifle cradled in his arms.

"That's far enough," he said softly. "State your business."

Jimmy Franks's heart skipped a beat. His pistol was in the pocket of his jacket. He should have known better than to walk up on a man without speaking first.

"Hey, hey, sorry mister," he said, and tried a smile, unaware that it made him look more like a weasel caught with a chicken in its mouth than someone friendly. "I was looking for the McKay place, but I think I took a wrong turn. They told me back in Austin how to get here, but they said the place was a distance off the road. It appears I'm not good with directions."

Carter's eyes narrowed. His name was on the mailbox right out on the side of the county road, and if this man had come from Austin, he would have driven right past it.

"Can't you read?" Carter asked.

Jimmy frowned and jammed his hands in his pockets, taking comfort in the gun beneath his palm.

"Hell, yes, I can read. What kind of a question is that to ask a man?"

"A real logical one, considering you drove right past the mailbox that said McKay, then took a road that had Mel Tupper's name on it, and drove right past Mel's empty house with a For Sale sign out front. Then you took off out into the pasture like you owned the place, and now you try and tell me you're looking for the McKays. I think it's time you state what business you have with them before I give the sheriff a call."

Jimmy had been watching the man's face while he was talking, and it occurred to him that he looked a lot like Wilson McKay, only an older version.

"Are you Carter McKay?" he asked.

Carter shifted the rifle, and his hand moved to the trigger. "Who wants to know?"

"You're Wilson's old man, aren't you?" Jimmy said.

Carter's stomach suddenly knotted. Jimmy wasn't the only one making a connection. Wilson had shown him and Dorothy a picture of Jimmy Franks when they'd found out he'd abandoned a stolen car in Austin. Admittedly, that man was supposed to be dead, but other than the fact that this man was bald, his face and the one in the picture were the same.

"And your name is Jimmy Franks. I'd heard you were dead. Maybe I need to see what I can do to rectify that situation."

Jimmy knew it was over. He pulled the gun from his pocket as Carter swung the rifle toward him. In his panic, the first shot went wild, sailing over Carter's head and out into the pasture, sending the herd of cattle into a stampede.

Carter was ducking as he pulled the trigger. His first shot went into the ground between Jimmy Franks's feet, but that was too close for comfort.

"Holy hell!" Jimmy shrieked, and made a run for the car as Carter shot again. The second bullet hit the front of the Honda right beside Jimmy's hip.

He swung back toward the rancher and fired

again, but Carter was already in his truck, where he threw the shift into Reverse and drove backward as fast as he could. A short distance away, he swung the truck around and stomped the accelerator.

Jimmy chose a similar strategy, getting back in the Honda and heading for the highway as fast as he could. He'd fucked this up royally. Now they knew he wasn't dead. Now they would be on the alert again. Damn, damn and double damn.

While Jimmy was making a run for it, so was Carter. All he could think was that he needed to get to the ranch and warn Wilson that Jimmy Franks wasn't dead.

Dorothy was sitting outside on the porch, rocking as she worked up the latest bushel of green beans, readying them for canning while poking at Old Tom with the toe of her shoe. The cat returned the favor by batting at the ends of her shoelaces.

She was smiling as she looked up and saw Carter's truck come over the hill and start down the road toward the barn. Her first thought was, *Oh good, he's back in time for lunch.* Then it hit her how fast he was driving. That wasn't like Carter at all.

She watched for a moment, then called out to Wilson.

"Wilson! Come here!"

Wilson was helping Cat put lunch on the table when he heard his mother call, and from the tone of her voice, he knew something was wrong.

He and Cat looked at each other; then he hurried outside with Cat right behind him.

"What's wrong?" he asked.

She pointed. "Carter! He's coming too fast. Something is wrong."

Wilson's frown deepened as he watched the dust boiling up behind his dad's old truck.

"What's going on?" Cat asked.

Dorothy's hands were clenched into fists. She didn't answer.

Cat moved up behind Wilson.

"Honey?" she said, sounding worried.

"Dad doesn't ever drive like that."

The cattle scattered as Carter's truck went barreling through the herd. His heart was hammering so loud against his eardrums that he couldn't hear the sound of the engine, and when he didn't see Franks behind him, he was afraid the man was already on his way back to their property by way of the highway. He kept thinking of Franks beating him back to the house and finding everyone dead. He was cursing himself for not taking his cell phone with him. Dorothy was always fussing at him about it, but he never liked the idea of being tied to the damn thing. Now he wished he'd listened to her.

The same mantra kept going through his mind: *Tell Wilson. Tell Wilson.* When he finally topped the hill and saw the ranch house and the outbuildings below, he thought he would be relieved, but his panic increased. And when that happened, a niggling pain he'd barely noticed in his neck and arm suddenly spread through his chest so sharply that he almost lost his breath.

"Sweet Jesus, please…" he whispered, and kept on driving.

The road was beginning to blur before his eyes, and it was growing harder and harder to breathe.

"Not like this. Not like this," he said, as he swung past the barns and headed for the house. He could see Dorothy standing on the porch, and Wilson and Cat beside her.

Just a little bit farther.

A hundred yards from the house, the people on the porch began to shift in and out of focus. Afraid he wouldn't be able to stop at all, he hit the brakes while he could still think and slammed the truck into Park almost fifty yards from the house.

"Wilson…tell Wilson," he mumbled, and tried to get out, but when his feet hit the ground, his legs went out from under him. He heard Dorothy scream his name, and then everything went black.

When Wilson saw his father clutch at his chest and then drop, he knew instantly what was happening.

"He's having a heart attack!" he shouted, and jumped off the porch and started running.

Cat came off the porch with him, but Dorothy had already gone into the house to call for an ambulance. Moments later, she came back out with her cell phone, talking as she ran.

Wilson's hands were shaking as he felt for a pulse in his father's neck. It wasn't there.

"He's not breathing," he said.

Dorothy screamed, then dropped to her knees and started to pray.

Wilson ripped his dad's shirt open, checked to make sure the airway was clear, then began CPR with a half dozen quick breaths into his father's mouth, before he switched to chest compressions. As he moved, Cat positioned herself to do the breaths. When Wilson paused, she didn't hesitate. She pinched Carter's nostrils together, then bent down. His skin felt clammy, and she tasted sweat as she touched his lips, then nothing, as she focused on her tasks.

She heard Wilson counting for her, then she went into a zone. Over and over—without stopping, without looking at each other, afraid to see failure in one another's eyes—they worked, keeping Carter McKay alive.

Beside them, Dorothy kept saying the same words over and over.

"Don't die, don't die. Please hear me, Carter. I love you. Don't die."

Finally, in the distance, they began to hear a siren.

"Oh, thank God," Dorothy sobbed.

The ambulance pulled up, and seconds later, one EMT took over for Wilson, while another grabbed a defibrillator. As soon as it reached full power, he yelled, "Clear!" and put the paddles on Carter's chest, then zapped him. Carter's body bucked from the electrical jolt.

All eyes went immediately to the readout, which still registered a flat line.

"Again," the paramedic said, then shouted, "Clear!"

Again the current coming through the paddles hit Carter's chest, and again his body rocked from the jolt, but this time…magic.

Within seconds, a heartbeat registered.

The EMTs quickly began to stabilize Carter for transport, putting in an IV, then strapping him to the gurney before pushing him toward the ambulance.

"I want to go with him," Dorothy begged.

"I'm sorry, ma'am, but we can't let you."

Wilson took his mother by the arm, holding her back as the driver slammed the door shut, then headed for the front seat.

"Don't worry, Mom. We'll get you there. Get in Dad's truck. We'll follow right behind them."

Dorothy was shaking so hard she couldn't walk. For once she was the one in need of comfort.

Cat took one arm, Wilson the other, and they helped her into the truck. They hadn't even cleared the yard before she began to cry.

"Oh God, oh God, I need to call the other kids."

"We'll call after we get to the hospital," Wilson said, then gave Cat a nervous look. "Are you okay? Are you up to this?"

She nodded. "Don't worry about me. I can throw up just about anywhere. Just drive."

"Shit," Wilson muttered, then stomped the accelerator all the way to the floor.

Fifteen

Another black mark had been added to Jimmy Dale Franks's rap sheet.

After looking through books of mug shots, Tita Little had made a positive ID on the man who'd abducted her. Trouble was, the Austin police department had already issued a statement regarding his death.

At that point Lieutenant Jakowski was forced to release an amended statement to the media stating that the dead man previously identified as Jimmy Dale Franks was in actuality a man named James Martin. Additional arrest warrants had been issued for Franks in connection with Martin's death, and the assault and kidnapping of area resident Tita Little. He made a call to the McKay home but got the answering machine. Reluctant to leave a message about this mess, he just left his name and number and a request for someone to call him.

Once that shit hit the fan, the national news media picked up on the story, and Franks's status as a no-account junkie had changed. If his intent had been to be remembered in history, he was well on his way, just not in the way his mother might once have hoped.

Jimmy Franks was cursing himself up one side and down the other. He'd gotten cocky, then gotten careless and almost gotten himself killed.

Bottom line was, he'd panicked. He wasn't half as confident about killing when someone fought back. Carter McKay's shot had taken the heel off one of his boots. A fraction of an inch closer and it would have gone into his foot.

Even worse, he'd been made. Shaved head, fake tattoo, leather pants and all, the son of a bitch had recognized him.

Now Jimmy was making his getaway off the property as fast as he could, aiming for the highway and heading for someplace new to lay low.

Wilson Carter's old man was sure to alert the authorities as to where he'd seen him and what he'd done. He was going to have to rethink his whole plan. But even in the midst of the mess that he'd made, it never occurred to him to just keep on driving and forget he'd ever met a man named Wilson McKay.

Luis Montoya was about an hour outside Dallas when he realized he needed fuel. He checked the map and took the next exit he came to, pulling into a mom-and-pop gas station with an attached café. It was well after noon, and his belly was grumbling from lack of food. He could fuel both his car and himself at the same time, then check on Conchita and Amalita before he got back on the road. His appointment with Detective Bradley in Dallas wasn't until three o'clock. He had plenty of time for a short break.

He began pumping gas, then stepped to the front of the car to use the phone, counting the rings until Conchita answered.

"Hello."

"Hey, honey, it's me. How are my girls doing?"

He heard her giggle before she answered.

"Oh, Luis, Amalita is so beautiful and so smart. Today I showed her two oranges, and she held up one finger on each hand and said *dos*."

Luis chuckled. "Counting already, huh? Pretty smart for such a little *niña*."

"It will be her birthday soon. She must have a

party. We'll invite all the family. It will be such fun. I saw a huge angel piñata the other day that would be perfect."

"Yes, perfect," Luis echoed, then heard the gas pump cut off. "Hey, honey, my gas tank is full. I've got to go pay and get something to eat. I'll talk to you tonight after I get to my hotel, okay?"

"Yes, yes, very okay," Conchita said, then disconnected.

Luis dropped his cell phone in his pocket and headed inside. It was amazing how someone so small as Amalita could make such a huge difference in their lives.

Inside, he paid for his gas, then walked through a breezeway into the café and chose a booth. He didn't bother to read the menu on the table behind the catsup and mustard. He knew what he wanted.

A waitress appeared with a pot of coffee, a cup and a glass of water.

"Want some coffee, hon?" she asked.

Luis nodded, then watched her pour. When the aroma hit his nostrils, his mouth actually watered.

"Do you know what you want to eat?" she asked.

"Yes. A hamburger with cheese, and French fried potatoes, please." Then he added, "And a piece of chocolate cream pie."

"A man after my own heart," the waitress said,

then flashed him a smile before leaving to turn in his order.

Luis settled back, satisfied that, at least for now, all was right with his world. His wife was happy. He was back on task with his case and was awaiting his favorite American foods: a cheeseburger and fries, and chocolate cream pie.

The McKay family was gathered in a room off the critical care unit, awaiting word on Carter's condition. All Carter and Dorothy's children, their wives and husbands, and even the grandchildren were unnaturally silent.

Dorothy hadn't said more than a dozen words to anyone since they'd arrived. The toddlers, who were always so sure of their grandmother's love, clung to their mothers in uncertainty. Every so often, Cat noticed Dorothy close her eyes, and even though she couldn't hear her, she knew Dorothy was praying.

Wilson pulled Cat closer, taking comfort in her presence. "She's praying," he said.

"I know. God…even worse, I know just how she feels."

Cat shivered, remembering how afraid she'd been when Wilson had been shot, and how the world had dropped out from under her when she'd witnessed his death. The fact that he'd been revived and lived to tell the tale gave her hope for Carter, because she couldn't imagine the family without him.

"I still can't figure this out," Wilson said, more to himself than to her.

"What do you mean?" Cat asked.

"This came out of nowhere. Dad didn't have any heart trouble, and I don't think he'd been feeling bad."

Cat slid her fingers through Wilson's, giving his hand a gentle squeeze to temper her words.

"Sometimes that's just the way life goes. One minute you're on top of the world, and the next thing you know, you're trying to crawl out from under the damn thing."

Before Wilson could answer, a doctor entered the waiting room.

"McKay?"

"Here," they all said, and jumped up en masse. Except Dorothy, who seemed frozen to her seat.

"Is he still alive?" she asked weakly.

Wilson's heart ached, for his mom and for all of them. Please God, let the answer be good.

"At the moment he's stable. We're giving him oxygen, and he has a heart monitor, so he might look worse to you than he actually is. I don't think he's suffered any lasting damage, but of course I can't promise. The next few hours are vital. We'll just have to see how it goes."

Dorothy sagged, then buried her face in her hands and wept.

Her children gathered around her, all talking at once, elated by the news.

It was Cat who realized the doctor was going to leave without someone asking the obvious question.

"When can we see him?" she asked.

"For now, I'm afraid only Mrs. McKay will be allowed in, and that will have to be brief. He won't know she's there, but—"

"I don't care," Dorothy said, and began swiping at her tears with the backs of her hands. "Please… take me to him."

The doctor nodded, and he and Dorothy disappeared behind a set of double doors, leaving the rest of the family looking at each other, a little uncertain as to what to do next.

It was Delia who noticed Cat's pallor and whispered in her ear, "Honey, are you all right?"

Cat sighed. "You tell me. I have good days and bad days. Sometimes I can't eat enough, and other days, like today, everything I eat wants to come up."

Delia hugged her. "Yep, you're all right. You're just pregnant."

"Who's going to stay with Mom?" Charlie asked.

"Someone needs to, even if she's the only one who can see him."

"I can," Wilson said, then gave Cat an apologetic look, as if just remembering she had to be considered.

"We can take Cat home," Delia offered. "She's not feeling well, and she looks like she's fading fast."

Everyone made sympathetic noises, which Cat quickly blew off.

Wilson's guilt worsened. He was torn between what he needed to do and what he wanted to do.

"Honey?"

Cat shook her head. "You absolutely stay, but I *am* going to take Charlie and Delia up on the ride. You'll be better off if you don't have two women to worry over."

Wilson just shook his head and hugged her. "Thank you, baby."

"Oh, Wilson, don't thank me. Your mom has been there for all of us. Now she's the one who needs you."

"And you don't?"

"I'll always need you, Wilson, but not now…not with things the way they are."

Wilson wrapped his arms around her, taking comfort in the steady beat of her heart against his chest.

"Call me if you need anything. I can be home in thirty minutes."

"I will," she said.

Delia slipped her hand under Cat's elbow.

"She can stay with us if she's afraid."

Wilson and Cat looked at each other, then grinned.

"What?" Delia asked. "What did I just miss?"

"You haven't seen her in action after a bail jumper. Cat's not afraid of anything on God's earth," Wilson said.

"Except tornadoes," Cat added.

Wilson brushed his finger against the back of her cheek. "Yeah, right. Except tornadoes." He smiled.

"I'll call you," he added.

"I'll be waiting to hear," Cat said. "Tell your mom I'll be saying prayers."

Then she was gone.

Jimmy was a bundle of nervous energy. He kept looking in the rearview mirror, half-expecting to see a cavalcade of cop cars pop over a hill with lights and sirens at full blast.

In his mind, he kept going over and over the run-in with the elder McKay, thinking how he should have handled it, how it should have gone down. If he had it to do over, he would have stayed his ground and emptied his gun into the bastard. If he had, he wouldn't be in this fix. And, he kept telling himself, he would have done that very thing if McKay's first shot hadn't come so close to taking off his foot.

But what was done was done, so he continued to move in a westerly direction, looking for a place to redefine his appearance and make a new plan.

In the end, Luis arrived at the Dallas Police Department half an hour late for his appointment with Detective Bradley, only to be told Bradley had been sent out on a case and wouldn't be back in the office before tomorrow.

It wasn't what Luis wanted to hear, but he had only himself to blame. He'd missed his exit off the freeway twice before he'd finally gotten reoriented. By the time he arrived, this was the result.

All he could do was leave his cell phone number on Bradley's desk, along with a short message and a note of apology, and wait for Bradley's call to reschedule. His next step would be to find a motel and a good place to eat dinner. He was about to leave when he realized someone here could probably give him an address on Cat Dupree, since she was actively involved in running down local failures-to-show.

The clerk at the front desk was handy. Since she

already knew what he'd come for and had been the one to tell him that Bradley was gone, he would start with her.

"Miss Sullivan, was it?"

"Yes."

"I wonder if I could trouble you for one more thing?"

"Certainly," Jennifer Sullivan said politely.

"There is a female bounty hunter from your city who might have some information regarding the case I am working. Her name is—"

"Cat Dupree. Everyone knows her," Jennifer said, then added, "Only it's McKay now."

"So you know of her? Do you know how I might contact her…maybe through her place of business?"

"Word is, she's quit chasing bail jumpers since she got married."

He frowned. "I see. Might you know where she's gone? Or…how to contact her?"

"Oh, after the tornado footage, we all knew where she'd gone. She's at a ranch outside of Austin."

"What footage? What tornado?"

"Oh my gosh," Jennifer said. "You've got to see it. It's the most romantic thing you've ever seen." She waved at a detective. "Hey, Joe, I'm going to take Detective Montoya to the break room to show him the Cat Dupree tape Shirley saved."

"Yeah, sure. I'll catch the phones for you till you get back."

"Thanks," she said, then added, "Follow me, Detective Montoya."

Luis followed, listening with only a passing interest as she rattled on and on about what he was about to see. As soon as they reached what was obviously the break room, she waved him toward a table.

"Pick a chair," Jennifer said. "I'll get it set up. Here's the deal. A few weeks ago we had one of our usual spring tornadoes. Do you have tornadoes in Mexico?"

"No, ma'am, hardly ever."

"Well, we get a lot of 'em, and this one was really bad. Three or four people were killed. Anyway, a lot of local news crews were out filming after it had passed. You know how it is."

He nodded, although he still failed to see why this was pertinent to his trip. But he was a polite man, and he continued to listen as she talked.

"Two crews, one in a chopper and the other on the ground, came upon a real-life drama in progress. They got every bit of it on film. We're about ready here. Would you like some coffee?"

"No, but thank you," Luis said.

"Okay, here goes." Jennifer punched Play. "The

man is Wilson McKay. He owns a bail bond business here in Dallas. The woman is Cat Dupree. And all this was filmed on the McKay ranch."

Luis began to watch with ambivalence, but was soon caught up in the panic and fear on Wilson McKay's face. And when the camera panned to the back end of a pickup sticking out of a stock pond and he realized McKay believed his woman was inside, he was hooked.

He watched McKay run into the water, then dive under. Every time he came up for air, Luis exhaled along with him, and when he went back under, Luis caught himself holding his breath and imagining the panic he would feel trying to find Conchita in the depths and darkness.

"How did the truck get into the water? Was there an accident?" Luis asked.

"No…no…there was a tornado, remember? The tornado dumped the truck in the pond."

Luis's eyes widened as his focus returned to the screen. Without thinking, he made the sign of the cross and watched as Wilson McKay finally crawled out of the water in obvious despair. Even though the only sound with the taped piece was the newsman's voice-over, when the camera closed in on Wilson's face, Luis felt physical pain from the man's silent scream.

"Ah...*Dios mio*," he whispered, watching as Wilson put on his boots and then began circling the pond toward the dam.

"Where is he going?" Luis asked.

"Just watch," Jennifer said.

Suddenly McKay disappeared off the side of the dam.

Luis thought he'd fallen. But before he could ask, the perspective switched to a view from the air. He saw McKay pick up a boot at the bottom of the dam, then clutch it to his chest. When McKay suddenly started walking away, Luis wondered if he had seen her body? No, wait. He knew she wasn't dead. Then what?

McKay pulled something from a bush. It looked like a piece of cloth.

Dear God, was that a piece of her clothing? Luis wondered, all the things that made him a good detective running through his mind. When he saw McKay suddenly look up, he realized the man had just become aware of the chopper. When he saw McKay turn and stare off into the distance, he scooted to the edge of his chair, watching as the camera panned the horizon, giving him the feeling that he was seeing everything through Wilson McKay's eyes.

It took a moment for Luis to realize he was seeing movement, then several more before he could tell he was looking at a woman staggering through the debris left by the storm.

The longer he watched, the more certain he became that, except for the mud on her body, the woman was naked. Then the camera panned back to the expression on McKay's face. The joy Luis saw was so vivid it brought tears to his eyes. He saw McKay running, and even though he couldn't hear him, he knew McKay was calling her name. By the time they embraced, Luis was crying unashamedly.

"Yeah," Jennifer said. "It does it to all of us… every time we watch."

"Jesus, Mary and Joseph," Luis said. "How did she get out of the water?"

"Oh, that's another thing. She was never in it. Said she woke up without a stitch of clothes, lying faceup on the windshield of the truck. They think she was sucked out of the truck when the windshield popped. She and the windshield went one way, while the truck did a swan dive into the pond."

"And she's all right?" Luis asked.

"Well enough to get married a few days later."

Luis didn't know what to say or what to think. He did know that he didn't want to find out later that this woman was guilty of anything but bad luck—or good fortune. It all depended on how one viewed what he'd just seen.

He stood abruptly. "I thank you for showing me this. Please make sure Detective Bradley has my apologies for my late arrival, and tell him I hope to speak to him tomorrow."

"Sure thing."

"Where did you say this woman is now?"

"On a ranch west of Austin. I'm friends with a woman who knows Wilson's secretary. She told my friend that McKay and Dupree are both quitting the bail bond business to live on the family ranch."

Once more Luis's suspicions returned. Quitting? Not many could afford to do that—unless they'd come into a bunch of money. Like the money Tutuola was reported to have had.

Was that what had brought Dupree back to Mexico the second time?

Now he *knew* he could not leave Texas without talking to this woman. Even if she had survived a terrible ordeal, as far as Luis was concerned, her troubles were far from over.

Jimmy Franks knew the minute he saw the old barn in the middle of nowhere that he'd found a good place to hide. The gate into the pasture was hanging on one hinge, with only a piece of baling wire holding it upright. The trail from the road to the barn was overgrown with weeds, which meant no one came here often. Privacy. Exactly what Jimmy wanted.

He was tired and hungry and needed a fix.

With one quick glance up and down the deserted highway, he opened the gate, drove through, then refastened it behind himself before heading toward the barn at a fast clip.

The main door was off the barn. He drove inside without caution, only to realize that he'd driven over something hidden in the weeds. By the time he got out, he could hear the air escaping from all four tires.

"Son of a freakin' bitch!" he screamed, and then walked back to see what he'd run over.

The iron teeth of a spring-tooth harrow looked a bit like the maw of a growling lion. He kicked all four tires, then the fenders and doors, until the car was as dented as the tires were flat.

"Great. Just fuckin' great," he cursed, then popped the trunk and dragged out his gear. He downed the last two sausage biscuits left over from breakfast and finished off the last two beers in a six-pack.

"Time for dessert," he said softly, as he tossed the empty cans aside, and pulled out what was left of a bag of crystal meth.

Five minutes later, he was so high he wouldn't have needed another vehicle for a getaway. All he had to do was spread his wings and fly.

Sixteen

It had been seven hours since Delia and Charlie dropped Cat off at the ranch. During that time, she'd mostly busied herself nervously doing whatever chores she could do and waiting to hear from Wilson again. He'd called her once about two hours after she'd gotten home, and now the silence was worrying her. The message regarding the false death report of Jimmy Franks was on the answering machine, but that was in the home office and she didn't see the blinking light.

When she'd first arrived, the silence of the usually lively home was telling. But, to her delight, she'd gotten a packet of wedding pictures in the mail from LaQueen and John.

She'd spent a good hour looking at them over and over, remembering that feeling and how certain she'd been that what she was doing was right. It was, however, a bit strange to see herself in that pink dress. It made her look like a woman. She rarely thought of herself that way.

What a difference the love of a good man could make in a woman's life.

To keep from thinking about what might be going on at the hospital, Cat had put away the food they'd been going to eat, fed the cats, put the jars of canned green beans in the cellar and snapped the last of the fresh ones that Dorothy had been going to can. She put them in the cooler on the back porch to stay fresh and then walked through the old house, listening to the silence.

The pictures on the walls and the love that held this family together were, for her, a physical presence she could feel in every room.

As she paused in the hallway, she began scanning the dozens of photos hanging on the walls. It was instinctive for her to search for Wilson's face first in each one. The progression of the years was recorded—from his first baby pictures to what appeared to be formal photos taken for high school graduation. Even as a little boy, Wilson had stood out from his siblings, as if he'd known he would walk a different path. In looking at them, she couldn't help but wonder if the baby she was carrying would look like Wilson or be a combination of both of them.

She thought of the pictures she'd had on her wall. Criminals, every one of them sporting every form of tattooed art a person could envision.

Without thinking, her hand went straight to her belly in a protective gesture. There were no baby pictures of Cat left in this world. No birthday photos where she was blowing out the candles on her cake or looking at presents piled on a table, with friends and family standing nearby. There weren't any pictures of her sitting with her family around the Christmas tree or running wild outside in the yard on an Easter egg hunt.

Emotion shattered her focus as she thought about all the growing up she'd done on her own. Without guidance. Without love. Most especially without love. Her jaw tightened, and her eyes narrowed, almost in anger.

"Don't you worry, my baby. You are going to belong to a big, loud family who might drive you crazy but who will never let you down. What happened to me won't happen to you. I promise." Her fingers clenched on her belly, as if trying to hold on to the beginnings of the tiny life inside.

Moments later, her cell phone rang. When she saw it was Wilson, she answered before he could ask.

"Hello. I'm fine."

The husky chuckle in her ear made her smile.

"Hello to you, too," Wilson said. "Dad's still out, but his vitals are good."

"What about your mom?"

She heard him sigh and knew that he was worried.

"As Dad would say, her fur is standing on end and her claws are out."

"In protective mode, I assume."

"You can't imagine," Wilson said. "She watches everything they do to him like they're trying to kill him, not save him."

"She's just scared," Cat said. "Believe me, I know the feeling."

There was a moment of silence as Wilson absorbed her words, only now realizing what she'd gone through while he was fighting for his life.

"Thank you," he said softly.

Cat frowned. "For what?"

"For fighting for me when I couldn't fight for myself."

Cat's vision blurred. "Oh, Wilson. You did the same for me, time and time again."

"Yeah…that's what people who love each other do."

This time it was Cat who got the message. "I know. I'm slowly but surely learning that, thanks to you and your family."

There was a moment of silence while he absorbed that, and then he asked, "Have you eaten anything?"

"Um…yes."

It was her hesitation that gave her away.

"Let me rephrase that. Have you eaten anything that's stayed down?"

"No."

"Mom says to tell you to have some tea and dry toast or crackers…and to sip the tea. It can be hot or iced, but no coffee."

A single tear rolled down Cat's cheek as she struggled with an answer.

"You take good care of your mother, do you hear me? Even now, when she's so worried about Carter, she's still thinking of others."

"Yeah, and I didn't know until I met you that we took all that love and attention for granted."

"Then we're good for each other, aren't we?"

This time it was Wilson's voice that broke.

"Baby…I've known that since the day we met. I just had a hard time convincing you I was right."

"So is this where I say thank-you for not quitting on me?"

"Yes."

Cat sighed. "I do love you, Wilson McKay."

"Right back at you, baby. Hey…Mom's got a look on her face that I recognize all too well. There's hell to pay somewhere. I'd better go see what's up. Take care of yourself, and call if you need me. Don't forget, I'm not an only child. There's a bunch of us. Any one of them can come and stay with her, too."

"Okay. Call me."

"You know it."

She was still smiling when the dial tone sounded. She dropped the phone back in her pocket, then moved into the living room. The sun was setting. It would be dark before long. She glanced out the front windows, scanning the area for a sign of something that didn't belong. Satisfied that all was well, she went to the kitchen to find something to eat.

She turned on the television to the local news, listening with half an ear as she dug through the pantry and settled on a can of soup to go with her toast.

But her culinary foray quickly ended when she heard a familiar name. She turned abruptly, then upped the volume, listening in disbelief until the bulletin was over.

"For the love of God," she muttered, then grabbed her cell phone and quickly dialed Wilson's number.

She expected him to think something was wrong, especially since they'd just spoken. She wasn't surprised when she heard tension in his voice.

"Hello? Catherine?"

"Yes, it's me. We've got a problem," she said.

"What's wrong?"

"Jimmy Franks isn't dead. The police are saying that the ID was premature, and that they have proof the man found beaten to death in his motel room was definitely not him. And they know he's on the run because he abducted a woman from a mall parking lot, then dumped her in a junkyard and took off to God knows where with her car. The only good news is that he didn't kill her."

"Damn it," Wilson muttered.

"Ditto," Cat said.

At that point the home phone began to ring.

"Hold on, Wilson. Someone's calling. Don't hang up."

"Okay," he said, his mind racing.

When she came back, he could hear the disgust in her voice.

"You'll be relieved to know that a Lieutenant Jakowski of the Austin police department thought it prudent to let you know that the man who tried to kill you in Dallas isn't dead after all. I told him we'd already heard it on the news and thanked him so very much for the warning, however late. He did say that he'd called earlier and left a message. I didn't check the answering machine. Maybe he had, but it's still a case of dragging their feet, not wanting to admit they issued a false death report."

Wilson had to grin. Cat's sarcasm was evident.

"They didn't have to call me, you know. It's not their job to pass along messages like that."

"I don't care. All they had to do was pick up a phone as soon as they knew for sure. For God's sake, Wilson. That creep could be anywhere, just waiting for a clear shot at your head."

"Just keep *your* pretty head inside, okay?"

"And you keep yours on your shoulders."

"Duly noted. I love you. Thanks for the update."

"I love you, too. You're welcome."

Then they both laughed.

"I don't know about you, but I feel better already," Wilson said.

Cat's chin jutted. "I don't, and I won't until that man is behind bars or six feet under, whichever the hell manages to come first."

"It's gonna be okay," Wilson said. "Charlie is on his way in, and I'll be heading home as soon as he gets here."

The tension in Cat's shoulders began to ease. She suspected Delia was responsible for the reprieve.

"Drive safe. I'll see you soon," Cat said.

"I will, and just to be on the safe side, make sure all the doors and windows are locked."

"I'm going to check them now," Cat said, and hung up.

Once she was satisfied that she was well and truly locked in, she ate her soup and toast, and was prowling for something else to eat when it dawned on her that she wasn't feeling sick anymore.

"So I have to be pissed to be able to eat now? What the hell is that all about?" she muttered, and moved into the living room to watch for Wilson's return.

Cat was in the shower when Wilson got home and didn't hear him until he was in the bathroom, calling her name.

"I'm in here!" she yelled.

He yanked the curtain back, then grinned.

Cat arched an eyebrow, then grinned back. He was stark naked and obviously happy to see her.

"Well…hello to you, too, mister. Are you looking for someone?"

Wilson grinned as he stepped inside, pulling the curtain shut behind him.

"Not anymore," he said, then cupped her cheeks and tilted her head upward. "Pucker up, baby… Daddy's home, hungry and hot for Mama."

Cat laughed aloud, slid her arms around his neck and turned him so that he was standing directly under the shower head.

"You'd better not drop me," she warned, as he pulled her legs up around his waist.

"Then don't let go," he growled, and smothered her lips with his own.

She heard him groan, then sigh, and knew exactly how he felt. No matter what went wrong with the world, this thing that was between them was strong enough to cure anything.

He started with kisses—hard and demanding, then soft and sensual.

"Put me down," Cat finally begged.

When she was on her feet, she took him in her hands, soaping then rinsing his erection in a slow, steady rhythm that nearly brought Wilson to his knees.

"Cat…wait," he mumbled, as he tried to hold on.

"Can't," she said, and knelt in front of him.

"Sweet mercy," he said, as she took him into her mouth.

She was one sweet lick from driving him insane when he thrust his hands into her hair and pulled her up, then out of the tub. He carried her to the bed and was about to lay her down when she flinched.

"Wait, Wilson…the bed…I'm wet."

His eyes were slits, his jaw hard and clenched.

"God, I hope so," he said, then laid her flat on the bed and slid inside her.

Cat arched up to meet him, and for a second their gazes locked. She saw his nostrils flare; then his eyes shut. After that, he made damn sure she lost her mind.

* * *

The next day, Luis Montoya was fifteen minutes early for his appointment with Detective Bradley. The same woman who'd shown him the tape of Cat Dupree was on duty again. She greeted him like an old friend, seated him in a waiting area with a fresh cup of coffee, and would have stayed and visited, but he reassured her that he was fine and she finally went back to her desk.

A few minutes later Bradley arrived, carrying a stack of folders, a cup of coffee and a fast-food sack with grease spots already showing through the paper.

"Morning, morning," Bradley said, as he led Luis back to his office, dumped the folders, then set down his breakfast. "Sorry I'm late."

"No, no. That's my line," Luis said.

Both men laughed. "Then we're even," Bradley said, and dug a paper-wrapped object out of the sack. "Sausage biscuit? I have two."

"No, thank you. I have had my breakfast. Please go ahead, though," Luis said.

Bradley took a big bite, then chewed while he talked.

"Please, refresh my memory. You're interested in the Mark Presley case…because…?"

"A few weeks ago a man was murdered in Chihuahua. His name was Solomon Tutuola. We had no leads except for a business card with Mark Presley's name on it. After a few phone calls, I discovered that Mark Presley was behind bars for murder."

"Yes, it was a big deal here in Dallas. Presley's wife came from old money. It was her father who built the business he was running. Mark Presley married into it, then couldn't keep his pants zipped. It was what brought him down."

"So I understand," Luis said.

"Now, how can I help you?" Bradley asked, as he downed the last of the biscuit and opened the second one.

"During my initial investigation, I discovered that Tutuola had been in possession of a very large sum of money, and by that, I mean millions. We are surmising that he was murdered for it, but we can't be sure. Someone pumped several bullets into his body, then set him and the fancy home he'd just purchased on fire and burned them both to ashes."

"Damn. Brutal way to die."

"The dead man's rap sheet wasn't much better."

"Hmm," Bradley said, as he downed the last sausage biscuit, "exactly how can I help you?"

"During my inquiries, there was a name that kept

popping up, and I must eliminate all suspects by, at the least, interviewing them."

"Yeah. And?"

"Cat Dupree. Do you know her?"

Bradley's eyebrows arched. "Oh, yeah. She was instrumental in bringing Mark Presley down." Then he grimaced. "Hell, if I'm honest, she pretty much did it on her own."

"Indeed? How so?"

"The woman Presley killed was her best friend, Marsha Benton. Benton worked for Presley, had an affair with him and was carrying his child when she went missing. Cat Dupree came to us, told us that Benton was missing and that Presley had killed her. Well, you understand our position. She didn't have any evidence, and we could hardly take her word for it."

"I see. So what happened to change things?"

Bradley shrugged. "She pretty much rubbed our noses in it, that's what happened. She went after him on her own. Found all the proof she needed. But Presley knew the noose was tightening and had himself a little mental breakdown. At least, that's what everyone thought. While he was in a hospital bed, supposedly unable to communicate, he was planning an escape. Dupree was on to him, though. When he made his escape from Dallas Memorial, she was right behind him. She followed him all the way into Mexico, with the aid of a fellow bounty hunter named Wilson McKay. Since no arrest warrant had been filed for Presley, there was no bounty on him. It was how she got around your country's laws against hunting bounty."

"Yes, I did find that much out. So she caught him and avenged her friend's murder. What happened after that?"

"Oh, Presley was found guilty. His wife divorced him. Life goes on, I guess."

"No, I meant…what happened to Dupree after that?"

"Oh. Hell if I know. She's something of an enigma, you know."

"No, I do not. Please explain."

"It has to do with her childhood. When she was six, she and her mother were hit by a drunk driver. Her mother died. She survived. Then, when she was thirteen, a man broke into their home and murdered her father with a knife. He slit her throat first, leaving her for dead. But she wasn't dead, and she watched the man stab her father to death, unable to cry out for help."

Luis was getting sick to his stomach. Once again this woman whom he suspected of murder, however reluctantly, was turning out to be anything but what he'd expected to find.

"How did she come to be a bounty hunter?"

"Art Ball, the owner of Ball Bail Bonds, hired her

to do paperwork. I think he just felt sorry for her. She'd just been turned loose from the foster system and didn't have anywhere to turn other than to odd jobs or living on the streets. One thing led to another and before you know it, she was a full-fledged bounty hunter. Damnedest thing... She turned out to be one of the best. Isn't afraid of Old Nick himself."

"Old Nick? I do not know this man," Luis said.

"Oh...yeah, sorry. It's an American phrase. It means she's not even afraid of the devil."

Luis exhaled slowly as he leaned back in the chair. So. A woman unafraid of the worst of men. Solomon Tutuola certainly fit that description. Every person he'd met along the way who'd seen Tutuola, even Padre Francisco, had referred to him as *el Diablo*.

"I am told this woman is married to the other bounty hunter...Wilson McKay, the man who was with her during the capture of Mark Presley. I am also told that they've quit their jobs and moved to McKay's childhood home. Is this true?"

"Yeah, only they didn't exactly quit. One of McKay's clients freaked out and tried his best to kill him. Shot him full of bullets. He just didn't die. Then, after Cat Dupree nearly died in that tornado, I think they both thought it was time to try something different."

"Ah," Luis said, more to himself than to Bradley.

It made sense. In such circumstances, both of them quitting their respective jobs did not necessarily mean they'd come into money, only that they had been given second chances at life and had chosen a different path. Still, he'd come this far. He wasn't going to leave until he'd met Cat Dupree. If nothing else, he was more than curious about such a woman.

"So if I wanted to talk to Cat Dupree, I would find her at the McKay ranch?"

"Yeah, that's what I hear. You can always call first to make sure they're there."

"Yes, I will do that. Do you by any chance have an address and phone number?"

"No, but I can get it for you pretty easy. Hang on."

Bradley swung around to his computer and in moments came up with all the info Luis needed. Bradley printed it out and handed it over.

"Thank you very much for you time and information," Luis said, as he pocketed the paper.

"Anything for a fellow detective," Bradley said. "Hope you find your doer. Nothing rankles more than to have an unsolved case go cold on you. I've been there a few times myself."

A short while later, Luis was on his way back to his motel to pack. It was early enough that he could easily get to Austin and out to the ranch. The sooner he got this over with, the happier he would be. But he wasn't going to call first and warn them that he was coming. He wanted the element of surprise to be in his favor. Most of all, though, he wanted to be home with Conchita and their new little girl. He wanted laughter and joy back in his life. Like McKay and Dupree, maybe it was time for him to rethink his occupational options.

Jimmy Franks was on foot once more, cursing thorn bushes, skunks and mean herd bulls with every breath. It wasn't as if he could just take off down the road walking in plain sight of God and everybody. Not after he'd pulled that stunt with Carter McKay.

So he'd been forced to stay off the roads and travel from one pasture to another, climbing through fences and ducking down in the tall grass or hiding behind the occasional stand of trees whenever a car would pass by. His only saving grace was that he was not in a heavily traveled area. It seemed that the only vehicles he saw coming and going were locals. Now he just needed to find one of their houses and get himself a makeover and a ride.

After about an hour of walking, he topped a small hill, stopped to take a breath and then smiled as he looked down into a shallow valley. At last. But there was good news and there was bad news.

Good news: He counted a truck, a car and an ATV, all within plain sight. That meant a new ride.

Bad news: No telling how many people lived there, but it appeared that they were all at home. That meant it might be a little difficult to get them to part with clothes, food and a vehicle.

Truth of the matter: None of it was their decision. He patted the gun in his pocket and kept on walking.

Journey Mathers was six feet, five inches tall, fifty-seven years old and deaf in both ears from a bout with measles at the age of six.

His wife, Arpatha Mathers, was of average height but weighed a good three hundred pounds plus, and had been deaf since birth.

She and Journey had married over twenty-two years ago, and she'd given birth to twin boys they'd named Bill and Will. Bill had died at birth. Will, who was now twenty years old, with the mental capacity of a two-year-old, had been put in a home for the handicapped after he'd gotten too big for Journey to lift.

In the grand scheme of things, Journey and Arpatha didn't have a lot going for them, but they managed, and most of the time they were happy.

They were both in the living room, watching TV and reading the captioned crawl at the bottom of the screen when Jimmy walked in the back door with his gun drawn. He heard the television and quickly moved into the hall. When he saw the size of the man and woman sitting in front of the television, the hair stood up on the back of his neck.

The man looked like Bigfoot, or what he thought Bigfoot would look like, if there was such a thing, and the woman was just plain huge. He palmed the pistol, making sure the safety was off, and then aimed it at the back of the man's head before yelling,

"This is a holdup! Get your asses down on the floor—now!"

Total denial of his existence was the last thing he expected. Confused, he yelled again.

"Get down, motherfuckers! Get down now!"

The man was making motions with his fingers and pointing to the television. When Jimmy saw the woman answer back in the same way, he nearly shit his pants where he was standing.

What were the odds of walking in on a houseful of deaf-mutes? He almost danced a jig. He could do as he pleased and they would never even know he was there.

Slowly he backed away, then hurried into the kitchen, quickly scanning it for some quick food and the possibility of a set of car keys.

There was a platter of fried chicken on the

counter, covered over with a paper towel, and a wooden plaque in the shape of a car hanging on the wall near the door. The catchy phrase that had been burned into it all but shouted *Here I am, help yourself.*

"'A car for keys and keys for a car.' Well, if that isn't just too cute for words," Jimmy muttered.

He glanced over his shoulder to make sure he wasn't being observed, checked outside to check the makes of the vehicles, then chose the keys to the Chevy Malibu sitting near the mailbox.

He grabbed the platter of chicken with one hand and the car keys with the other, then headed out the door, feeling smart enough about the situation to let the door bang behind him as he left.

He was almost at the car when a big dog came out of nowhere, barking and snarling.

Jimmy dropped the platter of fried chicken as he made a run for the car. It was all that saved him from a real ass chewing.

"Shee-it," he muttered, as he started the engine and spun out of the driveway as fast as the car would take him.

He was still hungry and still in skinhead mode, but he had wheels and Cujo had himself some fried chicken. All in all, it could have been worse.

Seventeen

"**P**aging Dr. Danvers. Paging Dr. Danvers. Dr. Danvers, pick up on line three."

It was the first thing Carter McKay heard when he began to wake up. He couldn't imagine what TV show Dorothy would be watching this early in the morning or why he couldn't smell coffee brewing. He did know, however, that she was nearby, because he could smell the scent of her lemon-verbena shampoo. She'd used that scent for almost as long as he could remember. He reached sideways, expecting to feel the softness of her hair against his palm and instead felt resistance, as if he were caught in an extension cord.

That didn't make sense.

Dorothy was nearby—his nose didn't lie—but he didn't know why things didn't feel right. Then he opened his eyes, recognized a hospital room and couldn't figure out how he'd gotten here.

He started to panic until he saw Dorothy dozing in a chair near his bed. Through a set of double windows, he could see Charlie standing out in the hall, nursing a can of Coke and talking to a doctor.

Okay. He was in the hospital. He looked down at himself, checking for stitches or casts. Nothing. Then he heard the steady beep, beep, beep of a machine and looked over his shoulder.

Hell. That looked like a heart monitor. He remembered what they looked like, because his dad had been hooked up to one after he'd had his heart—

Dear lord, he thought, remembering the pain in his chest. He'd been trying to get home. But why? Something urgent. Something vital to—Oh no!

He gasped, then started flailing at the wires hooked up to his body. What came out of his mouth was slurred and sounded as confused as he felt, but his mind was racing. He had to make them understand.

"Dorrie…wake…wake!"

Dorothy jumped up so fast, she was upright before her eyes were good and open. All she could think was that Carter was awake and talking. That had to be good.

"Oh, honey!" she cried, and ran to his side,

patting his face and kissing his cheek. "We've all been so worried."

"Wisson...talka Wisson."

The heart monitor was going haywire. A nurse came running into the room, saw her patient flailing on the bed and quickly grabbed his arm to keep him from jerking out his IV.

"Mr. McKay, you've got to calm down. You're going to hurt yourself."

Carter glared—as darkly and fervently as it was possible to glare from the flat of his back, with his bones feeling like rubber.

"I needa talka Wisson..."

A doctor came running into the room, issuing orders and grabbing at Carter's arms, restraining him while the nurse produced a syringe full of meds. Whatever she shot into Carter's IV put him under fast.

Despite that, Carter's last word was still "Wisson."

Dorothy didn't know why it was so important that their eldest son be present, but if that was what Carter wanted, then that was what he would get. The next time he opened his eyes, Wilson Lee would be at the foot of his daddy's bed or she would know the reason why.

She glared at the doctor, then sped past the nurse on her way out the door.

"Charlie!"

Charlie was so startled, he sloshed part of his Coke out of the can as he reacted to an oh-so-familiar tone.

"Yes, ma'am?"

"Call Wilson. Tell him his daddy is asking for him and to get here as fast as he can."

"Yes, ma'am. Is Daddy worse?"

"No. At least, I don't think so. Just do what I said."

"Yes, ma'am," Charlie said, and was already punching in the numbers to Wilson's cell phone as his mother flew back into the room and shut the door in his face.

It was after eleven. Wilson was just finishing up the chores, and Cat was grilling hamburgers outside. She wasn't much of a cook, but she could manage a grill, and when she'd offered to make hamburgers, he'd jumped at it. Now, the aroma of burgers grilling was in the air and making his belly growl.

When his cell phone rang, he flinched, then his gut knotted. When he realized the call was from Charlie, he was almost afraid to answer. Charlie was at the hospital. *Please God*, he prayed silently, *don't let anything be wrong.*

"Hello?"

"Wilson, it's me."

"I know. Caller ID, remember? What's up?"

"Oh. Yeah. Whatever. Anyway, I'm calling because Mom told me to. And I'm quoting her here. Charlie. Call Wilson. Tell him his daddy woke up and was asking for him. She said to tell you to get here as quick as you can. So I've delivered the message. You know Mom. I'd suggest you hustle."

Wilson was so scared he hated to ask, but he couldn't drive all the way into Austin fearing the worst.

"Is Dad…is he—"

"Oh. Hell. No, no. I should have said that first. She said he's okay. He's just asking for you." Then he snorted softly. "He always did like you better."

Wilson cursed beneath his breath. "Damn it, Charlie. I've heard you whine about that most of my life, and I can promise you, this is not the time to pull it out again. Tell Mom I'll be there as soon as I can, and if I hear that crap about who Dad's favorite is again, it'll have to have come up through your ass before it makes it back out of your mouth again."

"Point taken. See you later, bro."

"Count on it," Wilson said, and headed for the house, calling out to Cat as he ran.

She was just taking the last of the patties from the grill when she heard Wilson calling her name.

She turned with a smile, then saw the look on his face. Please. No more bad news.

"What?"

"Charlie just called. Dad woke up asking for me. Mom sent a message that basically means…get your ass here ASAP or suffer the consequences."

"Oh, no. Is he worse?"

"Charlie said he wasn't. I'm going to change into clean clothes and take off to the hospital. Want to come?"

"Oh, honey…the contractor already called. He's coming out to pick up a check. I told him I'd be here. Do you mind?"

"No. Of course not. Besides, knowing Dad, it's just some instruction about feeding cattle or the like. He probably thinks the place will go to hell in a handbasket unless he's running the show."

"Okay. You change clothes. I'll make you a burger to go."

Wilson kissed her quickly, then lingered for a second kiss. When he finally turned her loose, he groaned.

"Hold that thought," he said, then added, "And since I'm responding to a royal demand, please hold the onions on the burger, too."

"You got it," Cat said, and carried the plate of

burgers into the house as Wilson made a dash for their room to change clothes.

A few minutes later he was on his way to Austin, eating as he drove, leaving Cat behind to wait for the builder and eat her lunch in solitary splendor. Cat couldn't have cared less about eating alone. She was just grateful that today was a day when her food stayed in her belly where it belonged.

The contractor came and went, and the afternoon was wearing her down. She crawled onto the living room sofa and covered herself with one of Dorothy's afghans. Within minutes, she was asleep.

Jimmy Franks knew that backtracking in a stolen car was a risk, but he was through fucking around with Wilson McKay. Today was the day that it was going to be over and done with.

He drove with single-minded focus, never speeding, never calling attention to himself in any way. Just lessening the miles that he'd put between himself and the McKay household with every passing minute. By this time tomorrow, he would be out of the state, heading for points north. And at the first place he came to that had a bus stop, he would ditch the car and use public transportation to get himself out of the state.

He'd taken his last hit of meth on an empty

stomach and was as high as he could be without sailing through the roof of Arpatha Mather's Malibu. He was clutching the steering wheel so tightly that his knuckles were white. The bugs he felt crawling underneath the skin had to be the size of quarters, and he had an overwhelming urge to chew on his tongue. But he knew if he rode out the high in bliss, he would wake up in the ditch on a downer. You couldn't do any kind of business on a downer, and he was flat out of money to buy more meth until he made a withdrawal somewhere, preferably at the McKay ranch after he'd done them in. But, he wasn't going to be picky. First things first.

Kill McKay.

Kill McKay.

Kill McKay.

Luis Montoya once again missed the exit he had meant to take, this time the one that would get him to the McKay ranch. But he'd learned his lesson in Dallas. This time he didn't keep driving the wrong way, hoping something—like God and a miracle—would deposit him in front of the correct address, as he had done before. He got off at the next exit he came to and backtracked through the city streets, stopping twice at gas stations to make sure he was on the right track.

As he finally reached the correct road and aimed the car west, he made a silent memo to himself to buy a portable GPS before he did any more traveling. He wasn't sure how to use one, but it couldn't be any more difficult than what he was going through now.

As he drove, his mind kept going over and over everything he'd learned about Cat Dupree. If he was honest with himself, he would have to admit he was more than eager to meet this superwoman. But if it turned out that she was his killer, he wasn't sure he would be able to take down such an Amazon on his own. Besides, he knew that if he wanted to make an arrest in the United States, he would have to go through "channels." And the people who knew her seemed to hold her in high esteem, which meant the powers that be might be hesitant to send one of their own, so to speak, into a foreign country to do time. But, as his mother always said, trouble is a bad thing to borrow. He would just have to wait and see how the interview went.

Wilson got to the hospital in record time, only to find that his father had been medicated again and was sound asleep. Charlie had made an exit about five minutes before Wilson's arrival.

His mother was there, her face pale and drawn, but with a set to her chin he knew all too well. He slipped into the room and put an arm around her shoulder, surprising her with a soft pat and a kiss on the cheek.

"Hey, Mom. How's Dad?"

"Better…I think. But they shot him full of something before he could say what he wanted to say. I swear, all they had to do was—"

"It doesn't matter," Wilson said. "I'm here, and I'll be here when he wakes up. Then he can tell me to be sure and feed the old horse two scoops of sweet feed instead of one, and not to forget to band the new bull calves."

Dorothy sighed. "You're probably right. Still, it was really strange. I've never seen him so worked up."

Wilson frowned, thinking back over what Carter could possibly need to tell him that was so important, then knew there was no way to guess. They would just have to wait until he woke up to find out.

Cat was dreaming of little boys who looked like Wilson when she heard someone laugh. She thought she was still dreaming until she opened her eyes, and when she did, her heart stopped.

A man was standing less than ten feet away with

a gun pointed straight at her head—and she knew who he was.

"Well, hello, Sleeping Beauty. You should have waited a minute, so I could wake you up with a kiss."

"Like hell," Cat said, and swung a pillow and the afghan at him at the same time that she bolted.

She leaped over the back of the sofa and made a run toward the kitchen as the afghan flared, then settled over Jimmy Franks's head like a bullfighter's cape.

Surprised by the unexpected move, Jimmy ducked as he fired off a shot. The slug went into the ceiling. By the time he got the afghan off his head, the woman was gone.

"Bitch!" he screamed, then jumped over the sofa and ran after her.

Cat was running for her life and knew not to stop or look back. She'd seen too many booking photos to be fooled by a shaved head and biker gear. She had only two options now—outrun Jimmy Franks or outfight him. And while she would have loved to wipe that stupid grin off his face permanently, she couldn't stand empty-handed against a man with a gun.

She ran through the kitchen and was on her way out the door when she suddenly pivoted and back-tracked two steps toward the counter, grabbing a carving knife from the block before running out. Once outside, she flattened herself against the wall by the back door, waiting for him to exit.

Jimmy was screaming and cursing with every step as he chased after her. How was he to know that the bitch would not only fight back but outrun him?

When he reached the kitchen and still couldn't find her, he began to panic, thinking that she'd gotten away. He couldn't afford to leave another witness alive. It was like dropping breadcrumbs for the cops to follow. With his eyes on the horizon, he dashed onto the back porch.

He saw movement from the corner of his eye just as the screen door swung shut.

At the same moment that Cat swung sideways with the knife, Jimmy lunged backward just far enough that the blade missed the artery, slicing through muscle as it pierced straight through his shoulder. His roar of pain sent a shiver up her spine.

When the tip hit the wall, the knife vibrated like a tuning fork before flying out of Cat's grip when Jimmy yanked it loose. She heard it hit somewhere behind her and knew she couldn't outrun a bullet in time to get to it.

To her dismay, he was still upright and armed, and she was now without a weapon. Hoping that she'd wounded him enough to distract him, she made a flying leap off the back porch and started across the yard.

"You're mine!" he screamed, while blood poured down his arm, dripping through his fingers onto the porch.

"Stop now!" he shrieked, and fired off a second shot.

Cat heard the words just as the dirt between her legs suddenly exploded. She stopped—but only because she had more than just herself to consider.

"Turn around now!" Jimmy Franks screamed.

Cat turned to find him only a step behind her. He hit her cheek with the butt of the gun, and she went down.

When she didn't move, Jimmy cursed, then nudged her with the toe of his shoe.

"Get up!" he yelled.

She didn't move.

"Get up, damn it, or I'll shoot you right there."

When she didn't respond to that threat, it occurred to him that he might have hit her too hard. Fine. That would give him time to restrain her. He dragged her body to the porch, then, with blood dripping, dug through the laundry in a basket just inside the kitchen door, hunting for something to use as a rope. When he found a pair of pantyhose, he grabbed them.

Perfect.

Before the woman could wake, he had her tied to a porch post in a sitting position with her hands behind her back. Her long legs were sprawled and dangling down the steps. He stared at her long enough to get hard. That was when he made his last plan.

Cat came to in a panic, with a sharp, stabbing pain in her face, and unable to move. Before she even had time to remember why, Jimmy Franks walked into her line of vision. At that point she was hit with a double dose of fear. She bit on her lip, using the pain to focus, then lit into him with every ounce of strength she had in her, desperate not to let him see her fear.

"So you're the big bad Jimmy Franks. What a joke. Can't even take down an unarmed woman without cheating. You're a sorry—"

"Shut it!" Jimmy yelled.

He was stunned that the first words out of her mouth had been to berate him. She should be scared to death, begging for her life, not threatening his.

"You're in no shape to make threats, bitch. So shut your mouth or I'll just do you now."

"You don't have the balls to do yourself," Cat said, and then spat at him.

The spittle landed on the toe of his shoe.

He stared at her. "You're either the stupidest woman I ever met or you were born without a lick of sense."

"Why? Because I'm not afraid of you?"

Cat stifled the urge to weep and focused on anger instead. If she had any chance at all of surviving this, it would be because she kept him off guard.

Jimmy pointed his gun at her head.

Cat's heart stopped. *Dear Lord, no. Please. Don't let this be the way I end...not when my life is just beginning...not when my baby will die with me.*

Then she saw the glitter in his eyes, his dilated pupils, and realized he was not only mean and stupid, but he was higher than a kite. And she also realized that whatever he'd tied her hands with was stretching. She had another chance. She couldn't afford to blow it.

"Well, big man...where's the thrill in this?"

"Shut up!" Jimmy shouted.

Cat shrugged, then rolled her eyes. "Just like a man. When in doubt, shout."

Jimmy couldn't believe it. She was a bona fide nut. She had to be. Any normal woman would be afraid. He couldn't figure out what Wilson McKay saw in her. She was nothing but a freak.

"I'm gonna shoot you dead and fuck your ass.

How do you think you're old man is gonna feel about that?"

"Don't ask me, dumbass. I'll be dead. Did you ever think of that? Oh, by the way…thank you in advance for shooting me before you do me. At least I won't have to smell your stinky self all on top of me."

Jimmy picked up one of Dorothy's bowls that she used for her beans and slung it across the porch, shattering both it and what was left of his focus.

Now he couldn't kill the bitch first, because it would be letting her off easy, and he, by God, intended to make her life as miserable as possible before he put the gun in her ear and pulled the trigger.

"So you don't want to smell me? Too damned bad. You're not only gonna smell me, you're gonna feel me, too…jamming my cock inside your ass until you're begging to die. Do you hear me, bitch?"

Cat's hands were free now, but she needed him closer. She knew how she could take him down, but she wasn't sure what his reaction would be. Still, if she wanted to live, it was a risk she had to take.

"Answer me, bitch!" he screamed, and waved the gun near her ear.

Cat turned her head, looked him straight in the eyes, then answered without a hint of emotion.

"Boo. Hoo."

Jimmy went nuts. He jumped at her, intent on raping her where she lay.

Cat's hands came up and caught him around the neck just as he took her down. They fell backward onto the floor together. The gun went off, and again the slug missed her, hitting the wall beneath the porch roof.

Before Jimmy could move, Cat had her thumbs in his eyes. She pushed until she felt something pop, then kicked out from under him, rolled onto her belly and got up on the run.

Jimmy Franks went sailing, hitting his head against the porch post with such force that it loosened a mud daubers' nest, which fell out from under the eaves and onto his head.

Cat was running for the barn when she heard the shot. There was a burning sensation on her back that sent her staggering, and she heard four more shots as she went down.

Luis Montoya was feeling smug. Not only had he managed to stay on the correct road, but when he found Carter McKay's name on the mailbox and took the gravel road leading to the house, he felt certain his journey was coming to an end. One way or another, he should be on his way home by tonight.

He had to marvel at the beauty of a Texas spring, and the blue flowers blooming in the pastures and along the roadside as he passed. He had, however, also seen remnants of the tornado that had passed through this area. Bits and pieces of buildings were still lying about in pastures, and now and then a piece of metal siding was wrapped around a wire fence like a twist-tie from a loaf of bread.

When he topped a small rise in the road, the panorama below was like something in a painting. The bright green of new grasses, the white fences, well-kept outbuildings and a ranch house to be envied. The single-story home with the gray roof and white siding was neat and tidy, with flowers and blooming shrubs planted around the porches.

As he drove into the yard and pulled up, he suddenly realized a woman dressed in blue jeans and a T-shirt was running away from the house. To his horror, he saw a man go running after her, carrying a gun. When he saw the man stop and take aim, Luis bolted from his car with his own gun drawn. Before he could shout, the man fired. He saw a bright splash of red appear on the woman's white shirt.

He shouted, but the man didn't acknowledge him, and the woman was still running. When he saw the man taking aim again, he didn't hesitate. He fired four shots in rapid succession.

When Jimmy's first shot hit Cat Dupree and he saw blood splatter, he screamed,

"Yeah! That's what I'm talking about, bitch!"

He was taking aim again when something shattered his thoughts. A searing pain shot through his belly, then another and another. Before the last shot hit, he was already dead, facedown in the dirt with the gun still in his hands.

Wilson was standing just outside the door to his father's room when his mother began to wave at him to come inside.

He dropped his can of Mountain Dew into the trash and hurried in. Carter was already struggling against the needles and wires hooked up to his body, and Dorothy was trying to calm him down.

"Carter, you have to stop this," Dorothy said. "You're going to hurt yourself."

"Wisson…Wisson."

"He's here. He's standing right here beside me."

Wilson grabbed his father's hand. "Dad. Dad!

It's me, Wilson. I'm here, okay? You need to settle down before you hurt yourself."

Carter's fingers clenched around Wilson's hand, as if unwilling to let him go.

"Lissen…gotta lissen."

"I'm listening," Wilson said.

"Franks…Franks."

Wilson's heart skipped. Shit! He couldn't be talking about Jimmy Franks, could he?

"I'm here, Dad. I hear you. Are you talking about Jimmy Franks?"

Carter exhaled slowly, then nodded.

Suddenly Wilson began to understand. Somehow Franks was connected to what had happened to his dad.

"Did you see him?" he asked.

All the tension was leaving Carter's body. Finally he was getting his message out.

"Yes…fencing," he mumbled, then rubbed at his mouth.

"You saw Jimmy Franks when you were fixing fence?"

"Yes, yes…shot at me."

Dorothy gasped. "Dear lord…no wonder he had a heart attack," she said and started to cry.

"Did Franks know who you were?" Wilson asked.

Carter nodded.

Wilson was suddenly sick to his stomach. He'd left Cat alone at the ranch.

"Mom, I've got to go. Cat's out there alone. You call the sheriff. Tell him what happened and that I'm on my way home."

"Oh lord, oh lord," Dorothy moaned. "What if—"

"Don't say it," Wilson said. "Just don't…."

He couldn't finish his own thought. It was too horrible to consider. He left without saying goodbye and was running before he reached the elevator, calling home as he went.

There was no answer at the ranch phone, and when he tried her cell, he didn't get an answer there, either. He told himself it didn't mean anything, but he knew that wasn't true. Cat wouldn't ignore his call—not when everything in their family was so off kilter.

For the first time since she'd announced she was having his baby, he hoped to God she was in the bathroom, puking up her guts.

When Cat felt hands at her back, she came up fighting. It wasn't until she saw a stranger holding up his hands and backing away that she realized it wasn't Franks.

"Please, señora, I mean you no harm. You're safe.

You're safe. The man who was shooting at you is dead, and you are bleeding. Will you let me help you inside the house?"

Cat was lightheaded enough to want help but streetwise enough not to take it without an inquisition.

"Who the hell are you? How do I know you're not one of his buddies?"

Luis stared. She was bleeding from a gunshot wound. She had a terrible cut on her face, and her knuckles looked raw and bloody, but her eyes were on fire, her fists were doubled and she wasn't backing down.

He exhaled as if he'd just been punched in the gut. It had to be her. No other woman would react to what had just happened to her in such a manner.

"Is your name Cat Dupree?"

Her eyes narrowed, and her nostrils flared. "Like I said before…who wants to know?"

Luis wanted to smile. She was amazing. But he couldn't relent, not until he knew that she wasn't the killer he'd been trying to find.

"My name is Luis Montoya, and I am a homicide detective from Chihuahua, Mexico."

Cat froze, staring at his dark eyes and trim black mustache. Absently noting his hair pulled into a small ponytail at the back of his neck while watching his face for an accusation, looking for handcuffs, watching her life as she'd known it so far ending before her eyes. She wanted to scream. She wanted to fall on her knees before this man and beg him to understand. Instead, she lifted her chin and stared him down.

"So, Detective Montoya, I have you to thank for my life. However, since I seem to be bleeding, I hope you'll excuse me for not offering you some tea."

Then she grabbed her side, and when she looked down and saw blood on her hand, she said, "Dear lord, baby mine…I've taken you with me through hell and back one too many times. If I promise not to do this again, will you promise me that you'll be all right?"

Luis frowned. "Who are you talking to?"

She put her bloody hand on her belly, then let it drop to her side, unaware of the horrifying imprint she'd left behind.

"My baby. I'm pregnant."

Luis stared down past the bloody handprint to her still-flat stomach.

"Dios Mio."

"Ditto," she muttered. "I'm going in the house now to call my husband and then the police. They've been looking for this man for two murders, an attempted murder, and for assault and kidnapping. Congratulations. You've just made yourself a hero."

When she walked away without another word, Luis couldn't help but admire her spirit. She neither stumbled nor staggered as she strode past the dead body. When she didn't even bother to look down, Luis knew, with a sinking feeling, that he was watching a woman capable of murder.

He sighed, then followed her inside, to find her already on the phone.

"No, Wilson, I swear I'm all right. Yes, he's dead. I have company."

"Who's there, honey? The contractor?"

"No. It's the man who killed Jimmy Franks and saved my life."

"Thank God he arrived when he did. What's his name? Tell him to stay there. I want to thank him in person."

"Don't worry. I imagine he'll still be here when you arrive. His name is Luis Montoya. He's a homicide detective from Chihuahua, Mexico."

There was a long moment of silence; then Cat heard Wilson curse. At this point, there wasn't anything either of them could say.

"See you in a few," Wilson said.

She hung up, then turned around to see Montoya watching her.

"If you don't mind a bit of a wait, I'm going to find some bandages and a clean shirt. The sheriff is on his way, and knowing my husband, there will be an ambulance, too, but if Wilson sees me in this shape, there's a good chance he'll feed Jimmy Franks's body to the hogs before the sheriff can take him away."

Luis didn't know whether she was making a joke or stating a rather gory fact, but he knew he wasn't about to budge, so he nodded politely and took a seat at the kitchen table.

Cat looked him straight in the eyes, then nodded, as if satisfied.

"Give me a couple of minutes," she said, and walked away.

For some reason, it never entered his mind that she would run. Even if she was guilty, he knew she wouldn't.

Eighteen

Cat's hands were shaking so badly that she could hardly get her shirt over her head. The adrenaline rush that had kept her moving during Jimmy Franks's attack was crashing down around her in waves.

All the while she was digging through the medicine cabinet for bandages, she wanted to cry. Instead, she taped a wad of gauze to her side, then pulled a clean shirt over her head.

The walk from their bedroom to the kitchen seemed endless. She kept imagining cells on both sides of the hall and prisoners with their arms hanging through the bars, watching her pass.

In her mind, she heard someone say "Dead woman walking."

Her life was in tatters. There was the very real possibility that her baby would be born in a Mexican prison, and that she would never see it or Wilson again. Could she keep on living, knowing that Wilson and their child were in one country and she was in another, doomed to an existence behind bars?

She didn't know. What she did know was that she'd gotten herself here without anyone's help and had no one but herself to blame. She was scared out of her mind, but Luis Montoya would never know it. By the time she reached the kitchen, she had her game face on.

"Thank you for waiting. Would you please follow me? It's more comfortable sitting in the living room."

Luis was constantly amazed by this woman. There was a dead man out in her backyard, and she was talking to him as if he'd arrived for a friendly visit. If she was guilty, she was doing a masterful job of hiding the fact.

"I'm fine here," he said.

"I'm not," Cat said. "My back hurts like hell, and those chairs are hard. If you want to talk to me and you're not willing to shout, you'll have to move."

Once again her bluntness put him at a disadvantage. He quickly stood and followed her into the living room while stifling an urge to apologize for not understanding her pain.

Once they reached the living room, he realized that her fight with the dead man in the yard had begun here. The sofa was overturned, there was a bullet hole in the ceiling, and a lamp was broken. Before he could offer, she'd righted the sofa, picked up the broken lamp and seated herself in a large overstuffed chair.

When she sat, she eased herself down, not bothering to stifle a soft groan. He felt sorry for her in so many ways.

As he took the chair next to her, he was struggling with how to begin this interview, which was actually an interrogation. It was then that he noticed the huge ropey scar at the base of her throat and remembered how it had gotten there. No wonder she hadn't reacted to the dead man he'd left outside in the dirt.

Cat was tired and aching and wanted this over. As always, she chose to be the one in charge and began the conversation.

"So. You've obviously come a long way to talk. I assume it wasn't out of loneliness. I'm sure there are a lot of people you could visit in your own country, especially if you took the time to look for them."

Luis stifled a grin. She was a cool one.

"No, Miss Dupree, I—"

"It's McKay. Mrs. McKay, but you can call me Cat."

He bowed his head in acquiescence. "Is that short for Catherine?"

"Yes. And now that I've answered a couple of your questions, you get to answer one of mine. Other than saving my life, what the hell are you doing here?"

"Looking for the killer of a man named Solomon Tutuola."

To Cat's credit, she never blinked, but inside she was screaming.

"And you're asking me because…?"

Luis sighed. She wasn't going to help him. All right. He could work with that.

"A few weeks ago, this man, Tutuola, was murdered in our city. He was shot several times, and then his body and his home were burned to the ground."

Cat didn't comment. Didn't look away.

Luis shrugged. "We found a business card belonging to Mark Presley in his possession."

Now Cat's eyes registered an understanding. Son of a bitch. How ironic that the man she'd taken down for murder was about to do her in for the same.

"Ah…I see you recognize that name," Luis said.

Cat's disdain was obvious. "If you know anything about that man, then you know my connection to him. Of course I recognize the name. The sorry bastard killed my best friend and dumped her body into a ravine like a bag of trash. She was carrying his child."

Luis dipped his head slightly, as if acknowledging her grief.

"Yes. This I was told. I am sorry for your loss."

"So am I," Cat said. "What does Marsha's death have to do with your dead man?"

"I understand that you were in Mexico when you went after Presley?"

"Yes. We caught him in an abandoned hacienda outside Nuevo Laredo. You can check with the authorities there. The arrest was on the up and up."

"Yes, yes, this I also know."

Cat's brow knitted. "I still don't understand."

"We think that my dead man and your killer were together."

Cat's eyes widened. "Oh. Well…there was another man with Presley, but I never saw him. My husband… my partner at the time, was the one who saw him. They had a gunfight inside the hacienda while I was at the back of the house taking Presley into custody. The bastard ran out the back when the gunfire began in the front. You should talk to Wilson about him. He'll be here soon."

Luis was confused. If this woman was guilty, she was about the best liar he'd ever met. He needed to try this from another angle. The money. People always reacted to the mention of money.

"There was another thing. When Tutuola came to

Chihuahua, several people saw him flashing around money. Large amounts of money that he kept in a bag in the trunk of his car. Did you know anything about that money?"

Cat frowned. "Why would I? Maybe it was what Presley paid him for helping get him out of the States. You could probably get an interview with Presley if you requested it. They can't fry the bastard until all his appeals have expired."

Again Luis was confused. Maybe he'd been wrong all along about her.

"This money, Mrs. McKay—"

"Cat," she said, then winced when a wave of weakness washed over her.

Luis saw her go pale. "Are you all right?"

She looked at him as if he were sitting in the chair with his brains in his hands.

"No. Actually, I'm not. A shit-faced druggie pumped a bullet into me today, but do continue. It's helping me think of something but the pain."

Now Luis felt like a jerk. Maybe he should come back when she was better.

"If you wish, we can have this conversation later, say tomorrow, or the next day, after you've had a chance to recover a bit."

Cat leaned forward, fixing him with a cold, angry stare.

"In truth, I don't wish to have this conversation at all. It reminds me of a very painful time in my life. However, since you've come so far to have it, please go on. I'm sure I'll survive. I've been through worse."

"With regards to Tutuola's money, it was too much to be a payoff. I am speaking of millions."

Again Cat seemed to suddenly connect.

"Ah…then that might be the money Presley took out of his company safe."

The last thing he'd expected was for her to acknowledge the presence of a large sum of money. Especially if she'd killed to get it. Again, she'd confused him.

"And how do you come to know of this money?"

Cat shifted in her seat, trying to find a more comfortable spot but obviously not out of nervousness.

"When Marsha disappeared, I knew Presley had killed her, but I couldn't make the authorities believe me. So I hired a friend, who shall remain nameless, to bug everything he could that belonged to Presley. We bugged clothing and cars and everything we could get to in his office. My friend also told me that there was what he figured to be around two million dollars in the company safe."

Luis interrupted. "Your friend broke into Presley's safe?"

"He has many skills," she said, then continued. "He slipped a couple of bugs in between the stacks of bills. When Presley escaped, I followed him through a computer system connected to those particular bugs. I followed him all the way to Nuevo Laredo. As for the money, assuming he had it with him when the hacienda caught on fire, I figured the money burned with it."

Luis didn't know what to say. She had all the answers. And for some reason that bothered him. She had too many answers.

"The man who was murdered in my city had suffered recent burns."

"If all you say is correct, then what's left to figure out? You know where your dead man was injured. In that fire. You know where he got his money. From Mark Presley. Probably figured himself lucky when Presley got arrested and left it behind."

"But I still don't know who killed him or why— or where the money went."

Cat swallowed.

Luis saw the muscles work in her throat and in that moment knew he'd been right all along. She'd killed him. But how did he get her to say it?

While he was struggling with another way to go at her, his gaze fell back on her throat. He decided that if he got her talking about something else, she might lose her focus and let something slip.

He pointed to her throat.

"You have quite a scar. May I ask how you got it?"

Cat's eyes narrowed angrily. "That's a really rude question to ask a woman who's spent most of her life trying to ignore it. However, since you've asked so nicely, of course I would be happy to share a bit of my life history. When I was thirteen years old a man broke into our home, cut my throat and slashed my father to ribbons in front of me, and I couldn't call for help. I thought I would die. When I came to in a hospital and found out I was still alive, but orphaned, I was sorry that I hadn't."

For the first time in his life Luis felt shame for the questions he asked. He had to remind himself that this was his job.

"That is terrible. I am very sorry for what happened to you. Of course, seeing the perpetrator come to justice must have given you some satisfaction."

"They never caught him."

For a moment Luis didn't know what to say. "Are you serious? All these years and the case is still unsolved? Why? Did you not see his face? Could you not identify him?"

Cat's vision blurred.

He saw her eyes suddenly brimming. He saw her swallowing hard to keep from weeping. And when she managed to pull herself together without shedding a tear, he finally began to understand the depths of her strength.

"I see his face every night when I close my eyes."

"I am sorry. I didn't—" He stopped. How could he apologize when he'd meant to push her? "So the police never found him."

"No. The police didn't find him," she said, and it wasn't a lie. The police never found him, but she did.

"What led you to the business of bounty hunting?" he asked.

"It was a job that kept me apprised of criminals and their whereabouts."

Suddenly Luis understood. "Ah…the police stopped looking, but you didn't, did you? You never stopped looking."

"No."

"You must have seen thousands and thousands of criminals over the years, and many men look alike. What was it about him that helped you separate him from the others?"

Cat hesitated. If she told the truth, he was going to know. She thought about how to answer without giving herself away. She thought of Wilson, the baby, everything she would lose. Then an image slid through her mind: her father's face, twisted in pain. His eyes, beseeching her to forgive him for not being able to keep her safe. She couldn't lie. Not about this. She looked down at her hands, took a deep breath, then stared straight into Luis Montoya's eyes.

"He was tattooed. Many perps are, but it helped me sort through them."

Luis felt the blood drain from his face. Tattoos? He thought of the booking photo of Solomon Tutuola he had out in the car. Never had he seen so many tattoos on a man.

"I have a photo of Tutuola in the car. Would you mind looking at it?"

"I told you, the only man I saw at the hacienda was Mark Presley."

Luis kept pushing, aware that he was on the verge of the answers he sought.

"Yes, I remember. But you said you looked at booking photos of tattooed men. Why wouldn't you want to see if this man was the man you sought?"

Cat blinked and then, for the first time since they'd sat down together, looked away.

"Maybe because I'm sick and tired of the ugly side of life. Maybe because I'm going to have a baby that I don't intend to drag through the same kind of life that I was forced to live."

"You would want to let your father's killer live?"

"Hell, no!"

It came out before Cat thought. She took a deep breath, then closed her eyes. When she opened them, Luis Montoya was watching her every move. And then he attacked.

"So…this money that Tutuola had. It would have been nice to have some to put away for the little baby you carry."

The disgust in her eyes was unmistakable.

"Money? You think everything in life is about the money? In my opinion, Mark Presley's money is cursed. It's blood money. It was worth more to Mark Presley than my friend…even more than his own child. Why on God's earth would someone want that fucking money?"

Luis felt as if he'd just been slapped. He tried to pursue his previous tack, but his gut was telling him he'd had it wrong. All this time and he'd been chasing the wrong reason.

This woman had killed Tutuola. He would bet his life on it.

But not for money.

"So, Cat McKay…if you were me, what would you think happened to that money Tutuola had?"

"That it burned up in the fire with your dead man."

"By fire, I assume you mean the one outside Chihuahua?"

"It's a fair assumption," Cat said, then leaned back in the chair. Her back hurt. Her heart hurt. He knew what she'd done, and he knew that she knew it, too. But what he did with that knowledge remained to be seen.

"As I was driving through Mexico, backtracking Tutuola's last trip, I came upon a policeman and a priest who told me how you saved a baby in the desert. It occurred to me that this adventure was much later than when you were in Nuevo Laredo, capturing this Presley. Why did you come back?"

Cat gritted her teeth as a wave of pain swept through her. She stifled a moan but was unable to hide her suffering. God, she was pissed. About as pissed as she'd ever been in her life.

"Adventure? You call finding a dead woman being chewed on by coyotes an adventure? The baby she was holding was minutes away from becoming dessert."

Luis flushed. "Yes, yes, it was a poor choice of words. But you came back. Why?"

"As a rule, I don't much like people. Maybe you can understand why. If not, so be it. But I do like your country. The vastness of the mountains and desserts is calming and beautiful. But after I found the dead woman, it ruined the trip…if you know what I mean."

Her sarcasm was evident. Luis felt like a heel.

"Then I can assume your story is that you never saw Solomon Tutuola…in Nuevo Laredo."

Cat blinked. "Right. I never saw him there."

"And you are not a woman who would be willing to kill…for money?"

Breath caught in the back of Cat's throat. "No. Never for money."

"And that's what you want me to believe?"

Did she want that? "Yes."

When he stood abruptly, Cat thought that was it. This was where he arrested her—or at least took her in for questioning. It would only be a matter of time before they found people who'd seen her in Chihuahua. But she wouldn't go begging and screaming. When Luis stood up, so did she.

They were standing face-to-face.

Out the window, she saw Wilson coming down the driveway. She wanted to weep. She wanted to wail. Was this the last time she was going to see him as a free woman?

Luis moved toward her.

Cat had to make herself stand still. She'd never run from trouble before. She wasn't going to start now.

Luis reached for her hand.

Cat was shaking.

But instead of putting her in handcuffs, he took her hand. For a moment they stared—man to woman—eye to eye.

Then, to Cat's disbelief, he lifted her hand to his lips and kissed it gently, then let her go.

"I want you to know that never in my life have I met a woman with a heart as strong as yours. Your life has not been an easy one, but I believe you have lived it with honor. It has been a pleasure to meet you, and I wish you and your husband and your baby a very long and happy life."

Cat shuddered. Despite her best effort, tears began to flow.

"*Aiyee...gato pequeno,* now is not the time to weep."

Cat couldn't speak. Little cat. He'd called her little cat. She couldn't think past the gentleness in his voice. Was this it? Was he letting this go?

Behind them, the door flew open, hitting the wall with a bang.

Luis turned in time to see a tall, angry-looking man coming toward them. His hair was dark and short and standing on end. His face was strong, with a jaw that gave away the presence of a very stubborn streak. Then he saw the man's earring. A single gold hoop.

Outlaw?

Pirate?

"Wilson," Cat said.

Luis sighed. Ah…of course…only a man like this could handle a woman such as Cat Dupree McKay.

Wilson stopped in front of Cat, cupped her cheek with one hand and tilted her head to look at the deep bruise and cut on her face. What he knew for a fact was that this Mexican detective was not taking his wife anywhere. He would have to kill Wilson first.

"Franks is dead?"

She nodded. "You have this man to thank."

Wilson glared at Luis. "Thank you for saving my wife's life. Did you also make her cry?"

Luis shrugged, then smiled. "Sometimes a woman cries because she's happy," he said, then added, "Mr. McKay, your wife is a most remarkable woman. It was my honor to meet her."

Wilson wasn't sure what had just happened, but he managed to answer in a civilized manner.

"Thank you. Now maybe you'd like to tell me why you've come all the way from Mexico to talk to my wife."

Luis shrugged. "Most certainly. I was just tying up the loose ends of a case I'd been given. Your wife's information was most helpful, and now I'm ready to go home."

Wilson didn't bother to hide his relief. Ever since Cat had told him who was there, he'd had visions of losing her to a Mexican jail.

"The sheriff will want to talk to you about the shooting. He's on his way."

"Of course," Luis said, and walked outside to await the officer's arrival.

The door slammed behind him as he left.

"Sweet lord," Wilson whispered, and put his arms around Cat, then pulled her head down on his shoulder. "Oh, baby…I'm so sorry. That cut on your face is deep. Are you hurting? If you can't wait for the ambulance, I can drive you to the E.R. myself."

"No, it's not that," Cat said, and then started to sob.

He misunderstood. "I am so sorry that you had to go through this because of me."

She was crying so hard she was shaking. "No, no, I'm not crying because of that dead piece of shit in the yard. I'm not even crying because my side hurts like hell."

"Your side? What's wrong with your side?"

"Franks shot me."

Wilson's face drained of all color. He yanked up her shirt, saw the seeping blood and the makeshift bandage, and started cursing. Without stopping, he turned around, walked to the hall closet, took a pistol down from the shelf, jacked a shell into the chamber and stalked outside.

The deputy sheriff had arrived and was outside talking to Montoya. When he saw the gun in Wilson's hand, he was a bit startled.

"Wilson…hey, Wilson. Wait up. What's wrong? Where are you going?"

But Wilson wasn't talking. Rage was evident in every step he took. He circled the house with the men hurrying behind him. When he got to Jimmy Franks's body, he didn't pause, he just aimed the gun and shot.

The bullet went through the body and into the ground.

Wilson put the safety back on and turned around.

"What?" he asked.

"What in hell did you do that for?" the deputy asked.

"Because of what he did to Catherine."

Even as Luis knew he'd made the right decision regarding Cat, he was suddenly glad he hadn't had to contend with her husband, either.

"But he was already dead," the deputy said.

"Not dead enough," Wilson muttered. "I want his sorry ass to know that he's going to hell with a piece of my lead in him, too. And while I'm at it, where is that ambulance? Cat's been shot. Don't make me have to take her all the way into Austin in that kind of pain."

Then he walked back into the house.

The deputy looked at Luis.

"Uh...excuse me a minute. I need to double check on that ambulance."

"You have my name, phone number, badge number and statement. If you need more, I will be at the Austin hotel I mentioned earlier until noon tomorrow," Luis said, then got in his car and drove away.

Cat was still crying, but it was from relief. Finally, after all the years of living with the thirst for revenge, it was well and truly over.

Wilson came back in the house, put the gun on the shelf and took Cat in his arms.

"I heard a gunshot," she said. "What happened?"

"I put a slug in Jimmy Franks."

"But he was already dead."

"Not dead enough. Not until I gave him something to take with him."

"Oh, Wilson...I don't know how I got through life without you," Cat said, then grabbed her side, moaning softly as pain shot through her body again.

Muttering beneath his breath, Wilson picked her up and carried her to their bedroom. She wept with every step he took, which broke his heart.

"Catherine…baby… Oh God, please don't cry. I'm so sorry this happened. I'm so sorry you were hurt."

"That's not why I'm crying," she managed to say, and then shuddered, swept by a fresh wave of tears and relief. "He knew, Wilson. He knew, and he did nothing."

Wilson sat down on the side of the bed beside her, holding her hand. "The ambulance will be here soon. Just hang on, honey."

Cat groaned. "Wilson. Listen to me."

Wilson stilled. "What?"

"He knew. Montoya knew everything about Tutuola and figured out what I'd done. I saw it in his eyes, and still he did nothing. He just kissed my hand and walked away. It's over. Finally everything is over. Franks is behind us. Tutuola's death is behind us. Ever since my father's death, his face has been like a bad penny in my head, always turning up when I least expected it, never able to forget, never able to stop hating—not even for you."

Wilson sighed. All he could think was, *Thank God, thank God.*

In the distance, he could hear a siren.

"The ambulance is coming."

"Good. Tell them to give me drugs. It hurts like hell."

Wilson grinned. This was his Cat. This was the woman who'd stolen his heart.

"I'll tell them, baby…have no doubt. I'll tell them to give you whatever you want or they'll answer to me."

"Is your dad okay?"

"Yeah. Guess why he had the heart attack? He had his own run-in with Franks. Franks shot at him, and Dad wanted to warn me. Unfortunately, it came too late to help you." Then his eyes darkened. "Dad's going to be fine. I should have been here with you."

"However it went down, it's all good now. Your dad will come home. Life will go on. You should call your parents, let them know everything is okay."

"They'll know soon enough. Right now, you're my only concern."

There was a knock on the door.

"That'll be the EMTs. Hang on. I'll be right back."

Cat watched Wilson run out of the room, then closed her eyes against the pain. As she did, the images of her parents' faces suddenly slid through her mind. Always before, when she'd dreamed of them, it had been of the last horrible images that had been burned into her brain.

Her mother's still, lifeless face, staring blindly through a shattered windshield. Her father's face twisted in mortal agony.

But not now. This time they were smiling at her.

She could hear the sound of Wilson's voice and the hurried clip of his boots on the floor as he came running—running back to her.

Epilogue

Two little boys were slinging mud at each other from a puddle beneath their swing set.

Their mother was sitting on the back porch of an old, two-story ranch house, watching their impromptu war with humor and patience.

The baby in her arms stirred. The woman pushed off with the toe of her shoe, setting the old rocker into motion again. As she did, the baby settled.

"Sleep well, little girl. There will be plenty of time for running and playing when you're older."

The baby stuffed her little fist into her mouth, sucked it once, then sighed, her dark eyelashes fluttering on her cheeks as she slept, lost in whatever it was that constituted a baby's dreams.

A black truck was coming across the back pasture.

The woman paused, her gaze moving instantly to the man behind the wheel.

He'd followed her through hell and brought her to this place—to her heaven on earth. And even now, after five years, the sound of his footsteps on the back porch still made her heart leap. The touch of his hand in the middle of the night brought her to quiet ecstasy. The pride in his voice as he spoke of her and their children could bring tears to her eyes.

The truck pulled up on the outside of the yard fence and parked.

The two little boys, filthy from head to toe, stopped throwing mud at each other and screamed in delight.

"Daddy! Daddy! You're home."

He was laughing at them as he caught them up in his arms, mud and all, and carried them back toward the house and the woman waiting on the steps with their daughter in her arms.

"Daddy's home," he said softly, and leaned forward, kissed the baby's soft cheek, then kissed the woman on the lips.

Quick.

Hard.

For a brief moment their gazes met. And above the noise and the mess, a silent understanding came and went.

It had been love that brought them to this moment in their lives, and it would be love that got them through the years to come.

It would always be about the love.

REQUEST YOUR FREE BOOKS!

2 FREE NOVELS FROM THE ROMANCE/SUSPENSE COLLECTION PLUS 2 FREE GIFTS!

YES! Please send me 2 FREE novels from the Romance/Suspense Collection and my 2 FREE gifts (gifts are worth about $10). After receiving them, if I don't wish to receive any more books, I can return the shipping statement marked "cancel." If I don't cancel, I will receive 4 brand-new novels every month and be billed just $5.49 per book in the U.S. or $5.99 per book in Canada, plus 25¢ shipping and handling per book plus applicable taxes, if any*. That's a savings of at least 20% off the cover price! I understand that accepting the 2 free books and gifts places me under no obligation to buy anything. I can always return a shipment and cancel at any time. Even if I never buy another book from the Reader Service, the two free books and gifts are mine to keep forever.

185 MDN EF5Y 385 MDN EF6C

Name _____ (PLEASE PRINT) _____

Address _____ Apt. # _____

City _____ State/Prov. _____ Zip/Postal Code _____

Signature (if under 18, a parent or guardian must sign) _____

Mail to **The Reader Service:**
IN U.S.A.: P.O. Box 1867, Buffalo, NY 14240-1867
IN CANADA: P.O. Box 609, Fort Erie, Ontario L2A 5X3

Not valid to current subscribers to the Romance Collection,
the Suspense Collection or the Romance/Suspense Collection.

Want to try two free books from another line?
Call 1-800-873-8635 or visit www.morefreebooks.com.

* Terms and prices subject to change without notice. N.Y. residents add applicable sales tax. Canadian residents will be charged applicable provincial taxes and GST. Offer not valid in Quebec. This offer is limited to one order per household. All orders subject to approval. Credit or debit balances in a customer's account(s) may be offset by any other outstanding balance owed by or to the customer. Please allow 4 to 6 weeks for delivery. Offer available while quantities last.

Your Privacy: Harlequin is committed to protecting your privacy. Our Privacy Policy is available online at www.eHarlequin.com or upon request from the Reader Service. From time to time we make our lists of customers available to reputable third parties who may have a product or service of interest to you. If you would prefer we not share your name and address, please check here. ☐

BOB08R

NEW YORK TIMES BESTSELLING AUTHOR

ALEX KAVA

The cover-up was only the beginning... then came the nightmare.

Sabrina Galloway, one of the top scientists at EcoEnergy, makes an alarming discovery: someone has tampered with the production process, and an eco-disaster of staggering proportion is imminent. Toxic waste is leaking into the Florida waterways and the Gulf of Mexico.

In her determination to expose EcoEnergy's lethal secret, Sabrina is unwittingly drawn into a sinister plot that puts corporate greed and corruption above human life. She becomes the target of silent, faceless enemies—some of whose identities reach Pennsylvania Avenue itself.

WHITE WASH

> "Kava's writing is reminiscent
> of Patricia Cornwell in her prime."
> —*Mystery Ink*

*Available the first week of November 2008
wherever books are sold!*

MIRA®

SHARON SALA

32544 THE HEALER	___ $7.99 U.S.	___ $7.99 CAN.
32507 CUT THROAT	___ $7.99 U.S.	___ $9.50 CAN.
32352 NINE LIVES	___ $7.99 U.S.	___ $9.50 CAN.
66967 REMEMBER ME	___ $6.50 U.S.	___ $7.99 CAN.
66966 REUNION	___ $6.50 U.S.	___ $7.99 CAN.

(limited quantities available)

TOTAL AMOUNT	$ _____
POSTAGE & HANDLING	$ _____
($1.00 FOR 1 BOOK, 50¢ for each additional)	
APPLICABLE TAXES*	$ _____
TOTAL PAYABLE	$ _____

(check or money order—please do not send cash)

To order, complete this form and send it, along with a check or money order for the total above, payable to MIRA Books, to: **In the U.S.:** 3010 Walden Avenue, P.O. Box 9077, Buffalo, NY 14269-9077; **In Canada:** P.O. Box 636, Fort Erie, Ontario, L2A 5X3.

Name: _____
Address: _____ City: _____
State/Prov.: _____ Zip/Postal Code: _____
Account Number (if applicable): _____
075 CSAS

*New York residents remit applicable sales taxes.
*Canadian residents remit applicable GST and provincial taxes.

MIRA®

www.MIRABooks.com

MSS1108BL